2/2/2000

634.9

SMALL WOODS AND HEDGEROWS

LAND AND LIVESTOCK LIBRARY

SMALL WOODS AND HEDGEROWS

Valerie Porter

PELHAM BOOKS

STEPHEN GREENE PRESS

ACKNOWLEDGEMENTS

It is difficult to single out a few names from the many who have, directly or indirectly, helped me to understand about growing, caring for, harvesting, converting and admiring trees, but I am particularly grateful to the following: Paul Betteridge and Ron Hornet of Astolat, specialists in sweet chestnut coppice produce (Godalming, Surrey); Alison Tingley, FWAG adviser for Hampshire; Merrist Wood Agricultural College; Martyn New, horticultural lecturer at Sparsholt College of Agriculture, for an inspiring day about propagation of native trees and shrubs; Ann Griffiths, West Sussex County Council's countryside officer; Tilhill Forestry, whose managers (past and present) cared so well for Pallinghurst; Economic Forestry Group, Oxford; Forestry Commission at Alice Holt.

I should also like to thank a host of woodsmen who have been generous with their time and their talk over the years, especially Fred Goodall, George Quinnell, Sid Kingshott and the mysterious Alec.

PELHAM BOOKS/STEPHEN GREENE PRESS

Published by the Penguin Group
27 Wrights Lane, London W8 5TZ, England
Viking Penguin Inc., 40 West 23rd Street, New York, New York 10010, USA
The Stephen Greene Press, Inc., 15 Muzzey Street, Lexington, Massachusetts 02173, USA
Penguin Books Australia Ltd, Ringwood, Victoria, Australia
Penguin Books Canada Ltd, 2801 John Street, Markham, Ontario, Canada L3R 1B4
Penguin Books (NZ) Ltd, 182–190 Wairau Road, Auckland 10, New Zealand

Penguin Books Ltd, Registered Offices: Harmondsworth, Middlesex, England

First published 1990

Copyright © Valerie Porter, 1990

Printed and bound in Great Britain by
Butler & Tanner Ltd, Frome and London

A CIP catalogue record for this book is available from the British Library.

ISBN 0 7207 1868 6

CONTENTS

	ACKNOWLEDGEMENTS	4
CHAPTER I	TREES	7
CHAPTER II	RENOVATION	13

Options. Valuable Timber. Windblown Trees. Softwood. Uncommercial Woodland.

CHAPTER III	MANAGEMENT TECHNIQUES	22

Cleaning. Brashing. Thinning. Enrichment. Conversion of Coppice. Felling. Measuring and Marketing.

CHAPTER IV	NEW WOODS	31

Options. Assessment. Site Preparation. Vegetative Competition. Browsers. Old Stumps. Planting. Maintenance.

CHAPTER V	PROPAGATION	61

Seed Collection. Dormancy. Storage Methods. Storage of Different Species. Sowing. Undercutting. Cuttings. Natural Regeneration.

CHAPTER VI	COPPICE MANAGEMENT	79

Options and Effects. Managing Established Coppice. Neglected Coppice. New Coppice. Access and Extraction Routes. The Coppice Harvest. Stacking. Sweet Chestnut Coppice. Hazel Coppice. Willows.

CHAPTER VII	COPPICE PRODUCE	91

Fuel. Fencing. Creative Outlets. Walking-sticks and Crooks. Brushwood. By-products.

CHAPTER VIII SPECIAL TREE CROPS 116
Christmas Trees. Willows. Poplars.
Eucalyptus. Sea Buckthorn.

CHAPTER IX HEDGEROWS 124
Uses. Hedge-trimming. Laying. Hedgerow Trees. Shelter Belts. Hedge-Planting.

CHAPTER X MULTIPLE LAND USE 138
Options. Agrosilviculture. Trees and
Livestock. Working Horses. Poultry.
Game in Woodland. Games in the
Woods. Nature Conservation.

APPENDICES: I GRANTS 158
II ORGANISATIONS 161
III RED TAPE 166
IV MEASUREMENTS 168
V SPECIES NOTES 170
GLOSSARY 184
BIBLIOGRAPHY 188
INDEX 190

I

TREES

In an urban age it is easy to forget that Britain is essentially silvan.
Woodland is the natural blanket for these islands, as it is for many
other lands, but humans have sought to exploit and dominate the
trees. We are dendroclasts. Yet we are also dendrolaters: trees
command our respect, admiration and love, and never more so than
when they are going or gone.

October, they say, is the 'season of mists and mellow fruit-
fulness' – very evocative of trees – but it can also be awesome. On
16 October 1987 thousands of people trembled in their beds during
the early hours of that phenomenal Friday morning as the storm
that some described as a hurricane raged relentlessly for several
long, dark hours over southern England. Very few slept through its
mighty, majestic onslaught, and at first light many of us crept half-
fearfully out of our homes to face the aftermath.

At six that morning the scene in my own valley was overwhelming.
Although only an hour from London, this is a well wooded area
and many local people are directly employed in small wood-based
enterprises like family sawmills, coppicing and the working up of
coppice materials, rustic or fine-quality furniture, fencing and firewood. Others make use of farm woodland and game coverts or simply
enjoy strolling in the woods and studying wildlife. Most of those
that live here accept the woods as a familiar scenic backcloth and it
was perhaps these less involved people, even more than those with
a practical interest in the trees, who were most appalled by the
devastation they saw that Friday morning. Hundreds of trees –
perhaps thousands – had been uprooted or jaggedly snapped in two
and lay scattered as if a giant had carelessly emptied a matchbox
over the valley and its sheltering slopes.

The labour and financial outlay required to clear the roads, retrieve
blown-away sheds and mend broken houses and barns were considerable; but these caused less general despair than the enormous
sense of loss and, yes, grief for the trees. As in most parts of southern

England that day, many people had tears in their eyes and it was not the wood-smoke that precipitated them. The local papers were full of poems expressing desolation, written by undisciplined hands in styles which might be mocked by the literati but which were all the more powerful in conveying the emotions of ordinary people.

As it often is for those who grieve for dead friends, the sense of shock was delayed for many but built up within them over the next few days or weeks, surfacing now and then when triggered by the sight of the shattered, undignified arboreal corpses that still littered the countryside on the first anniversary of the storm. And whenever the winds began to rise again in that first year, many of us experienced a sense of dread and foreboding as we waited for the storm's second coming.

This is a practical book, but trees are like livestock. Those who tend them, even if solely for profit, will only succeed if they have a natural empathy for their charges and the ability to wonder at them.

The book is not about forestry, which is essentially the management of trees for the production of timber on a commercial scale and perhaps only incidentally the management of woodland as part of the landscape and as a habitat for wildlife (though forestry attitudes are changing rapidly in those respects). Nor is it about growing high-quality timber trees, though that can always be an ultimate dream. Rather, it is about trees on a small scale: it is about making the most of those little pockets of woodland and copse which are scattered islands in a sea of agricultural land or wasteland or urbanisation; it is about copses and spinneys, and the controlled linear woodland of hedgerows that often link them. It is about conservation and landscape.

However, it includes, and seeks to combine, the possibility of modestly profitable harvesting and imaginative craftwork along with a sympathy for the environment, because woodland in all its guises is an ecosystem which is capable of supporting a grand diversity and richness of life. In particular it is about the infinite adaptability of coppicing, that traditional, personal-scale system of making the best use of the utilitarian and decorative qualities of wood. Woodland is never simply a stand of trees: it has a vegetative understorey too, and is home to all manner of living creatures, warm-blooded and cold, and it is the smaller patchwork of carefully coppiced woodland that is often the liveliest and most welcoming.

There is great diversity in woodland life, and there is also great diversity in the ways in which you might choose to use your woodland. Keep an open mind and consider possibilities other than the obvious ones. There are so *many* possibilities:

Table 1
SOME WOODLAND USES AND SYSTEMS

Amenity value

Animal browsing, pannage and shelter

Animal enterprises: deer parks, rare-breed settings, forest poultry

By-products: leaf compost, bark, muka, distillation, sawdust, wood ash for potteries

Chip production: bedding, fuel, heat heaps, mulches, gallops, playground surfaces, packing, horticulture

Christmas trees

Conservation of wildlife, nature trails

Co-operative enterprises: timber/coppice production, sawmills, horse teams, workshops, chipping machines, willow harvesters

Coppice: pure or mixed stands, or coppice with standards

Craft centres: coppice and other rural crafts, turnery, wood-carving, fencing-making, tools and implements, woodland museum

Employment: local skilled and unskilled

Food from trees: fruit and nuts, resins, leaf protein, wines, spruce beer, preserves, gourmet meals, fungi

Fuel centres: firewood, chips, faggots, charcoal, stoves, biofuel/gases

Game cover: pheasants, deer, fox coverts

Green education (and not only for children) and interpretation centres

Hedgerows, spinneys, copses, field-corner planting, shelter belts

Landscape, and landscape ideas for other landowners and gardeners

Leisure activities: adventure trails, camps, log cabins, fitness trails, sports, war games, woodland walks

Multiple land use: agroforestry, silvopastoral systems, forestry and fruit, multi-storey home gardens

Nursery of native seedlings, local provenance

Nurse crops and shelter for buildings/crops

Orchards: fruit, grazing, bees, chickens, pigs, vegetables

Timber production: high-quality veneer, carving woods; bulk softwood for pulp, etc.

Underwood production

Willow plantations: basket osiers, charcoal, energy crops, cricket-bat willows

Woodland park with fishing lake, museum, tea-room/restaurant, camping, sale of rustic furniture, firewood, pea-sticks and bean-poles, tree seedlings, hedging plants etc.

Tables 1 and 2 give an idea of the generosity of trees.

Of course, there are many limitations on your choice of woodland enterprise (and here 'enterprise' is defined broadly as an undertaking

Table 2

WOODLAND PRODUCE

Basketwork and trugs	Gates
Bark (tanning, mulch)	Pea-sticks, bean-poles
Barrels, boats, wagons, wheels	Props (clothesline supports, hop-
Brushwood (besoms, jumps,	poles, mining timber)
faggots)	Pulpwood, matchwood
Building materials (roundwood or	Rustic furniture, rustic poles,
sawn), roofing shingles	bird-tables, sheds, Wendy
Cellulose, lignin, chemicals	houses, plant containers
Charcoal	Sawmill timber
Chips	Seeds, seedlings, transplants
Fencing (posts, stakes, panels,	Thatching spars, clothes pegs,
hurdles, poles, rails, palings)	rake tines, walking sticks
Firewood	Turnery, carving, kitchenware
Foliage for florists (eucalyptus,	Veneer
conifers)	
Furniture	

with full initiative, rather than specifically as a business concern): there are fundamental restrictions imposed by the site which may be immutable, or expensive or inappropriate to counteract; there are the restrictions of personal inclination, resources, skills and finance; there are the restrictions imposed by society in general and by local government and your neighbours in particular.

You might not have noticed it but we are in the throes of a revolution, especially in rural areas, and popular concepts are, as they should be, persuading governments to respond. Farmers, for example, after many years of being challenged and aided to increase productivity and efficiency, are now gripped by uncertainty, unsure of their future role and unsettled by the public's apparent determination to bite the hands that have been feeding it. This uncertainty is reflected (and often propagated) by government policies and the Europeanisation of Britain. Because the attitudes are changing, so is the legislation, and any specific advice in this book about, say, tree-planting grants and set-aside schemes could be superseded within months. It is therefore important that you obtain up-to-date information on the red tape of woodland management, and the most obvious source is the Forestry Commission (FC). Although the Commission is by its nature concerned above all with timber production, its officers will give unbiased and up-to-date advice on all aspects of woodland management, including uncommercial matters like wildlife conservation, and at the time of writing the initial general advice on site is given free of charge.

Table 3
FACTORS AFFECTING YOUR CHOICE OF WOODLAND ENTERPRISE

Accessibility Getting into and out of the woodland – roads, rides, tracks, ground conditions, undergrowth. Getting produce to markets, or buyers to produce. Distance to loading points

Advice from sound sources – Forestry Commission, Farming and Wildlife Advisory Groups, Nature Conservancy Council, county council, private consultants

Emphasis Priorities and combinations – amenity, coppicing (for own use, or for sale raw or worked up), commercial timber production, nature conservation, landscape, income (regular or eventual), employment, sporting value, screening and shelter (livestock, buildings, crops, motorways), multiple land use, special crops

Environment Effect on landscape and view; local pollution; disturbance of neighbours/wildlife; public rights of way; national park, area of outstanding natural beauty, site of special scientific interest, nature reserve, ancient monument, tree preservation orders, conservation area, etc.

Existing potential Extent, nature and condition of existing woodland (ancient, mature, neglected), coppices, hedgerows, spinneys, thickets, scrub, shelter belts, plantations, specimen trees, amenity plantings

Finances

History Previous uses for the site (check for indicator species, ancient banks and other earthworks, suggestive old names, old maps etc.; also more recent use, e.g. arable pasture, coppice, reclaimed marsh)

Labour Availability and cost – own labour, family, employees, local self-employed woodsmen and forestry workers, contractors, co-operatives, volunteers. Seasonal or regular

Land Soil, climate, altitude, aspect, terrain, etc.

Markets Suitable species (pure stands or mixtures) for local outlets or major markets. Ages, sizes, shapes, extent of package, location (*see* **Accessibility**)

New plantings Possibilities for new woodland, coppice, hedges, small-group plantings, special-crop plantations

Skills and equipment Managerial, manual, advisory, marketing and tool/equipment-handling skills; learning abilities and opportunities; power equipment (tractors, ATVs, horses, power tools), hand tools and skills, transport, craft tools and skills

Time factor Long-term and short-term

There are also numerous private forestry and woodland con-sultants and you should be able to obtain a choice of recommended names from your local FC office if you explain roughly what your

Small Woods and Hedgerows

aims are, whether commercial, selfish or altruistic. There is a great deal of expertise on tap: make use of it in the context of your particular case.

At present everyone wants to encourage tree-planting. Appendix I gives details of the main national grant schemes in operation at the time of writing. In many parts of the country it is possible to obtain valuable support (advisory, practical and financial) from local councils, especially for amenity and conservation enterprises, though some might object to your ideas on the basis of local planning policies if they affect the general landscape, for example, or if you are considering a public enterprise like woodland camps or war games.

There are several major organisations willing to offer advice (though less often financial aid) with conservation schemes – for example, the Farming and Wildlife Advisory Group (FWAG), Men of Trees and the Woodland Trust – and their names, addresses and activities are set out in Appendix II. If you want to remove rather than plant trees, woodlands or hedgerows, you will probably need permission from someone somewhere – for example, a felling licence from the FC – and there are details of such regulations in Appendix III.

You will probably seek some kind of return from your woodland and hedgerows. This might be merely personal satisfaction with an environment or the bonus of the wildlife it attracts, or it might be the practical value of having your own firewood and fencing materials readily available, or it might be more ambitiously commercial in exploiting small-scale specialist plantations (Christmas trees, willows or walking-sticks, for example) in which case you need to consider markets and marketing. As with any kind of product, study your potential market thoroughly, find a niche and then exploit it. There are plenty of other people trying to do exactly the same thing but, with good advice, good contacts and good sense, you should be able to find your marketplace.

The Bibliography mentions several books concerned with more commercial woodland management and also with the history of forestry and of our ancient woodlands. These histories are the context within which we need to consider woodland today. As John Ruskin (1819–1900) wrote: 'God has lent us the earth for our life. It is a great entail. It belongs as much to those who come after, as to us, and we have no right by anything we do or neglect, to involve them in any unnecessary penalties, or deprive them of the benefit which is in our power to bequeath.'

If you become involved with trees, you become involved with history and with posterity.

II

RENOVATION

Trees *want* to grow: why not let them? And then, why not manage them to suit your purposes?

On most holdings there are patches of woodland and pockets of what hardly merits the name 'woodland' at all. In the context of renovation, take a look at the holding in its entirety and, as a first step, draw up a map showing all your potential 'woodland' areas, including high forest (standard trees grown mainly for timber), spinneys, old coppices, scrubby areas, shelter belts, avenues, hedgerows and bits of land which are difficult to use for pasture or crop-growing because they are damp or the soil is difficult or they are in awkward corners or on fairly steep slopes.

During the survey you should, of course, try to identify the species of tree and shrub in each site (easiest when they are in full leaf and bearing fruit or flowers) and whether the site is a jumble of all-sorts or is more or less dominated by two or three species, which would make management easier. Take note of the ages of the trees, whether the block is fairly uniform and clearly planted at more or less the same time or is a pleasant plethora of self-regenerating woodland. Take special note of unusual native trees like the wild service, and seek to protect and encourage them.

Typically, a piece of woodland has been left to its own devices for some time until a new owner, or its present owner inspired by a new sense of urgency and purpose, looks at it with a more critical eye and decides vaguely to 'do something' with it. Before that intention can be turned into even a half-hearted plan, there is a need for an overall philosophy on priorities. Do you need the quickest possible financial returns, or an instant 'amenity', or are your aims more long-term and leisurely, whether in terms of profitable cropping or enjoyment by future generations or conservation of a landscape or an area for wildlife?

With these very broad principles in mind, bring in an expert to help you assess the potential and guide your ideas on management. Incidentally, do not assume that neglect is ideal for wildlife: conservation woodlands need just as much management as commercial plantations, but with different emphases.

Go to the local FC station and ask for one of their officers to inspect the site and give a free consultation (ask for the private woodlands officer, or for a conservation officer if that is your priority), or request that they recommend a suitable and trustworthy private consultant; alternatively, approach your county council's countryside department, or talk to FWAG about conservation.

The first assessment will probably look at the following points.

VALUABLE TIMBER

Are there any hardwood trees on the site which are of a species sought by the timber market and, if so, are any of them good specimens either for felling now or for growing on for harvesting in due course? (Terms like 'hardwood' are defined in the Glossary; hardwood timber comes from broadleaf trees as opposed to the softwood of conifers and the word does not necessarily reflect the hardness of the wood.)

To be of value, a hardwood tree needs first of all to be of a useful species. Table 4 summarises the main commercial markets for hardwoods and softwoods, and Appendix V gives greater details for each species. Note that the most valuable outlets for large broadleaf trees are as veneer and saw planks. Veneer stems fetch the best prices but need to be of exceptional quality.

The most valuable specimens for planking have a long, 'clean' trunk with a minimum of knots, no forking or twisting, and a good, straight growth with a fairly uniform diameter which does not taper rapidly. The minimum length of this clean stem is 3–5m, and the longer the better. The yield of a tree is generally a measure of the volume of its stemwood, which includes any part of the trunk more than 7cm in diameter, or more specifically in broadleaf trees the stem to the point at which the trunk is no longer visible in the crown, and before it branches. To achieve a long, clean stem, the tree needs to grow among other trees: in competing to reach the light (which is the goal of any woodland tree) it will have concentrated its energies in growing upwards rather than expanding its trunk and branching out in all directions like a parkland tree.

The big, old parkland oaks with their massive, squat trunks and huge crowns are not much good for sawn timber but they could be valuable sources of veneer. A good veneer specimen has a substantial and consistently fat butt. A large diameter is much more important than length of stem – though there is a minimum acceptable length of, say, 2.2m – but quality is even more important than bulk. The veneer buyer looks for an attractive grain, especially in the decorative woods like walnut and yew. If your parkland or hedgerow tree has ever been used as a fencing post, the nails and staples driven into it

Table 4

COMMERCIAL TIMBER

MAIN COMMERCIAL MARKETS

In order of quality/value, starting with the best:

Veneer Especially oak, cherry, walnut, other hardwoods, yew

Saw planks Timber stored and seasoned by sawmills for sale to manufacturers of furniture, building materials, etc. Hardwoods and softwoods, but only the highest quality for joinery and turnery

Sawn fencing Especially oak, chestnut, treated softwoods (panels, feather-edge, palisades, posts, etc.)

Chipping wood For chipboard, etc. – quality less important than bulk of supply; hardwoods and softwoods

Pulpwood Hardwoods for cardboard, softwoods for paper (major demand is for newsprint, especially white-wooded spruces) – quality even less important than for chipping, but this is a mass-market business and bulk is important

Firewood Sold locally either to merchants or direct to public; mostly hardwoods from thinnings or lop-and-top or coppice – opportunity for 'added value' crop if you cut logs to size, split if necessary, and season before selling to individual customers

MAIN HARDWOODS	MAIN SOFTWOODS
Ash	**Douglas fir**
Beech	**Sitka spruce**
Birch	**Norway spruce**
Cherry	**Larches**
Oak	**Scots pine**
Poplar	**Corsican pine**
Sweet chestnut	
Sycamore	
Walnut	

years ago by a thoughtless farmer will immediately detract from its value, as they will in the case of a planking stem. Not only will the scrap metal have been engulfed by subsequent annual rings so that the chainsaw will unsuspectingly come to grief during the felling (even worse if barbed-wire has been swallowed into the tree) but there is also every likelihood of such wounds, and other wounds caused by livestock and careless use of machinery, having become infected and letting rot into the stem. For these reasons, most timber buyers will automatically reject the lower 1.5m of a hedgerow tree.

Whether or not it will be worth trying to sell isolated specimens of these hardwood trees depends on factors like their individual value, accessibility and the degree of interest of a local buyer. If you have a really superb veneer log, or if you can combine with neighbouring woodland owners to offer a large enough volume of timber in one package, your chances of finding a buyer are much higher.

Your consultant will advise on such marketing factors and will also provide a time-scale. It might be that some specimens are already overmature, or that some are mature enough for immediate felling, which you can only regard as a bonus. There may be other trees which are worth encouraging to maturity and which need only sensible management to enhance their development for harvesting in the years to come.

That is where you come face to face with the fact that trees are for the future. Any landowner involved with trees needs to be concerned with coming generations more than the present one. In its diamond jubilee publication, *Trees: Sixty Years Towards the Future*, published in 1982 – sadly, in the year of the death of its founder, Dr Richard St Barbe Baker ('St Barbe'), at the age of ninety-two – that unique organisation, the Men of Trees, printed the stories of several inspirationally altruistic tree-planters. St Barbe had founded his dream with the help of Chief Josiah Njonjo at Muguga in the Kenyan highlands, an area then too close to the encroaching Sahara Desert. The little book told of Elzeard Bouffier, a shepherd in Provence, who always carried an iron rod and a sack of carefully chosen acorns which he planted wherever he and his flock roamed. In the three years before the First World War he planted a hundred thousand oaks, expecting ten thousand of them to sprout and survive the ravages of rodents. A land previously barren of trees became what everyone believed was a natural forest (Bouffier was a solitary man who did not boast of his plantings) which ultimately proved of great benefit to the valleys below.

Softwoods

Softwoods (essentially coniferous species) are the backbone of commercial forestry. They grow fast, they grow close together, they grow almost anywhere; and their timber is much in demand for general building, joinery, fencing, propping, a wide range of particle boards and, of course, enormous mountains of paper pulp.

No farmer, and certainly no smallholder, can hope to compete with the commercial softwood growers and any conifers you do find during assessment are unlikely to be of much value on the market, though there will always be uses for them at home. However, if you have a genuine plantation of conifers, seek advice on their degree of maturity and the best methods of managing the crop until it can be harvested. In the meantime you will be able to take thinnings at intervals to help cashflow as well as to improve the final crop.

WINDBLOWN TREES

The 1987 storm blew down more than fifteen million trees in England and an estimated four million cubic metres of timber in the south. A lot of the trees were in small woodlands or scattered here and there in hedgerows, gardens, town streets and parks. Half the volume was broadleaf and suddenly there was a huge amount of windblown timber lying around the countryside, and no one knew quite what to do with it. Those few violent hours had felled the equivalent of about a third of the normal entire annual production for the whole of Great Britain. The most abundant casualties were pines (1.25 million cubic metres) and beech (0.7 million cubic metres) – not the kind of trees that can be left until there is more time to handle them and a reasonable market for the wood. Snapped or bark-torn pine, for example, rapidly submits to fungal attack and staining, and the white wood of beech is soon stained as well.

The Forestry Commission quickly set up a Windblow Committee and produced guidelines for dealing with these trees. The broad principles are set out below not in the expectation of another catastrophe on such a scale but as sensible advice for dealing with occasional storm damage and also as an excellent management plan for taking in hand any kind of neglected woodland.

(a) *Carry out a survey and assess the damage*
Timber markets and prices are affected by the species of tree, its size and its timber quality. Use a large-scale map (1:10,000) to illustrate the areas to be managed, dividing larger areas into units if necessary, then assess the volume of windblown trees in each area or unit. Calculate each species in each area separately.

(b) *Decide on priorities*
Priority emergency clearance should be given to species which, because they are susceptible to attack by fungi and insects, degrade relatively quickly after being blown. Their timber becomes increasingly difficult to market as it develops staining and decay. However, if the roots or part of the root system remain in the ground, a tree will still live, and the greater the proportion of root in ground contact, the longer its prospective life and the more likely it is to resist insects and fungi for perhaps a year or more.

The more valuable timber is also a priority in a windblow situation: the fresher it is sold, the better it retains its value. But against this you need to set the state of the market. In the winter of 1987 it was,

Table 5

PRIORITIES FOR REMOVAL OF WINDBLOWN TREES

1 Clear any road blocks, threats to power lines or property, or other dangers to public.
2 Clear broken or shattered trees.
3 Clear uprooted but largely intact trees with their roots still in some contact with the soil.

PRIORITY BY SPECIES

1 **Pine** (likely to harbour insects and suffer from staining very quickly):
(a) Clear those with high proportion of snapped stems first.
(b) Then clear other pine.

2 **Beech** (also suffers from stain): clear after pines.

3 Then clear any other species with a high proportion of snapped stems, concentrating first on pale-wooded hardwoods:
sycamore, poplar, ash, lime, plane, birch.

4 Next, clear the conifers:
(a) **Spruces** and **silver firs.**
(b) **Douglas fir, western hemlock.**
(c) **Larches.**

5 Finally, clear the three most durable hardwoods, which can be left for up to five years if intact:
Sweet chestnut, oak, yew.

of course, saturated and it was sensible to defer trying to sell good timber if its value could reasonably be expected to last a while. For example, it is possible that blown oak or sweet chestnut would remain saleable for up to perhaps four or five years, whereas 'white' hardwoods like beech, ash and sycamore have a much shorter market life, even if they still have some roots intact. On the other hand, if you have quite a lot of mixed trees to shift, you might find a better market for a 'job lot' clearance all in one rather than keeping the best separate. Remember that 'the best' is the biggest and straightest – long, clean, straight stems with the largest possible diameter. The FC booklet *Guidelines for Dealing with Windblow in Woodlands* suggests ways of minimising the degradation of windblown timber in its appendices.

The timing of extraction of timber will of course depend to some extent on ground conditions. Other site factors affecting the timing include the likelihood of damage to natural regeneration, if that is something you wish to encourage, and other uses for the woodland such as the remunerative letting of sporting rights.

GUIDE TO PERISHABLE AND DURABLE SPECIES

(Based on heartwood being in contact with damp soil and remaining free from visible rot. Note that the major types of degradation are from stain, rot and insect damage.)

PERISHABLE (will probably degrade within twelve months):

Alder	Holly	Plane
Ash	Hornbeam	Poplar
Beech	Horse chestnut	Sycamore
Birch	Lime	Willow

NON-DURABLE (rot appears in less than two years):

Apple	Douglas fir	Corsican pine
Elm	Noble fir	Lodgepole pine
Red oak	Norway spruce	Scots pine
	Sitka spruce	

MODERATELY DURABLE (rot-free for up to five years):

Cherry	Larch
Turkey oak	Lawson cypress
Walnut	Western red cedar

DURABLE (can be rot-free for more than five years):

Sweet chestnut	Yew
Oak (sessile and pedunculate)	

There is also the conservation angle to be considered, in the interests of which there is quite a strong case for leaving some of the fallen trees where they lie. A fallen tree is not necessarily a dead tree and two years after the October storm many trees are still living, though flat on their backs or snapped in two – they are reacting as if coppiced, pollarded or layered, and sending up new shoots. Appearances can be deceptive, however: in the summer of 1988 some trees which were prone but still had roots in the ground sprung into a magnificent burst of leaves and flowers in the spring but the new growth withered and died later. Even so, a large fallen tree can be of considerable benefit to wildlife. First of all, its fall creates a gap in the woodland canopy which lets in the light and creates a glade for butterflies, while encouraging the growth of young trees and ground flora like bluebells and primroses. The fallen crown gives cover to nesting birds and small animals; the prone trunk is a hibernation site for reptiles, amphibians and hedgehogs; a large, dead limb can be colonised by fungi and insects which are food for other creatures; and the uprooting creates a damp, sheltered cavity which can be a habitat for moisture-loving plants and shelter for animals like deer, foxes and badgers.

Then you must consider the obligations you should fulfil before removing the timber. Statutory obligations may include the need for a felling licence, respecting Tree Preservation Orders (TPOs) and Sites of Special Scientific Interest (SSSIs) and keeping open public rights of way. There is also the question of commonsense obligations to neighbours and tenants who might be affected by the taking out of the timber or by obstruction from windblown trees.

(c) *Harvesting*
The principles and practice of harvesting timber are outlined in Chapter III. There is a choice of selling the trees as they lie (or standing, if some have been damaged or made dangerous by the collapse of their neighbours) or from a collection point where they have already been trimmed and properly stacked either by a contractor or by yourself if you have the heavy equipment and skill needed – but take great care: hung-up trees can be very dangerous, and windthrown trees under tension could whiplash unexpectedly when they are cut. You might prefer to store the extracted timber somewhere until the markets improve, but storage and seasoning require space and expertise.

(d) *Restocking*
Do not panic. A lot of people rushed into replanting after the storm, making the most of the numerous offers of financial help thrust upon them by councils and conservation groups, but with trees you should always take plenty of time to consider before you act. Take years if necessary. Remember the bitter little rhyme from the 1970s:

> Plant a tree in '73;
> Plant some more in '74;
> Few alive in '75;
> All dry sticks in '76.

In the meantime, read one of the books by that famous woodland historian and philosopher, Oliver Rackham, just to get a sense of perspective. Then, looking well ahead, consider the extraordinary possibilities of the 'greenhouse effect' which, some predict, could give Britain such a warm climate by 2030 that spruce plantations on today's cold Scottish uplands will not be able to thrive. It might already be time to start searching for new species from more southerly lands. The forester's problem has always been one of prediction, though usually of social factors affecting future markets rather than dramatic changes of climate.

UNCOMMERCIAL WOODLAND

If your site has little of commercial value in the way of good timber trees, you have plenty of options – depending partly on your philosophies and partly on your pocket. Your consultant, if a forester, will probably suggest clear-felling the lot, stacking it up as firewood (which you can use yourself or sell when it is seasoned) and then replanting to take advantage of any grants which might be available. Note that most of the grant schemes are applicable only to blocks of replanting, generally in areas of at least 0.2ha, so that you might not receive aid if you decide to take out a few trees here and there and then replant the gaps, a system known as 'enrichment'.

However, if you are not desperate for grant aid it could be sound practice to let in the light judiciously, in order to give existing trees a better chance, to encourage the understorey and natural regeneration, and to provide a better habitat for a wider variety of life.

For a replanting scheme it will be necessary to destroy all the old stumps. In theory you could do that mechanically, ripping them out or even blowing them out with explosives, but in practice most people use the easier option of chemical stump-killers. If the stumps are not destroyed, they will regenerate into a thicket of coppice regrowth and that might or might not suit your purposes, depending on the species. For a piece of woodland which you want for firewood, or a fairly pure stand of a practical species like sweet chestnut or ash, creating a coppice could be just the answer. Other alternatives include less commercial approaches such as using woodland for conservation, or indirectly commercial enterprises like letting the area to a shoot.

Some woodlands are worse than neglected: they are effectively derelict. These are areas which have been clear-felled in the past and then left with little or no management to regenerate as they will – which tends to be as scrubland. The prospects for such areas are daunting: you will need to put in quite a lot of money, a lot of work and a lot of time to train them into something that you can justly call woodland, and it might be better to turn them into conservation areas, applying only the most gentle management techniques.

III

MANAGEMENT TECHNIQUES

Neglected woodland has been described as an overgrown wood, overstocked with poor-looking trees that have not been thinned, so that their canopy denies light to most species of ground flora but does not deter what a forester would call weed species – like birch, the great opportunist which was one of the first to invade the clean, bare aftermath of the retreating glaciers at the end of the last Ice Age.

Neglected woodland, unlike derelict woodland, can be rescued but it takes time, good planning and skilled labour. The techniques include judicious thinning to let the better specimens breathe and grow, the removal of unwanted species, a planned felling programme stretching over many years, and all possible methods of invigorating the area which might include, for example, a thorough overhaul of the drainage channels.

A generation ago men like C. P. Ackers, at Huntley in Gloucester, and the unique Wilfred Hiley at Dartington with the support of those famous original thinkers Dorothy and Leonard Elmhirst and the Dartington Hall Trustees, were practising 'opportunist' forestry. This involved the cultivation and nurturing of natural seedlings, suckers and coppice shoots in order to reduce planting costs, with the use of shade-tolerant species for underplanting and enrichment, and the full utilisation and intensive marketing of 'irregular' opportunist thinnings of the crop, even where the aim was a profitable final crop. For example, you might have a woodland containing patches of hazel coppice for pea-sticks and bean-poles sold locally, with birch supplying nearby turneries, short-rotation poplars, ash high forest for cleft stakes, rails and tent pegs, some sweet chestnut coppice for fencing and a limited lime coppice for propping up clothes-lines and fruit trees and for making handles for the besom brooms created from birch brushwood. On top of that there could be a small outlet in Christmas trees, foliage for florists and sporting rights. The keys to the whole system are diversity, imagination and marketing – that is, opportunism. The tradition continues today: look at John Makepeace's marvellous ideas in the setting of Parnham House at Beaminster, Dorset (which he bought in 1976), and his new school for craftsmen in wood at Hooke Park a few miles away. Makepeace has a vision: he is a furniture maker but he also seeks to revitalise the British timber industry not only by creating furniture and training craftsmen but also by growing trees himself and finding new uses for 'waste' timber like small-diameter roundwood. Go to Dorset if you seek inspiration!

Creativity apart, there is plenty of hard work in managing woodland on any scale. Whatever that scale, and whatever the situation, here are some of the basic techniques you will probably need.

CLEANING

If you want to give some promising individual trees or stands of trees the chance to grow well, you can help them by cleaning their immediate environment of unwanted and competing growth. This usually consists of climbers like woodbine (honeysuckle) or old man's beard, or the regrowth of coppice shoots which sprout so fast that they quickly outgrow everything in sight, or the saplings of invasive woody weed species such as elder, willow, birch, thorn and rhododendron. Some of these can be tackled with slasher and saw but others are very persistent and will need either chemical treatment or rooting out. (Rhododendron is particularly awkward in woodland.) However, before you get carried away with clearing, think about the wildlife. A fairly messy-looking patch of woodland often offers more niches than a tidy one for wild creatures of all kinds.

BRASHING

Young woodland is typically thickety; brashing means in effect pruning – it involves removing the lower branches. It is more often done for convenience than to promote good growth: it gives you access and a better view of the situation, and it also reduces the risk of fire. A stand of conifers might be brashed when the trees are perhaps 7–8m tall, and all the twiggery is removed up to about head height on each trunk, leaving them nice and clean. Some people brash when the trees are perhaps only half this height. If you want to encourage a clean hardwood stem, you need to deprive it of its lower branches and sproutings before they get a chance to reach any size. The earlier you prune them, the smaller their diameter and the smaller the resulting scar; the tree's subsequent annual rings will grow over the scar in due course, and it will become a knot within the grain of the timber. Use a curved pruning saw for the job, which is almost impossible to mechanise and is therefore often ignored. In due course the canopy closing above the trees shades out the side growths so that they will die off naturally if the planting is close enough. There is no need to paint the small wounds caused by brashing with Stockholm tar or other compounds: they will heal much better of their own accord by the natural formation of callus.

THINNING

Thinning is a major factor in helping potentially good trees in a neglected wood to achieve that potential. A tree can readily be restricted in its crown or even killed by too vigorous a neighbour taking all its light, and the first thinning is generally taken when the trees close the woodland canopy. In general you might take your first thinnings from a conifer crop when it reaches twenty to twenty-five years of age and thin thereafter every five or six years; and from hardwood perhaps the first thinnings at thirty to thirty-five years old; but it will depend on the initial spacing at planting, and you will also have to exercise your own judgement in the case of mixed woodland and in the light of your ultimate aims and philosophies.

The first thinnings will probably be good only for firewood, though second thinnings might be quite marketable. Be reasonably methodical: use a dash of tree paint to mark the most useless trees – those that are diseased, dying, damaged, growing very close to each other, poorly shaped or (if you are aiming for good long timber stems) forked, twisted or knotted. Felling might be difficult as there might be very little room in which to operate and you also need to plan how the felled trees are going to be removed without making a filthy mess of the site. This is where a good heavy horse comes into its own.

Be judicious in your thinning. If trees have been growing fairly close together all their life, those that remain after thinning could miss the physical support of their neighbours and begin to bend over or even be uprooted or snapped off by the first puff of wind. They could also suffer from bark scorch because of their sudden exposure to the elements, and indeed if the bark of a clean stem is freshly exposed to light its dormant adventitious buds will suddenly start sprouting lots of little whiskery shoots (known as epicormic growth) which need to be shaved off unless you are specialising in burred oak.

If you are dealing with areas of considerable natural regeneration, where you decide to retain a percentage of the young volunteers but to thin out the rest in order to give the chosen few a better chance, you will probably find that the new isolation of the latter draws the attention of browsing predators like deer so that the young trees might need individual protection. Clearance which opens the canopy in a young plantation could also encourage plenty of unwanted weed growth: light is the great stimulant.

Another type of thinning is group felling, which is taking out a patch of trees completely here and there to let in the light and allow enrichment of the wood by small group plantings or natural regeneration. Each group will probably cover perhaps 0.1–0.3ha and the fellings can be progressive, opening up new areas perhaps every five years or so.

ENRICHMENT

'Enrichment' is filling in gaps with new plants. You might want to plant up the odd gap in the wood, either a natural glade or a patch left after group felling or windblow. As a rule of thumb, it is not even worth trying to replant a gap unless its diameter is greater than one and a half times the height of immediately surrounding trees, because there will be far too much competition for the young plants to survive and thrive.

Even if the gap is nominally big enough, avoid planting at its edges: leave an empty fringe equivalent to at least half the height of the encircling trees. Thereafter keep a careful eye on the young trees to ensure that they always have some open sky above them – and that will probably mean thinning out some fringe trees in due course.

CONVERSION OF COPPICE

God bless the man who first realised that a felled broadleaf tree was not a dead one but that its stump could throw up a multitude of new stems which, properly managed, were a bounty of great richness!

A close look at many neglected patches of woodland often reveals that the area was originally a methodically cropped coppice; that is to say, a single plant was encouraged, by cyclical cropping, to produce continual multiple flushes of new stems which could be harvested again at regular intervals and put to endless practical uses – fencing, firewood, tool handles, tanning bark, charcoal and heaven knows what else. Instead of waiting a whole lifetime or more to harvest one stem of timber, the tree's exploiter could chop off a walking-stick or a bean-pole within three years or let the multiple stems grow for five or six times as long to produce fencing posts time and time again, and all without having to replant new trees.

All broadleaf species can in theory be coppiced and even a long-neglected coppice can be restored to production if it has been worked at some stage in the last few decades (say, thirty years for hazel; at least twice as long for other species). This kind of renovation brings quick returns and, with careful rotation, does not disrupt the overall environment in the way that clear-felling and replanting does. Alternatively, some of the stools (the coppice stumps) could be converted into timber trees by thinning out all but one straight, strong stem on each stump and leaving it to grow on as a single tree.

FELLING

Do not be tempted to do your own felling unless you have the equipment (including safety equipment) and the expertise. You can get appropriate FC training through your local agricultural training board – and for your own sake you really must, especially for trees of large enough diameter to require a chainsaw.

There is an excellent series of handbooks published by the British Trust for Conservation Volunteers which describe in step-by-step detail the techniques for every possible kind of labour their volunteers are likely to undertake, including how a team should set about minor fellings. Here are some of the points to be borne in mind.

Fell in winter – from October to March – whether you are thinning or taking a final crop or clearing old woodland. If you are dealing with useful timber, this winter timing is especially important. In summer, a tree's sapwood is full of sap: the higher the ambient temperature, the greater the tree's transpiration through its foliage, and that draws up the sap through the tree by capillary action. Sap is an ideal sugar-and-starch medium for fungi, so that timber cut when full of sap will be wide open to infection by fungi and thus to rot in due course. In winter, with lower temperatures and (in deciduous species) no foliage, there is less transpiration and therefore no rising sap. The less sappy the wood, the easier it is to handle (though not necessarily easier to cut) and the sooner it will season.

Another major reason for cutting in winter is that you can see what you are doing. Most of the undergrowth has died down; and deciduous trees have shed their leaves, which makes them much less cumbersome. The drawback is that the ground is likely to be wetter, and if the site tends to be damp it is best to time the felling for late summer or early autumn. If the area is important to wildlife, time your felling to cause minimum disturbance to the wood's residents: bear in mind in this context that bats often overwinter in hollow trees and hedgehogs and some other creatures hibernate in secret places, but for most other wildlife winter is probably the best time for disturbance, if disturbance there must be, because the mating and rearing seasons are over for the year and any fruit and nuts will already have fallen or been devoured or stored.

Clear any undergrowth around the trees and along the extraction route before starting felling work, and plan your escape route before you tackle individual trees. Work out exactly where you want them to drop and look out for hung-up trees and large branches nearby which might be dislodged by the felling. Estimate the full length of the tree and beware of letting it drop over impediments like stumps, boulders or lying trees: it will kick back and break either its own back or yours. Obviously watch out for power-lines, buildings, valuable trees and so on; tell the electricity board if you do have to fell near one of their lines – they might arrange to switch off the supply in the meantime.

Bear in mind that felling causes profound physical and chemical changes in the environment, especially if done on a very large scale where it could lead to soil erosion and rapid fluctuations in water-table levels, with effects a long way downstream from the site. On any scale felling dramatically alters the immediate habitat for flora and fauna, and you will find that many people are angered by felling, however minor and however necessary, simply because they do not like a change in a familiar landscape. Check whether or not you need a felling licence and whether there are any tree preservation orders or other legal restrictions (see Appendix III).

MEASURING AND MARKETING
Note that the FC uses metric measurements but many other people, especially those dealing with coppice and broadleaf trees, continue to think in imperial units.

How to Measure Diameter at Breast Height (DBH)
To measure the DBH of a tree, use a pole 1.3m long. Hold the pole vertically against the trunk with one end resting on the ground, then measure the circumference of the tree where the upper end of the pole touches it. To measure the circumference, use a forester's girth tape, which allows you to read the diameter directly and saves you having to work it out with the formula $2\pi r$. If the tree is on a slope, measure the DBH from the upper side of the trunk.

How to Measure Windblown or Felled Stems
To measure windblown or felled stems for the market, you need to know that high-quality timber is priced by volume, and low-quality by tonnage. For good timber trees, measure each log separately:

Length (L): Measure a conifer from its base to the point where its overbark diameter is 7cm.
Measure a broadleaf from its base to where the main stem branches into forkwood and becomes indistinguishable. In each case, measure to the nearest 0.1m for stems up to 10m long, or to the nearest metre for longer stems.

Diameter (D): You need the average diameter – that is, the over-bark diameter at the midpoint of the timber length L. Measure the diameter to the nearest centimetre.

Volume (V): The volume, in cubic metres, equals the square of the diameter in centimetres, multiplied by the length in metres, multiplied by a factor (0.0000785) – that is:

$$V = D^2 \times L \times 0.0000785$$

There are published mensuration tables to help with these calculations. Some broadleaf trees are still measured imperially in hoppus feet, which are larger than cubic feet (1 hoppus foot = 1.27 cubic feet; see Appendix IV).

It is worth measuring all individual trees with a DBH greater than 30cm one by one, but in the case of smaller trees just measure a representative sample.

How to Estimate the Full Height of a Standing Tree
(a) Ask someone of known height to stand next to the trunk, or put a measured pole against it, then stand well away and use your eye to estimate how many times taller the tree is than the person or pole.

(b) Stand a vertical pole of known height some distance from the tree. Visually align the top of the pole with the top of the tree. (In theory, you should lie flat on your stomach so that your eye is more or less at ground level!) The height of the tree is equal to the height of the pole multiplied by the distance from your eye to the tree's base, divided by the distance from your eye to the base of the pole. For greater accuracy, use a 45-degree hypsometer and a touch of trigonometry, or for a rough calculation use the simple pencil method shown in Figure 1.

Calculating Weight
Fresh-felled timber weighs approximately a tonne to the cubic metre, reducing to a tonne to 1.2–2m as it dries out – see Table 20 on page 93 for more details.

Standing Crops
If you are trying to sell a standing crop, bear the following points in mind:

Conifers will be readily saleable as sawlogs in parcels with a mean DBH greater than 16cm, or for pulpwood and stakes (at lower prices) at more than 12cm, unless you have a particularly good local market for smaller stems. Individual trees need a diameter of 18–30cm to be considered for sawlogs. A 'log' is generally over 18cm in diameter; less than that and it is 'small roundwood' (down to a minimum of 7cm diameter overbark), which is generally too small for sawmills.

Broadleaves need to be more than 30cm for sawlogs, or 12–30cm

Figure 1: Estimation of tree height

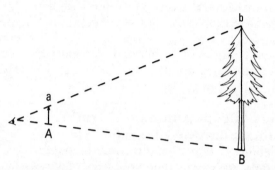

(i) Hold a pencil vertically at eye-level so that the tip of the pencil (a) aligns with the top of the tree (b), and the base of the pencil (A) with the base of the tree (B).

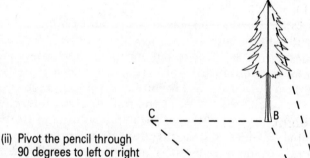

(ii) Pivot the pencil through 90 degrees to left or right so that it is horizontal, keeping its base (A) at the same point, i.e. aligned with the tree base (B).

Make a visual note of the point (C) at which the pencil tip corresponds to a point in a parallel plane horizontally from the tree base. This is where the top (b) of the tree would reach if the tree is felled in that plane. The distance BC is roughly equal to the full height (Bb) of the standing tree and can be measured on the ground.

as firewood. Individual trees should have a diameter of perhaps 45–60cm to be considered for sawlogs or veneer, and oak should be even larger for veneer.

Parcels of less than 100 cubic metres are less valuable because of the purchaser's setting-up costs, and if they are less than 50 cubic metres – forget it! Alternatively, combine with a neighbouring producer to present a more substantial parcel. Timber merchants are mostly interested in bulk quantities of uniform trees; contractors need expensive equipment to fell and transport trees large enough for the timber market and will naturally charge you at a higher rate the lower the volume of timber involved.

Other Factors Affecting the Sale of Timber

Apart from the size, species, age and condition of the log and the volume available, other factors affecting the potential sale of timber include the ease of extraction: you need a good road and hard standing for a loading lorry, for example. You have an advantage if the woodland is reasonably close to, say, a fencing treatment plant, a sawmill, a pulp mill, a chipboard mill or other local industries, but bulk is what most of them look for and you might do better to create your own market – perhaps working up the raw material yourself in some way.

You also need expertise to select the right trees for felling, and to harvest at the right moment, and to find the right market and price – expertise which, if you need to pay for it, always comes more expensively for smaller volumes. If you are fairly near a port, you might be fairly near a pulp mill, and if you have a silver tongue you might be able to persuade the buyer at the mill to give you a bulk quota, as long as you can guarantee a reasonable volume of timber *regularly*. 'Reasonable' depends on the buyer's definition of the word, but is likely to be substantially more than small farms, smallholders or even co-operatives of smallholders can produce. However, it is worth finding out about the FC's joint tender scheme with Timber Growers UK Ltd (TGUK; see Appendix II for the address) and it is also worth talking to a group like the National Farmers Union (NFU) or your local Ministry of Agriculture (MAFF) adviser: increasing numbers of farmers are turning their attention to productive woodlands, and there are more and more opportunities for co-operative marketing.

IV

NEW WOODS

They say that a forestry 'year' is a five-year cell and that the forester's vision is fifty or a hundred years. Don't let that put you off planting new trees, even if you are pessimistic enough to believe that the living world could be wiped out by nuclear warfare or pollution or some other man-made catastrophe before your grandchildren have a chance to reap the rewards (financial, practical or sensual) from your foresight in planting for future generations.

Should your motives be less altruistic or you do not have that typical human urge to perpetuate your own brief life by living on as a memory in a forest, there are trees you can plant which will give a relatively immediate return and will continue to do so at intervals over the years. However, not all these options will be open simply because they appeal, nor is it always better to plant from scratch. You must make a careful assessment of your objectives, then you need an equally diligent assessment of the potential site. If you are interested in serious forestry, get a copy of the 1:250,000 soil maps and reports of the soil survey of England and Wales or of Scotland.

Next is the question of what to plant. Table 7 gives guidance on the soils most favourable to various species of tree, but it is only guidance: some species are tolerant of a wide range of conditions, and some fail where in theory they should thrive. Quite apart from the species, you also need to consider the race within the species, and the provenance of the plant – that is, where its parents came from. Appendix V gives more detailed information about different species.

Native species generally look better in the landscape, though they will not necessarily have the practical or commercial advantage over introduced species. However, they certainly support a much richer natural fauna, and this variety will be even greater if monoculture is avoided. Table 8 shows which species are the true natives that established themselves after the last Ice Age (nine or ten thousand years ago) but before the erosion of the cross-Channel landbridge (five thousand years ago), either by natural migration or as a result of introduction by migrating tribes. Many more species were introduced in very early times, well before the Romans (who also brought new species), for fruit and cattle fodder. From then until

Table 6

FACTORS TO CONSIDER WHEN CHOOSING A SITE FOR A NEW WOOD

Soil Texture, pH, drainage, subsoil

Rainfall Broadleaf species not particularly affected but conifers strongly influenced

Altitude Affects economic productivity

Latitude Many species are at extreme of their range in Britain; some will not grow well further north. Summer warmth is necessary to several species: for example, sweet chestnut, walnut, black poplar – confine to south

Exposure Only a few species are suitable for maritime areas or other very exposed situations; also, trees on the edge of a wood or plantation do not grow as fast or produce as acceptable timber stems as those sheltered within the wood – they tend to be shorter and more branched

Winter cold/duration Restricts planting of several species: for example, eucalypts and southern beech. Some species very hardy and frost-tolerant: for instance, Norway spruce, alder. Could mix more vulnerable broadleaves in a nurse crop of conifers. Spring frost can be dangerous until young trees are well established; avoid frost pockets

Existing species Useful guide to what grows well locally

Terrain Accessibility for maintenance, harvesting, extraction – the more difficult the terrain, the greater the deterrent to regular management, and could also seriously affect sale of standing crops; steep slopes or very boggy land create special problems at harvest; consider aspect of slope also

about 1600 there was a steady trickle of introductions which are by now so well established that they hardly count as aliens.

After 1600 written records help identify new introductions and the seventeenth and eighteenth centuries saw a flood of them from North America, the Mediterranean and the Far East. In the nineteenth century it was the turn of conifers from all over the world and also increasingly exotic species from Japan and China. The diversity of our trees would be rather restricted if the population were limited to the original natives.

It can be seen from the table that we have very few native coniferous species (only Scots pine, juniper and yew) and this is perhaps one of the reasons why conifers tend to jar in the landscape when they are introduced as fast-growing commercial crops. Another problem is that individual conifers have an exceptionally uniform

Table 7
SOIL TYPES PREFERRED BY VARIOUS TREE SPECIES

HARDWOOD SPECIES	CHALK	CLAY	SAND	PEAT	UPLAND	COAST	DAMP
Alder, common		✓		✓	✓		✓
Alder, grey		✓	✓				✓
Alder, Italian	✓						
Ash (very fussy)	✓	✓				✓	(✓)
Beech (mild, sunny site)	✓		✓		✓		
Birch			✓	✓	✓		
Cherry	✓	✓		✓			
Hazel		✓	✓				
Holly	✓	✓	✓				
Hornbeam	✓	✓	✓				(✓)
Horse chestnut		✓	✓				
Lime (high pH)	✓	✓	(✓)				
Maple	(✓)	✓				✓	
Oak		✓	✓			✓	✓
Poplars (fussy)		✓	✓			✓	✓
Southern beech (sheltered site)		✓	✓				
Sweet chestnut (southern Britain)		✓	✓				
Sycamore	✓	✓		✓	✓	✓	
Walnut (southern Britain)		✓					
Willows		✓		✓	✓	✓	✓

SOFTWOOD SPECIES	CHALK	CLAY	SAND	PEAT	UPLAND	COAST	DAMP
Cypress, Lawson		✓					
Fir, Douglas (well drained site)		✓	✓	✓	✓		
Fir, grand (sheltered site)		✓					
Fir, noble		✓			✓		
Larches (annual rainfall >750mm)	✓	✓	✓	✓	✓		
Pine, Corsican	✓	✓	✓	✓		✓	
Pine, lodgepole (north and western Britain)			✓	✓	✓		
Pine, Scots			✓				
Spruce, Norway	✓	✓		✓	✓		✓
Spruce, Sitka (northern and western Britain)		✓			✓		✓
Western hemlock (shady site)				✓	✓		
Western red cedar (southern and western Britain)	✓	✓			✓		
Yew	✓	✓	✓				

Table 8
SPECIES OF TREES FOUND IN BRITAIN

Species are listed in their likely order of arrival in Britain.
Latin names are given in Appendix V.

TRUE NATIVES

Common juniper	Common oak	Midland thorn
Downy birch	Wych elm	Crab apple
Silver birch	Rowan	Wild cherry
Aspen	Sessile oak	Strawberry tree
Scots pine	Ash	White willow
Bay willow	Holly	Field maple
Common alder	Hawthorn	Wild service tree
Hazel	Crack willow	Large-leafed lime
Small-leafed lime	Black poplar	Beech
Bird cherry	Yew	Hornbeam
Goat willow	Whitebeam	Box

INTRODUCTIONS BEFORE 1600 AD

VERY EARLY	PRE-ROMAN
True service tree	English elm
White poplar	Smooth-leafed elm
Grey poplar	Cornish elm
Medlar	Plot's elm
Wild pear	Walnut
Almond	
Myrobalan plum	
Peach	ROMAN
	Sweet chestnut
	Swedish whitebeam
	Sycamore

pattern of growth, exaggerated by the way in which they have been planted in massive, rigid, monotypic blocks that are quite alien to the surrounding countryside. There are also other problems with these species: for example, they tend to dry out soils; their acid needle-litter can have an adverse effect on water quality; and they are often so closely planted that there is no other life at all at ground level beneath their cathedral-like, columned gloom. Even the FC has in recent years begun to encourage the retention and planting

c. 1500	1500–99	
Holm oak	Common laburnum (1560)	Scotch laburnum (1596)
Maritime pine	Bay (1562)	White mulberry (1596)
Stone pine	Cherry laurel (1576)	Oleaster (1597)
Mulberry	Turkish hazel (1582)	Judas tree (pre-1600)
Norway spruce	Eastern balsam poplar (1589)	
Italian cypress		
Oriental plane		

INTRODUCTIONS SINCE 1600 AD

c. 1600 Common lime	1681 Sweetgum	1753 Pagoda tree
1603 Common silver fir	*c.* 1685 London plane	1754 Madenhair tree
1616 Horse chestnut	1691 Scarlet oak	(Ginkgo)
c. 1625 European larch	pre-1683 Norway maple	1758 Lombardy
1636 Locust tree	pre-1699 Cork oak	poplar
1639 Cedar of Lebanon	1724 Red oak	1759 Corsican pine
1640 Swamp cypress	1734 Bully Bay	1760 Zelkova
1650(?) Tulip tree	1735 Turkey oak	1780 Grey alder
1656 Red Maple	1751 Tree of heaven	1796 Chinese privet
		1797 Monkey puzzle

NINETEENTH-CENTURY INTRODUCTIONS

1827	Sugar pine, Western yellow pine, Douglas fir
1831–3	Grand fir, noble fir, Sitka spruce, Monterey pine, Digger pine, big-cone pine
1838	Monterey cypress (macrocarpa pine)
1843	Coast redwood
1850–4	A few Chinese species from treaty ports
1851–5	Many conifers from western American slopes
1853	Giant sequoia
1861	First major influx of Japanese plants
1878–90	Second Japanese influx (interior mountains)
1888	Chinese interior species (major influxes from central and western China 1901, 1907–8, 1910–35; Dawn redwood from central China discovered 1941, here by 1948)

of broadleaf woodland species rather than conifers, and it is also promoting the revival of coppicing in areas where this has been traditional.

Different conifer species grow in sheltered and exposed sites on the same soil, and broadleaves are suggested for sheltered sites only. Exposed sites are not necessarily on hillsides: think of the open, flat lands of East Anglia or coastal sites swept by salt-laden winds. If you are planting a shelter belt, clearly you must select species which are tough enough to become established in the face of the weather, or else you need a temporary windbreak to protect the plants for the first few years, but even then you should choose species which will be resistant to storm damage as they mature, or which are planted in such a condition that they can remain resistant. For example, if the soil cover is thin, the tree's root system will be shallow and the tree could be vulnerable, but in a perpetually exposed situation in the teeth of a prevailing wind the roots have an amazing capacity to develop in such a way that the tree is firmly anchored by great arms of roots which often arch right out of the ground on the windward side.

However, the depth of the root structure is determined above all by the water-table. A tree's roots would rot if it had its feet permanently in water, and thus the root system spreads above the level of the table, so that the system will be shallow if the table is high. If the table is under a layer of rock, the roots will penetrate down through any crack they can find, but they do so for the sake of water and not for the sake of keeping the tree stable. The feeding roots need to penetrate no further than the top few inches of soil for nutrients; it is water that is the controlling factor.

Incidentally, it is rarely necessary to apply artificial fertilisers to growing trees except in situations where nutrients are badly leached. In fact fertilisers are more likely to promote the growth of weeds than of trees, and if used near watercourses they could have a eutrophic effect, completely altering the balance of water life downstream. Some trees have root nodules, like clover and other legumes, which can fix their own nitrogen supply; these include alder, laburnum and robinia.

Then how about the drainage? Very often, areas are afforested because the soil is so wet that no other crops can be grown successfully. The great ancient Andreasweald forest of southern England grew its oaks on wealden clay so damp and heavy that for hundreds of generations humans did not even attempt to clear and cultivate the land or settle on it. That is not to say the oaks prefer wet land, simply that they can tolerate it. Other species are more fussy about drainage: sweet chestnut, for example, definitely dislikes damp conditions and is happier on well drained, fairly acid sandy soils.

Peaty soils are also poor-draining and in many places foresters use the trick of creating a drier microsite by planting on ridges or upturned turves. However, established trees are efficient drawers of water and can suck the impermeable soils so dry that the earth cracks open like the Dakota Badlands in miniature, and indeed tree-planting can help dry out the soil and reduce the level of the local water-table if desired. However, it is often necessary to allow some degree of water movement through the soil by cultivating compacted subsoils, and this can be a particular problem on those odd corners of a farm where trees are planted in awkward angles or on headlands where regular tractor-turning has created a pan. In such circumstances the subsoil should be thoroughly ripped before trees are planted, or they will fail.

Drainage is a complex subject, with ramifications of which you might be unaware. Always remember that, by interfering with an existing water system by digging or cleaning out drainage channels, you will affect an area considerably more extensive than the one you are managing, especially downstream.

Another negative reason for choosing to plant trees on a site is that the slope is too difficult for the annual management of food crops or pasture. In my own valley, for example, the slopes of the surrounding hangers are generally planted with sweet chestnut or conifers. This is not necessarily because the chestnut prefers the slopes (though it does like a southerly aspect into the sunshine) but because the nineteenth-century landowners could not think of anything else to put on them. And now, as the coppice craftsmen gradually age and their hand-tools are rejected by the mechanised younger generation, some of these coppice slopes are beginning to show signs of neglect. No one likes the hard work of felling and extracting from such sites; tractorwork is dangerous on the slopes, and the collecting lorries get themselves stuck in the clay tracks at the foot of the hangers. The situation is ripe for horsework but, shortsightedly perhaps, today's woodsmen consider that to be a backward step.

This little cameo serves to highlight the importance of the site's setting as well as its soil, drainage and degree of exposure. If you are growing any kind of crop, it requires management, even if as with trees that is a spasmodic activity in comparison with the annual cycle of grain-growing. The more difficult it is to get at the site, or to work on it, the more likely it is that it will be neglected. To some extent, that can be an advantage to wildlife, but even conservation areas need management if they are to remain as rich habitats.

The setting is part of the landscape, and that is a key feature too often overlooked. In the planning stages stand well back from the site – take a really long-distance view of it, from the neighbouring parish if possible, so that you can visualise the effect of any new planting on the general landscape. Then plant *with* the landscape rather than in defiance of it. New trees either blend and flow with the land, or they create new landscapes themselves. Follow the shape of the land: take photographs of the wide view and use overlays to get a better idea of how your plans will affect it, and remember the

Table 9

INDICATOR PLANT SPECIES IN ANCIENT WOODLANDS OF SOUTHERN ENGLAND*

TREES	SHRUBS	GRASSES
Aspen	Alder buckthorn	Wood barley
Wild cherry	Bilberry	Hairy brome
Crab apple	Blackcurrant	Bearded couch-grass
Wych elm	Butcher's broom	Giant fescue
Field maple	Redcurrant	Wood meadow-grass
Midland hawthorn	Field rose	Wood melick
Holly	Guelder rose	Wood millet
Hornbeam	Spurge laurel	Creeping soft-grass
Small-leaved lime		
Sessile oak		
Wild service tree		

FERNS	SEDGES	RUSHES
Hard fern	Pale sedge	Wood clubrush
Hard shield-fern	Pendulous sedge	Forster's woodrush
Hart's tongue	Remote sedge	Great woodrush
Lemon-scented fern	Smooth-stalked	Hairy woodrush
Polypody	sedge	
Soft shield-fern	Wood sedge	
Wood horsetail	Thin-spiked wood	
Oldest woods only:	sedge	
Narrow buckler-fern		
Scaly male-fern		

* The Nature Conservancy Council's 'South' region, which is effectively central southern

differences of winter and summer appearances. However small your plantation or group, do try to avoid a regimented shape. For ease of management you will probably plant in rows, but at least have the outline of the plantation pleasantly irregular rather than square. There are no straight lines in nature. Keep the whole feature in scale with its surroundings, neither overwhelming them nor stuck there like a ridiculous pimple.

ASSESSMENT

Looking more closely at the site itself, what grows there already? Cataloguing the resident species is an important part of your assessment. You should also check the history of the site, either from records or from observation.

Major sources of information on ancient woodlands and hedge-

FLOWERING PLANTS

Wood anemone	Pignut
Yellow archangel	Yellow pimpernel
Nettle-leaved bellflower	Primrose
Betony	Ramsons
Large bitter-cress	Three-nerved sandwort
Bluebell	Sanicle
Black bryony	Saw-wort
Columbine	Opposite-leaved
Common cow-wheat	golden saxifrage
Daffodil	Slender St John's wort
Early dog-violet	Solomon's seal
Wood everlasting pea	Wood sorrel
White climbing funitory	Wood speedwell
Long-leaved helleborine	Wood spurge
Narrow-lipped	Barren strawberry
helleborine	Small teasel
Purple helleborine	Toothwort
Herb paris	Tutsan
Stinking iris	Vetch (bitter, bush, wood)
Lily-of-the-valley	Marsh violet
Narrow-leaved lungwort	Water avens
Meadow saffron	Woodruff
Moschatel	Wood garlic
Bird's-nest orchid	Golden rod
Early purple orchid	Goldilocks
Great butterfly orchid	Broad helleborine
Orpine	Green hellebore

unties excluding the South-west and South-east and the Midlands.

rows are Saxon land charters, early maps at county records offices, and modern maps (especially the 1870 Ordnance Survey 1:10,000 series) for parish boundaries and old tracks. Place names can tell you plenty: for example, 'hurst' is early Saxon for a wood or wooded hill, and 'leah' is late Saxon for a glade, grove or light woodland, usually on the heavy clays. Look for old banks, ditches, earthworks, lynchets and burial mounds. The oldest woodbanks are big, broad and sinuous, while later ones are steep, narrow and straight. The scientific examination of pollen samples in peat and pond-mud can give an intriguing record of the types of trees which have grown on a site over the centuries, and the wild vegetation now growing there can also be a revealing indication of the area's history. Flowering plants, for example, colonise new woodland at different rates – some within decades, some not for many centuries even from adjacent woodland (oxlip has still not colonised medieval woods in some places) but the rate of colonisation varies according to region. Ask the Nature Conservancy Council or your county council's countryside department for a list of indicator species in your own region and then count how many different species are present in the wood. Most ancient woodlands have between fifteen and thirty indicator species and the richest sites have between forty-five and sixty-four. Table 9 gives a list of indicator species for ancient woodlands in southern England.

Look particularly at species growing in the surrounding area: they will give guidance on what does well locally according to soil, aspect, climate and so on. If the site or its immediate surroundings are bristling with thriving regenerative seedlings, clearly the conditions are good for that species, but it does not necessarily follow that those particular saplings should remain on the site. There might be genetic weaknesses in the local stock, for example.

SITE PREPARATION

There are many types of potential site for planting trees. In view of set-aside, the area might have been under cultivation for grain crops or pasture, in which case preparation is simple – use whatever means are suitable to destroy or subdue weeds and grass. You might be trying to reclaim scrubland or wasteland, which is more difficult, or, very typically, a site will have been clear-felled of a previous tree crop and will be full of fresh stumps, some of them already sprouting with coppice regrowth and probably bestrewn with lop-and-top. Sort out the lop-and-top: reclaim the firewood and burn the rest on site – and do so at felling rather than leaving the job until later when the undergrowth tangle makes it more awkward. However, it is possible to plant through conifer lop-and-top, or you could use a brush chopper if there is no danger of murdering wanted natural regeneration. In fact there can be adverse effects in removing or burning all the lop-and-top: it can eventually lead to a less healthy, less fertile site. There will also be a reduction in the organisms that depend on dead and dying wood, and as these are often at the start of the food chain there can be a resultant general decrease in the woodland wildlife.

The broad principles in the rest of this chapter apply on almost any scale, whether you are planting one small group of trees, a small plantation, a glade, a 'useless' corner, or something more ambitious altogether.

Before setting to work on site preparation, stop and consider why it is that trees fail. Assuming that you have chosen species appropriate to site conditions in the first place (which is more practical than trying to adjust the conditions to suit the species), and assuming that you have good, healthy plants to start with, the main hazards to their successful establishment and growth will be these:

- Bad ground conditions at the time of planting.
- Bad planting workmanship and techniques.
- Competition during establishment: weeds and scrub; closed canopy; browsing predators; insects and fungal diseases; pollution.

It is this competitive group that needs to be considered right now, before you make the first cut with the slasher or the first thrust of the planting spade blade. It is better to control competitors in advance, and then continue to keep them under control, than to take fire-brigade action later. For that reason, let's forget about temporal sequence and leave the actual planting to the end.

VEGETATIVE COMPETITION

Weeds, including both the herbaceous and the woody types, will have to be controlled to some extent until the young trees have outgrown them or are able to compete on equal terms. Table 10 shows the effects of competitive undergrowth of this kind. As the new trees grow and mature, they will rise above the undergrowth and, by means of their own canopy, will begin to suppress it – if they get that far. Beech, for example, is notorious for the barrenness of its understorey: not many plants like growing in the drip-shade of beech.

Table 10

WEED COMPETITION

Among very young trees, weeds:

- Compete for light (especially tall weeds)
- Physically damage young trees when they fall (tall weeds)
- Harbour bark-gnawing rodents (voles)
- Compete for soil nutrients
- Compete for soil moisture
- Lose more moisture by transpiration
- Reduce survival and growth rate of newly planted trees, especially in first spring and summer
- Continue to impede growth of new trees for several years

As any gardener knows, it is easier to deal with weeds by controlling them *before* planting, so that the tree has a chance to make early root growth before a new crop of weeds starts competing with it, but that may not be simple on tree sites. For a start, if the area has recently been clear-felled the whole environment has undergone a sudden and extreme change, and seeds which have lain dormant in the soil for many years will suddenly wake up. Coppicing gives many examples of this phenomenon: in the year or two after a rotational crop has been harvested, and before the regrowth takes over, there will be a profusion of plants like foxglove, primrose and bluebell, and a rash of tree seedlings, where apparently there was none before. Indeed, this profusion of new life is one of the bonuses of coppicing, and before you attempt to eradicate the lot, stop and think about what you are trying to achieve. There is a place for everything – in its place.

Some might be inclined to make a clean sweep and spray the whole area with herbicides in the summer months before planting, which could have unexpected effects by altering the natural flora and thus the dependent fauna, and is also very dangerous to water life affected by run-off. Others might try burning off, which will regenerate an amazing crop of dormant species that actually *need* fire to germinate their seed. Others will vaguely slash and hope. It would be much better to concentrate instead on each planting station: clear an area of at least 1m across and *keep* it clear after planting. Start weeding early in the year, whether before or after planting: April is the very latest time for your first weeding of the year, especially in the first spring after planting, because if the weeds get any chance to set seed – well, one year's seed is seven years' weed. Continue to control weeds for at least the first three years of the new tree's life on the site.

The main methods of weed control are:

- Careful hand-hoeing. A laborious job: it stimulates weed germination and therefore has to be repeated six or seven times during the year, unless there is a drought. Take great care not to damage the tree with the tool.
- Chemicals. The 'easy option' and the most practical on a commercial scale, but despised by the organic grower among others, and it might even let in a different crop of weeds.
- Mulch. A very good way of both suppressing weed growth and retaining ground moisture (and thus helping the tree's uptake of nutrients), but not for waterlogged sites.

Grasses are major competitors in a well-lit site: they take a lot of moisture away from a young tree's roots and need to be carefully controlled in the rooting area. It is no good mowing the stuff: that simply encourages it to grow more thickly. You could try taking off the top layer of soil at the planting station (it will be full of weeds or potential weeds in any case) and then rotovating to bring up deeper seeds and let them germinate so that they can be killed off, chemically or mechanically. By the way, pigs will do an excellent job of digging and turning a site, and manuring it at the same time, and they will clean up all manner of unwanted plant roots, grubbing out brambles and bracken for example.

Once the land is clean, you could resign yourself to the fact that *something* is going to grow anyway, unless you are an assiduous sprayer or hoer, so you might as well deliberately sow a low-maintenance mixture of, say, fescue and bent which will keep low of its own accord and give the tree a chance. But you still need to keep the area of each planting station fairly free of growth. If you have left nothing but subsoil, you will find that native tree species are tough enough to grow well in it but herbaceous weeds on the whole will not.

Mulches

There are various ways of mulching to suppress weed growth. A number of different materials have been the subject of FC research: biodegradable paper and card tend to rot down too quickly and make a nice planting medium for weeds; perforated materials let weeds grow through; clear or translucent materials tend to let enough light through to allow the weeds to grow so strongly that they push up the mat, and also create an overwhelming greenhouse effect which can kill the tree roots. Thick-gauge black plastic sheeting, treated to avoid brittleness from ultra-violet degradation and cut to form 'spats' or mats around each tree, seems to be the best form of mulch.

Clean the planting station of weeds, then lay a suitable piece of plastic flat on the ground to protect an area about a metre across. Cut a slit from the edge to the centre so that you can fit it around the tree at the time of planting, and make sure that the edges overlap each other when the spat is in place: the aim is to stifle potential weeds and deny them light. You should also dig in the edges of the sheet and weigh it down with turves to anchor it from invasion by tunnelling voles, who find nice dry nesting places underneath and also a secret approach to nibble the tree's bark – and once they start tunnelling, curious foxes and cats start digging after them. Do not use plastic sheeting if there are any livestock likely to eat it: it will do them no good at all, and could kill a lamb or calf. You could cover the sheeting with bark or gravel if you do not like the look of it. An added advantage of the mat is that it will help to protect the tree from cack-handed slash-wielders and sprayers, who will have no reason to go anywhere near the tree itself.

Small Woods and Hedgerows

Traditional mulches, with a similar effect to that of plastic sheeting, were of compost or well-rotted farmyard manure mixed with straw, but they now tend to be of woodchips or coarse bark fragments (not too fine or they will blow away). Make sure that the woody material is not contaminated with, say, the dreaded honey fungus, and avoid conifer bark, partly because of its associated fungi and partly because of its acidity. Spread the material about 10cm thick and compress it down to about 7.5cm. At that depth, the mulch should effectively suppress grasses for about three years, which is long enough for the tree to become well established.

BROWSERS

Some time around the twelfth century a small, furry mammal was reintroduced into Britain as an important provider of meat and fur. The coney, as Chaucer called it, was protected from poaching and the laws made it clear that it was 'gentleman's game': a third offence for a night-time poacher meant seven years in Australia, a land where the animal arrived in the mid-nineteenth century and thrived beyond its own wildest dreams.

At about the same time, the British were gradually realising that the gentleman's game and the poacher's pot-filler were the farmer's affliction, but it was not until 1954 that the rabbit was legally defined as a pest. A year after this, the familiar little bundles of lean protein had almost disappeared from Britain: more than 99 per cent of the entire rabbit population had succumbed to the terrible ravages of myxomatosis. Yet twenty years later it was probably causing almost as much damage as it had in its century-long heyday before the 'myxy', and today rabbits are rife again.

Unfortunately for tree-growers, rabbits do not restrict their grazing to pasture weeds and corn crops. They also nibble trees, especially newly planted youngsters or fresh, tender shoots, and they strip the bark from saplings in hard winters and late springs. A rabbit can reach to perhaps 0.5m up a tree, or even higher from a snowy platform. Ring-barked trees die, and your nibbled new trees will either be killed or permanently stunted and certainly unintentionally coppiced if the rabbits can get at them.

Apart from controlling rabbits by the constant vigilance of trapping, shooting, snaring and ferreting, your best non-violent defence is either to try to keep them completely out of the planted area by fencing it or to protect individual trees. If you fence a plantation, you will possibly keep out rabbits but you will also keep out other creatures. Pheasants, for example, will never fly if they can walk and a rabbit fence is a sure deterrent to them. This is bad news if you want to encourage the birds in your woodland. Pheasants will also

Table 11
BROWSING MAMMALS

BARK-STRIPPING
DEER (RED, SIKA, FALLOW)

Deer strip off bark for food, using lower incisors against hard pad of upper gums: vertical parallel tooth-marks (**red** 9.5mm wide, up to 1.7m above ground level; **fallow and sika** 6.4mm wide, up to 1.1m; **roe** stripping is rare, up to 0.6m).

Time of damage: mainly January–March, especially in snow and hard weather.

Favourite species: Norway spruce, lodgepole pine, most hardwoods (especially young elm); sometimes firs and young sitka spruce, Scots pine, larch.

Brashed trees are more vulnerable to stripping.

Note that domestic livestock, especially sheep, sometimes strip young trees too.

RABBITS AND HARES

Rabbits and hares strip off bark for food: the signs are four narrow furrows rather than two (they have two top incisors as well as two bottom ones) and usually diagonal marks rather than vertical, less than 3.2mm wide, well below 0.6m above ground level unless heavy snow gives them a platform to reach higher up the trunk.

Time of damage: mainly winter and early spring, especially in snow.

Damage often in places inaccessible to deer, e.g. in hedges.

Rarely serious or widespread damage.

SQUIRRELS

Bark stripped off trunk or main branches of trees ten to fifteen years old in summer as follows:

(a) Hardwoods starting at ground level.

(b) Hardwoods at several points above main boughs, on boughs and trunk.

(c) Conifers in last ten years of growth, high up on main stem.

Often leave bark in coils, strips and chips.

Grey squirrel likes sycamore and beech and will also attack pines, oak, ash, larch, hemlock, birch, maple; damage can be very serious.

Red squirrel prefers Scots pine, occasionally larch, lodgepole pine and Norway spruce; much less damaging than grey as the population is much lower.

Table 11 cont'd

VOLES

Field vole strips bark in winter just above soil level on young trees in tussocky grassland – tiny tooth-marks (less than 1.3mm) in small patches; tunnels through grass; damage can be very serious.

Water vole causes similar type of damage occasionally on stems and exposed roots of waterside trees but fairly harmless.

Bank vole gnaws away lengths of bark from angle between stem and branch on small or young trees 60cm–2m above ground level (perching posts); not serious.

BROWSING
DEER (ALL SPECIES)

Stems generally left torn and ragged, and severed shoots always consumed.

Peak time of damage: January–May when other food scarce, but deer also find buds and young shoots delectable at any time.

Nibble on newly established trees in particular, resulting in multiple leaders or reducing conifers to well-clipped shrubs. Side-shoot browsing might be acceptable but leader browsing can be very damaging.

Choice of favoured species same as for stripping, and especially soon after planting in deer's grazing glades.

Trees eventually grow out of reach (**muntjac** 1m, **red** 2m).

Do not plant or replant in deer's favourite established browse areas: they are very habitual.

RABBITS AND HARES

Clean, oblique cut across stem very distinctive; shoots often clipped off and left lying, unconsumed.

Up to 15cm above ground level (higher from platform of snow).

Time of damage: mainly winter and early spring, especially in snow.

Can be severely damaging.

FRAYING
DEER (MALES OF ALL SPECIES)

Male deer of all species:

Roe March–August

Others August–November, and to some extent in spring.

Males rub antlers on stems and foliage (territorial behaviour and sexual aggression). Note hairs on trees, and accompanying ground scrapes.

Table 11 cont'd

Damage especially to aromatic trees, or individual trees with different scent from majority of crop, or trees near the places where deer come out into the open, or trees standing alone uncluttered by undergrowth.
Muntjac: up to 40cm above ground level, often stems only, often in open woodland; often leave tooth-marks as well; mostly thin stems (25mm diameter); August–May.
Roe: up to 75cm; undersides of branches damaged; cause more serious damage than other species because of different behaviour patterns - fraying continues for months and is widespread because of territorial distribution.
Fallow: thicker stems (75mm) up to 1.2m high; thrashed stems up to 2m.
Red: thick stems, severe damage to branches and tops; no ground scrapes.

get trapped against the netting by dogs and foxes. (My vegetable patch is vaguely fenced against rabbits with wire mesh less than 1m high: at least once a week one of my half-tame pheasant hens takes refuge there from a passing dog and then spends the rest of the day wondering how to get out again. The possibility of flying out simply does not enter her head!)

If the rabbits do not get at your trees, the deer will. Deer love woodland, especially mixed woodland bordering on farmland and well furnished with warm, secret glades: it gives them somewhere to lie up and plenty to nibble – nuts, leaves, twigs, bark and shoots. Whereas rabbits cut a shoot diagonally and very cleanly, as if someone had taken a sharp pair of pruning secateurs to the plant, browsing deer leave a more ragged edge and they also have the habit of fraying: the males erode the tree bark and break off twiggery by rubbing their antlers and faces against the stems to mark their territory, and you will often notice a sprinkling of deer hairs or scrapings in the earth close by. Several species, especially red, fallow and sika, also deliberately strip off bark with their teeth during severe winter weather and can devastate quite substantial saplings.

Fencing to keep out some of the browsers needs regular inspection and maintenance and can be expensive and laborious to install initially. The FC recommends a fence 1.37m above ground level to keep out rabbits and deer, with another 15cm turned outwards at the base and buried or held down by turves, and a strand of barbed wire 15cm above the top of the netting for good measure. Use rolls of 1m galvanised 8-gauge hexagonal netting with 31mm mesh for the lower half of the fence, including the turned-out footing; then you can use a bigger mesh size (which is cheaper) of woven field fencing for the top half. For the sake of the deer I abhor the use of barbed wire: I have heard innocent young deer screaming in fright and pain as they meet its thorns.

Put up your fencing at least three months before planting. When it is first installed, you will need some one-way rabbit gates to let out those that find themselves inside once the netting is in place. It is rather more difficult to shepherd out the deer, who panic easily and blunder into the new netting time and time again in a desperate attempt to escape. Please be gentle with them: they do manage to break a leg all too easily and are quite capable of dying of fright at the proximity of humans. Is it worth it for a tree or two?

Table 12
FENCING

AGAINST RABBITS

Height of fence: 0.75–0.9m above ground level
End posts: 2–2.3m long × 10–13cm diameter, 200m apart
Stakes: 1.7m × 5–8cm, 10–14m apart
Struts: 2m × 8–10cm
Mesh: Hexagonal, maximum 31mm mesh
Baffle: Turn out base of mesh at right angles to form 150mm apron either pegged or held in place with turf to deter digging under (e.g. 1050mm roll: 150mm turned out, 900mm above ground vertically)

AGAINST DEER

Height: 1.8–2m
End posts: 2.8m × 10–18cm, up to 400m apart
Stakes: 2.5–2.6m × 5–10cm, maximum 15m spacing (10m better)
Struts: 2.5m × 8–13cm
Mesh: High-tensile deer netting (HT 13/190/15) or stock netting (C6/90/30). Hexagonal mesh (31mm, 18g) for lower half of fence only but not adequate for top half (except perhaps for roe) which should be welded or woven rectangular mesh.

ELECTRIC FENCING

(a) Electric netting could be used against rabbits temporarily.
(b) Three-wire electric fencing for rabbits on short stakes – top wire at about 250mm above ground level.
(c) Electric scare wires as further deterrent to deer and livestock at rabbit or stock fencing: offset wire about 450mm from main fence at two-thirds of animals' height (say 1.2m); decorate with fluttering coloured tape to attract deer to investigate and receive shock.

Tree-guards and Tree-shelters

The more versatile protections used today, especially in conservation areas, are tree-guards. Some people have tried chemical repellents but they have never worked for me against either rabbits or deer; they also need frequent re-application and if you use that white 'paint' it actually seems to draw attention to the very plant you are trying to protect. In Germany they hang up bags filled with human hair, the smell of which deer are said to dislike so intensely that they keep well away.

Tree-guards can be cylinders of wire or plastic mesh to ward off mammalian browsers, or simply spirals of plastic tape which you wind up the stem to fend off rabbits (there are holes in the tape to let the tree breathe). However, today's tree-guards are more sophisticated in that they have at least three roles. Their primary use is still to protect the new tree from browsing but they also deter weeds immediately around the tree and provide a microclimate to encourage its fast growth: they are effectively miniature vertical greenhouses. These guards are known as tree-shelters or tree-tubes and they are widely used to grow broadleaf trees.

Most tree-shelters are translucent or transparent plastic tubes, preferably the former. They come in various designs and colours: some are square in cross-section, some round, some have vertical ridges, some have horizontal spirals. If you take a drive along the Hampshire roads through Alice Holt Forest, home of the Forestry Commission in England, you will see thousands of shelters in all sorts of colours – yes, colour does have a role to play. Most people seem to use white at present but in fact deer tend to fray white more often than other colours, and also row upon row of white tubes standing like sentinels in a plantation completely spoil the look of a place, though at least they remind you where the young plants are. Greens usually fail to be 'natural'; browns tend to blend better and are less likely to be frayed.

Experiments continue, not only to judge the effects of different colours but also to try out different shapes and materials. It is early days yet to draw firm conclusions for the tubes were first introduced only in about 1979. Apparently there is no truth in the idea that by encouraging much faster growth and protecting the tree from every kind of vicissitude the shelters produce an ultimately weaker tree, but they have not yet been in use long enough to prove or disprove theories about their long-term effects. Nor are they yet bio-degradable and though they tend to split off (especially square ones, and often much too soon) the bits still have to be picked up and removed from the site. Someone suggested to me that they should be designed to 'grow' with the tree and ultimately degrade when no

Small Woods and Hedgerows

longer needed, so that the countryside is not littered with a new kind of rubbish. However, it is admitted that 'a tree-shelter should be left around the tree until it disintegrates naturally, which should be after five to ten years. Premature removal before adequate stem thickening has taken place may lead to stem snap or the need for some continuing support of the tree.' (DOE Arboriculture Research Notes). It is also possible that a shelter could make a fast-growing tree spindly in the stem and top-heavy in the bush so that it would be vulnerable to windblow when the shelter is removed.

Table 13

TREE-SHELTERS

IN FAVOUR OF TREE-SHELTERS

- Protect new trees from browsing mammals.
- Increase height growth-rates for most tree species: provide greenhouse effect for first two or three years, and then continued support and protection while stem thickens.
- Cheaper than rabbit fencing for areas of more than 2ha or of awkward shape.
- Allow pheasants, etc., free access to woodland.
- Reduce planting losses.
- Enable establishment on exposed sites.
- Identify planting stations.
- Show public that trees have been planted.
- Deter weeds from immediate environment to some extent.
- Protect trees from mechanical weeders and spray drift.
- Avoid need for geometrical outline to plantation.

AGAINST TREE-SHELTERS

- Have only been used since 1979: could be unforeseen problems.
- Premature removal or loss of shelter exposes tree with thin stem and heavy crown; will need additional support. Shelters must remain in place for five years.
- Alien in the landscape, especially in geometrical rows, or in white or unnatural colours.
- Not biodegradable: old or broken shelters need to be removed from site by hand.
- Brittle if handled in cold weather: could break.
- Plastics need ultra-violet light inhibitors to slow rate of breakdown in sunlight.
- Older types tend to split and fall apart.
- Some colours attract deer, especially for fraying.
- Some designs rub and fray tree bark after emergence.
- Staking can be difficult to secure and needs adjusting.

Table 13 cont'd

• Weeds inside shelter difficult to remove. Shelters are *not* an alternative to weeding.
• Can provide too warm a microclimate (up to 48°C inside the shelter) and up to 100 per cent relative humidity.
• Can trap small birds.

MATERIALS AND DESIGNS

(a) **Corrugated polypropylene** Square or hexagonal tubes, folding flat for transport and storage. Danger of corner-splitting. To avoid rubbing, buffer with straw or soft string.
(b) **Extruded tubes**
   (i) Smooth rigid 'drainpipe' type.
   (ii) Ribbed flexible 'field drain' type.
   (iii) Twin–walled type with stake niche and flared top.
Bulky to transport but strong. Short stake (0.8m) is adequate for rigid types.
(c) **PVC sheeting** or **pre-formed PVC cones**
(d) **Mesh with plastic film** (wire netting and polythene, by the roll) for small-scale use.

HEIGHTS TO DETER BROWSERS

Rabbits – 0.6m	Sheep – 1.2m
Roe deer – 1.2m	Cattle, horses – 2m
Fallow, red, sika deer – 1.8m	

Taller protection will be needed on slopes and in snow.

INSTALLATION

STAKES
Use round (chestnut) stakes – they rub less than sawn.
Must be robust size. The taller the shelter, the stronger the stake necessary.
Drive in at least 0.3m or until firm.

SHELTERS
Push into the ground 1–4cm for stability, to retain shape, to reduce vole damage, and to prevent low-springing shoots from growing out.

PRE-FORMED
Slide over tree; fasten to stake with wire or staples.

SHEETS
Staple to stake first; wrap around tree and stake; then lap the joint.

Table 13 cont'd

GROWTH RESPONSES TO TREE-SHELTERS BY DIFFERENT SPECIES

(*Based on Forestry Commission experiments to 1987*)
Source: Arboricultural Research Note 63/87/SILS: Treeshelters

VERY GOOD

Beech (but occasionally slow or poor)
Hawthorn
Small-leaved lime
Pedunculate oak
Sessile oak (but often one or two trees fail to respond)
Sweet chestnut (rapid initial response only)

GOOD

Ash (limited experiments but generally most successful)
Crab apple
Large-leaved lime (often very good)
Field maple (variable)
Norway maple (variable but can be most successful)
Sycamore

VARIABLE OR POOR

Italian alder
Eucalypts (develop oedema on leaves)
Horse chestnut

SUCCESSFUL

Alder   (initially good but not
Birch   enhanced after early
Cherry   emergence)
Holly
Hornbeam (variable: site sensitive)
Larch (initially most successful, not necessarily sustained)
Holm oak
Rowan
Southern beech (but very variable and site sensitive)
Walnut (very site sensitive)
Western red cedar (site sensitive)
Douglas fir
Corsican pine (branches constricted)
Norway and sitka spruce (both very variable response)
Yew (but still very slow to grow!)

Whitebeam
Grand fir
Scots pine
Western hemlock

In their favour, the shelters do encourage growth and deter browsers. But, if using them, be a little careful about weeds: if the ground is not clean when you plant the tree, some weeds will thrive in the vertical greenhouse along with the tree. Make sure too that the tube is wide enough to allow the tree to breathe and not to harbour disease. You can make your own shelters using plastics with built-in ultra-violet inhibitors so that they do not disintegrate at the first touch of spring sunshine.

OLD STUMPS

The stumps of felled broadleaf trees or cut-back weed trees and shrubs of almost any species will very quickly shoot with new growth like any self-respecting coppice stool. If that is what you want, fine – but the regrowth will be very fast, abundant and bushy and could rapidly overwhelm carefully planted treelings. In the words of Dr Oliver Rackham, a transplanted tree is always an injured tree, whether planted by foresters, conservationists, gardeners or civic dignitaries, and in order to flourish it needs tending, whereas the regrowth from an established stump is a much more robust organism with its own very healthy root system ready to support a veritable thicket of its own.

If regrowth is not wanted, you will either have to kill the stump or remove it. Uprooting stumps is extremely hard work, and so rarely considered practicable that most foresters would automatically use chemical herbicides to destroy the regrowth and then plant around the stump later, or use highly toxic chemicals to disintegrate the stump itself. Most chemicals on the market are sprayed, painted or pasted on within twenty-four hours of felling, and replanting is usually delayed for at least three months after application.

Those who object in principle to the use of chemicals, or who have practical reasons for not using them (for example, the risk of run-off into a watercourse or access by livestock), can either have the stumps blown up by professional explosives engineers or 'gobbled' by a contractor's machine which reduces stumps to chips, or they can start digging. Use a mechanical excavator for large or numerous stumps, or try hand-grubbing smaller ones – but even a long-established small shrub takes more rooting out than you might imagine. Do not try to chop into the heart of a stump: dig around it to loosen the roots and then lever or winch it out. It will be easier if a metre of trunk was left intact at the time of felling so that there is something to get a rope or cable around. You could also try weakening the regrowth by encouraging the stump to rot naturally: make its top dished to retain rainwater, for example.

Stump extraction leaves holes, especially in wet sites, and you might need to plough the area to make it reasonably uniform in the interests of future maintenance work.

PLANTING

The prime planting time is probably November. Avoid the dormant season: you want the roots to get going into soil still warm enough to encourage establishment. Do not plant in frosty, very dry or waterlogged conditions, and watch out for March winds if you decide to wait until early spring.

You have probably decided on the species or mixture of species you wish to plant, but have you considered the age and condition of the transplant, or even the possibility of planting actual seeds? The subject of growing from seed is discussed in Chapter V, which also explains how bare-rooted nursery trees are regularly transplanted or undercut to stimulate the development of compact, fibrous root systems. Plants are described in terms of the number of years they have spent in different situations at the nursery from the time of germination, and the code shows first of all how many years the plant has been in the seed-bed, and then at what stage it has been undercut ('u') or transplanted ('+'). Noting that a 'season' generally refers to the growing season from germination and sowing in spring, and that transplanting and undercutting generally occur in the early winter, here are some examples of the code:

Seedlings

1+0: One season in the seed-bed, not yet transplanted.
2+0: Two seasons in the seed-bed without transplanting: that is, eighteen to twenty-four months since germination.

Transplants

1+1: One season in the seed-bed, then transplanted, then one season in the transplant lines.
1+2: One season in the seed-bed, then transplanted, then two seasons in the transplant lines.
2+1: Two seasons in the seed-bed, then transplanted, then one season in the transplant lines. 2+1 or 2+2 is ideal for planting up a new coppice.

Undercuts

1u0: One season in the seed-bed, then undercut.
1u1: One season in the seed-bed, then undercut, then a further season in the seed-bed.
2u1: Two seasons in the seed-bed, then undercut, then a further season in the seed-bed.
1u1u1: One season in the seed-bed, then undercut, and undercut again after another season, then a third season in the seed-bed.

A transplant or undercut plant two or three years old will be a sturdy thing, with lots of roots and plenty of potential. Do not be put off by its above-ground size, which might in some cases be as little as 30–60cm: roots are much more important, and such a plant will generally grow well enough to overtake bigger plants and will be all the healthier too. It will also be cheaper, but it does need protection from browsers and good maintenance for the first three to five years. The minimum height for tree transplants is about 20–25cm for most species, with a minimum root-collar diameter of 4–6mm for broadleaf species or 2.5–3mm for softwoods. The root collar is the 'tidemark' at which the plant was embedded in the nursery soil and it is essential to plant to the same depth so that the root collar is at ground level. The stem above the root collar has been 'hardened off' by exposure to the air, but if it is engulfed by the new planting medium it will be susceptible to rot. Planting too deep is almost a passport to failure.

A drawback to bare-root plants is the danger of the roots drying out during transit unless they are wrapped in damp straw and hessian. You can buy container-grown plants instead, which are increasingly popular with gardeners. They are more expensive than bare-root plants and not necessarily any better, though they can be planted out at most times of year, ground conditions permitting, so that you are not tied to the calendar. There is little further advantage in containers for hardwood trees but they are good for conifers transplanted when more than 90cm tall. However, the shock of a less friendly soil than the comfort a container-grown plant is used to might deter its root from exploring the new environment, especially on clay, so that it will be rather slow to establish – and that is a considerable drawback. Root establishment is the primary aim in planting new trees of any kind.

Whips, Feathers and Standards
At a minimum of 90cm, whips are a lot taller than most transplants; they are also less sturdy and more expensive. They are single-stemmed and their lead shoots are probably out of reach of most browsing lagomorphs, though not of deer. Feathers are even taller – perhaps 1.2–1.5m or more – and look like untrimmed semi-standards. Standards have a minimum stem length of 1.5m and a total height of perhaps 2–3m. They need good support, are more difficult to establish and are particularly vulnerable to drought. They are also very expensive and are really considered only for instant amenity planting.

Cuttings
Poplars and willows strike easily as cuttings: you simply push a twig into prepared, cultivated ground and it will usually root with no trouble at all – a very cheap method of propagating, and a very easy way of planting.

Spacing
If you are planting a crop, the points to bear in mind about the initial spacing of the trees are these:

● As the years go by, the trees will gradually be thinned out, either because of failures or because of a planned thinning programme through which you can achieve some returns during the long run-up to crop maturity.

● Every site has its maximum potential for production. You cannot increase the total volume of timber from that site but you can fail to realise its full potential by understocking or by mismanagement. It is up to you to exploit the site by the correct choice of species and the best management to promote the best trees for the best possible quality timber. You might decide to plant a thousand trees for harvesting fairly quickly as, say, fencing stakes or firewood, but you would ultimately achieve the same total volume of timber from a fraction of that number of trees grown on the same area as timber standards and well managed until they are mature enough for felling. Although it might seem more lucrative to get cash in hand from your crop as early as possible to write off initial costs, in fact it is generally worth waiting for prime timber instead, even if you will not benefit from it personally.

● Wider-spaced trees increase their stem diameter more quickly than closer-spaced trees: you get a fatter trunk, but sometimes it will taper more readily. Closer spacing encourages a faster *upward* growth, with longer, cleaner stems: side-branching is quickly suppressed so that the timber has smaller knots. (The closer the trees, the more quickly the canopy closes.)

● Wider spacing means fewer trees to buy and plant initially, and bigger trees at the thinning stage for a better return. It is also easier to work and gain access between more widely spaced trees. Note that grants might not be available for very widely spaced plantings.

In general the tendency is to plant at 2–3m apart for conifers, 2m for broadleaf trees, but at least 5m if you want to encourage a good undergrowth for wildlife. For group planting – perhaps in an odd corner or for shelter belts – try rows a little more than 2m apart, and plant the individual trees within the rows 2.4m apart in all directions: the rows should be staggered. Parkland trees need to be at least 9m apart.

Nurses
The plantation spacings given above are for clean sites: they can be wider if there is an existing nurse crop to help draw up the new trees. Nurse crops are often planted simultaneously with the main crop and it is customary to plant fast-growing conifers either to protect broadleaf species on an exposed site or to draw up the more valuable hardwood which is intended as the final crop. The nurse

Table 14

NURSE CROPS AND MIXTURES

Oak with: Norway spruce on heavy, damp. acid clays
European larch on lighter loams or alkaline clays
Scots pine on freely draining soils
Ash and cherry on good brown earths or clay over chalk

Ash with: European larch on drier sites
Norway spruce on wetter sites
Sycamore and sweet chestnut

Beech with: European larch on free-draining sites
Western red cedar
Lawson cypress
Scots or Corsican pine
Cherry
Japanese larch with: Scots or Corsican pine

species also supply thinnings at an earlier stage. A typical combination is beech with larch on a free-draining site, or oak with Norway spruce on heavy, damp sites. The nurse crop is thinned after perhaps twenty or thirty years, during which time the slower growing hardwood has striven to keep up and therefore has good, long stems. The second thinning is of the hardwood species, leaving it at more or less its final crop spacing to grow on to maturity. Make sure that the nurse trees do not swamp the main crop, especially in the early stages. On the other hand, on soils with a high pH the broadleaves could suppress the conifers instead.

The 'coppice with standards' system, which is not nearly so much in favour today as in the past, effectively used the coppice species as a nurse for the standards, to the detriment of the coppice, which was eventually shaded out.

Planting Up

Choose the time of planting with great care: it could be crucial to the success of your trees. Depending on latitude and local climate, hardwoods are generally planted from late October to December and softwoods in September or October in sheltered places but otherwise in late March or early April. Avoid January, February and most of March for any species.

Conditions are ideally mild and damp. Do not plant in ground which is frozen, bone-dry or waterlogged, and do not thrust the poor transplant out into a desiccating wind. Always be wary of the wind: if it is blowing while you are planting, it will be more uncomfortable for the trees than for you, especially if you are planting bare-rooted specimens. It is vital to avoid desiccation of the roots before and during planting. Although you might have enough sense to avoid icy, chilly winds for your own comfort, you need to be aware that a light wind on a pleasantly sunny winter's day can be just as drying. Keep bare roots covered and in the shade while they are waiting to be set but beware of using something like black plastic bin-liners in sunny weather because the unplanted trees will probably die from overheating, even in winter.

Assuming that you have acquired healthy stock which has been carefully lifted from its nursery bed, the other main dangers to the tree at planting time are mechanical damage to its roots or bark by careless handling and planting, the use of unsuitable backfill material (especially impermeable clay or soil from the permafrost layer), planting too deeply, and firming or watering too much or too little. Always plant with the root collar at ground level.

Notch Planting

On free-draining soils, the quickest way to plant lots of trees is either to cut a single vertical slit with your spade and then waggle the blade to widen the gap a little before popping in the tree, or cut twice into the turf in either a 'T' or 'L' shape so that you can peel back a flap, put in the tree, replace the flap and tread it back into position. Alternatively, you can skim off the entire piece of turf and invert it to keep the roots warm.

Pit-planting

Larger plants and amenity trees are usually pit-planted. At each station, dig out a pit large enough to accommodate the roots comfortably, then break up the soil at the base and add well-rotted manure or compost if you want to give the tree a really good start, incorporating it into the broken soil. Put in a stake before you plant the tree: position it on the windward side of the tree, with its top level with the standard's first branch. Then plant your tree, backfilling with reasonable soil and treading at intervals to ensure the roots are well in contact with the soil and securely planted. Leave the surface even: you do not want a hollow where water will collect and rot the stem at ground level. Use expanding tree-ties on the stake, one at about 30cm above ground level and another perhaps 15cm down from the top of the stake. Make sure that the tree will not rub against the stake.

Stumping Back

After planting a tough little transplant, decapitate it. Slice off all that splendid top growth down to ground level. In that way you will relieve stress on the roots which are trying to support the top, and you will encourage the new plant to produce a straight new stem if it is not already doing so. Unlike a well-established coppice plant, a young transplant does not have the kind of substantial root system which would allow it to throw up multiple stems at this stage but it will rapidly put out a single new shoot. In the old days they used to grow tree seedlings in a mixture with cereal crops and then scythe the whole lot to the ground at harvest, leaving each tree seedling to send up a clean new stem and grow on from there. It might seem heartless to murder that new little tree, but very often it is the kindest cut of all, especially if the original stem has been slightly damaged during transplanting.

MAINTENANCE

Your main tasks in helping the newly planted tree to become well established are to fend off weeds and browsers by techniques already described and to retain adequate soil moisture by mulching. Concentrate on that square metre around the plant for at least three years, keeping it clean for the sake of the tree by one means or another. If you are reduced to using a strimmer against the weeds, take great care not to ring-bark the tree with its cord.

Inspect all ties, guards, shelters and fences regularly, and after the first winter check that the tree is still firmly planted: tread back any frost-lifted ground.

Beating Up

Keep an eye on early planting failures and try to work out why they died so that you do not repeat the mistake. 'Beating up' means replacing early failures with new plants if necessary.

Thinning

Conifer plantations are usually first thinned when they are perhaps twenty years old and thereafter at five-yearly intervals, though larch is generally thinned at ten years old and thereafter triennially. Broadleaf trees are not usually thinned until they have been standing for perhaps twenty-five to forty years in a forestry enterprise but thinnings for firewood and stakes can be taken earlier, depending on the vigour of the stand. The longer the interval between each thinning, the greater the volume of each harvest. With broadleaves, the aim of thinning is to leave the best to grow on for good timber in due course: you want even, well-balanced crowns on your final crop.

Small Woods and Hedgerows

Note that ash and oak need more light than, say, beech or sycamore, but that heavy thinning could depress height growth and encourage too branchy a crown spread.

Pruning

There is plenty of pruning in nature: if lower branches are denied light, they eventually die and are shed by the tree. Prune to remove already dead or dying branches, and also take out some of those at the very bottom of the crown. You need to strike a balance: the tree needs ample leaf area for its own growth. Most people still prune flush to the tree, which is the age-old practice and looks much cleaner, though some prefer to cut outside the branch bark-ridge that you can see in the fork – but do not leave a stub as long as your thumb because it will die back and will not readily form callus, and it is callus which protects the wound from invasion by fungi and disease, and ultimately does so much more successfully than anything you can paint on it. Many people like to apply artificial protection until the callus can form, and to encourage it to form, but they might be making matters worse rather than better. Prune when a branch is small enough not to leave a large wound anyway; prune in late winter or early spring to make the most of the more active callus-growing period (it is negligible from autumn to mid-winter); and above all use very sharp tools for a clean cut with no tearing.

V

PROPAGATION

Propagation is fun! And it is also as much an art as a science. The aim of this chapter is to encourage you to make the most of nature's bounty: it discusses how to raise native trees, woodland shrubs and hedgerow plants for your own use from hand-gathered berries, nuts and seeds. It might even inspire some people to think more seriously about propagation as a source of income, but for that you need to be very careful in your choice of seed stock and you need to consult the regulations about registered seed sources. By EC decree, no forest reproduction material (whether seed, cones, cuttings or plants) can legally be *marketed* for *forest* use unless its source is registered and inspected by the Forestry Commission. However, that does not prevent you from growing for your own use. Think how many miles of hedge you could plant from one good year's crop of wild berries!

The commercial prospects are limited not only by EC rules but also because, for example, hedgerow harvesting is so laborious; indeed, many nurseries prefer to buy in their seed rather than pick it themselves. The whole business is often too expensive for the commercial grower but could be well worth the while of a private individual or a conservation group whose motives are less to do with income than satisfaction.

The Hampshire Wildlife Trust is a typically practical conservation group which has set up its own nursery, raising locally harvested seed in order to sell good plants of local provenance to local farmers and councils. Hampshire County Council, incidentally, is one of those which, on behalf of the Countryside Commission, provides grants for small plantings but only of native trees and shrubs, and preferably those of local species, which are more suitable in the landscape and to which the wildlife of the area is better adapted. Local species generally have a greater chance of succeeding in the area – that is why they are local.

Whatever the eventual destination of the new plants, it is important to know something about their parentage. Naturally you need to identify the species but you must also check that the parents are healthy specimens, partly in order to obtain viable seed and partly to avoid propagating serious genetic defects. Many native species have become rare because of disease problems, and this needs to be borne in mind when you are considering the reintroduction or encouragement of local trees. For example, look at the wild service tree, *Sorbus torminalis* – if you can find one. Its underrated fruit is delicious if eaten when 'bletted' (rotted) like a ripe medlar: it tastes like acid raisins and also makes good wine, but is far too precious in its rarity to be wasted. The tree is a genuine native but now has its last toehold in southern England and south Wales. The species has major problems with a parasitic wasp which invades the seed, and the grubs have rendered unviable almost all the seeds produced on wild service trees in southern England in recent years. In addition, the tree is susceptible to a vascular disease on badly drained land and, if you do succeed in germinating good seeds, you could find your whole crop wiped out by the disease, even when quite tall, if your nursery beds are not really well drained. Nor is the tree particularly vigorous on its own rootstock and many commercial nurseries graft it on to other rootstocks or, even worse, import foreign seed. What a way to conserve a local species! If you do find a healthy wild service tree, you might be better advised to take cuttings than to fail with seed – and you have an almost bounden duty to try to propagate such a rare tree.

The wild service has been taken as an example because it is a historic tree which is in trouble and because it is also attractive. It is one of a group of trees that are the subjects of folklore, which adds to its appeal. It is of the natural family *Rosaceae*, and its genus includes the common whitebeam and the mountain ash (or rowan), which has always been a powerful charm against evil. The wild service gets its name from the Latin *cerevisia*, meaning beer, and it was sometimes called the chequers tree: its bark is patterned with squares. Chequer berries were sold in Sussex and the Isle of Wight for eating when they were half-rotten, and the fruits were also recommended in medieval times as a cure for gripe, while a distillation of the flower stems and leaves was used for consumption, earache, and 'green sickness in virgins'.

There is more about medicinal and culinary uses for our various wild fruits in Table 22 (page 113). Now let's get down to the practical business of propagation.

SEED COLLECTION

Collect from plants in a recognised stand if possible: you do not know where isolated specimens have sprung from. A forester would collect only from trees of a good type and form with naturally clean stems and all the other qualities sought in forestry, but ecologically you can be much less fussy and can happily mix up seeds from lots of different blocks. Do not be deterred because a tree looks stunted: it might have been dwarfed by its environment (for instance, salt-laden winds) rather than by its genetics. There is an argument that by being selective at all you are interfering with the natural order of things and weakening the genetic stock by narrowing the gene pool, but if you are completely unselective you might also be perpetuating characteristics which are in the long run detrimental to the species. The whole subject of selective 'breeding' is one for the philosophers.

Long before the harvest, make a survey over a wide area to find good fruit-bearing trees. This might have to be over a period of years rather than months because many species are periodic seed-producers. Oak, for example, might have a good acorn crop only every three or four years, and with beech you might have to wait six years for a good mast season. Be observant and be ready to collect the crop before it is naturally dispersed.

In principle, collect seed when it is ripe; that is to say, when there will be no further increase in the seed's dry weight. In general, autumn is the most practical time to collect, assuming that you have made a visual assessment of the trees in full growth during the preceding months, and that the crop is dry and not yet dispersed. However, in the case of many fruits wildlife will beat you to the harvest if you do wait till autumn.

There are many methods of gathering fruit from trees. A commercial concern might use a mechanical tree-shaker to bring down a crop of beechmast or walnuts, for example. Cones are generally hand-picked, but hand-picking small berries can be either a chore or an idle pleasure. It is often easier to snip off a twigful of fruit with good secateurs and then strip them at home as you would bunches of black currants. Be judicious in your abusive pruning of the plant, however.

The term fruit, incidentally, includes single or bunched berries, top fruit, nuts, winged seeds which vary in size from ash and syca-more keys to the little winged nutlets of birch, and the tiny gossamer-trailing seeds of the sallows and poplars.

DORMANCY
In temperate climates many seeds which drop from plants in autumn remain self-protectively dormant during winter and will not ger-minate until conditions are right in the spring. Some species stretch this dormancy into the second spring, eighteen months after fruit-fall, and some can remain dormant for years until circumstances are more favourable to successful germination and establishment. Dormancy might be protected by chemical inhibitors or by mech-anical factors such as a very hard seed coat which does not easily break down.

Table 15

TREE SEED PRODUCTION AND COLLECTION

SPECIES	AGE AT FIRST GOOD SEED CROP (YEARS)	AGE OF MAXIMUM PRODUC-TION (YEARS)	AVERAGE INTERVAL BETWEEN GOOD CROPS (YEARS)	RECOMMENDED COLLECTION PERIOD
BROADLEAVES				
Ash	25–30	40–60	3–5	Aug for immediate sowing; Oct for 16–18m stratification
Beech	50–60	80–200	5–10	Oct
Birch	15	20–30	1–2	Aug/Sept
Horse chestnut	20	30	1–2	Oct
Oak	40–50	80–120	3–5	Oct
Sweet chestnut	30–40	50	1–4	June
Sycamore	25–30	40–60	2–3	Sept/Oct
CONIFERS				
Western red cedar	20–25	40–60	2–3	Sept
Lawson cypress	20–25	40–60	2–3	Sept
Douglas fir	30–35	50–60	4–6	Sept
Grand fir	40–45	(poor)	3–5	Aug/Sept
Noble fir	30–35	40–60	2–4	Aug/Sept
Western hemlock	30–35	40–60	3	Sept
European larch	15–20	40–60	3–5	Feb/Mar
Other larches	15–20	40–60	3–5	Sept (Nov in Scotland)
Corsican pine	25–30	60–90	3–5	Dec
Lodgepole pine	15–20	30–40	2–3	Aug/Sept
Scots pine	15–20	60–100	2–3	Jan
Norway spruce	30–35	50–60	Rarely	Oct
Sitka spruce	30–35	40–50	3–5	Sept/Oct

(Based on Forestry Commission Bulletin 14: *Forestry Practice*)

Table 16
SEED TYPES

FLESHY (BERRIES, DRUPES AND FALSE SUCCULENTS)
All the shrubs whose names end in 'berry' plus:

Blackthorn (sloe)	Maidenhair tree	Wild service tree
Buckthorn	Medlar	Spindle
Cherry	Mulberry	Strawberry tree
Cotoneaster	Pear	Wayfaring tree
Currants	Plum and bullace	Whitebeam
Dogwood	Privet	
Elder	Quince	
Guelder rose	Wild roses	
Hawthorn	Rowan	
Holly	Sea buckthorn	

NUTS	CAPSULES AND PODS
Beech	Box
Hazel	Broom
Oak	Eucalypts
Horse chestnut	Gorse
Sweet chestnut	Laburnum
Walnut	Robinia

WOODY CONES
most of the conifers (except as mentioned above), that is:
Cedars, cypresses, firs, hemlocks, larches, monkey puzzle, pines, redwoods, spruces.

OTHER WINGED SEEDS	WINDBLOWN HAIR-TUFTED SEEDS
Alder ('cone')	Aspen
Ash	Plane
Birch	Poplars
Elms	Willows and sallows
Hornbeam	
Lime	
Maples	
Sycamore	

WINGLESS CONIFER SEEDS
Juniper: fruit referred to as 'berry' is in fact several small, hard, wingless seeds in a scaled cone similar to that of the cypresses.
Yew: very primitive conifer with *succulent* fruit, each berry containing one wingless seed.

Table 17

SEED DORMANCY (Period Between Ripening and Germination)

QUICK GERMINATION

Alder (on damp mud)
Ash (if keys picked while green; becomes dormant if picked brown)
Wych elm (germinates within weeks of falling after May ripening)
Oaks (acorns germinate readily in mild, damp autumns)
Poplars (very short viable seed life indeed and cannot be stored; must be sown within a few days of ripening and will germinate in six days on damp soil in the wild)
Willows as poplars

SHALLOW DORMANCY

Reluctant rather than unable to germinate: generally stored to protect from rodents until sown in spring. Includes most of the temperate conifer species.

DEEP DORMANCY

Includes most broadleaves to varying degrees. They must be exposed to low temperatures before they can germinate.

GERMINATION IN FIRST SPRING

Beech	Norway maple
Birch	Red oak
Butcher's broom	Privet
Wild cherry (if bird-voided)	Wild service tree (sometimes)
Hazel	Spindle
Holly (if bird-voided)	Sweet chestnut
	Sycamore

GERMINATION IN SECOND SPRING OR LATER

Ash (if picked brown)	Juniper
Blackthorn (after twenty-four months)	Field maple (erratic; after fifteen to twenty-four months but eighteen months on average)
Wild cherry (if not bird-voided)	
Hawthorn	Limes
Holly (if not bird-voided; may be anything from twelve to twenty-four months)	Rowan
	Wild service tree
	Whitebeam
Hornbeam	

Most of the temperate conifers are shallow-dormancy species but some of the broadleaf trees and shrubs are deep-dormancy species which need to be exposed to low temperatures before they can germinate. When these long-term sleepers do germinate, they often come up like weeds: they have a high potential rate of germination, whereas the quick-germinating species tend to be much more erratic. Some species, especially oak, germinate almost as they hit the ground under the tree, needing only a little moisture and gentle ground warmth to start pushing out a radicle – their dormancy factor is nil.

A major problem with dormant seeds is that you need to store them during their dormancy in such a way that they are neither eaten by predators nor rotted in the meantime. Some can have their long-term dormancy broken by extremes of heat or cold (fire or freezing) or by chipping at their hard coats. But dormancy is a fact of life, so what is the rush? It really is easier to wait until they are ready to germinate in their own time. Those involved in any way with trees are patient people with long-term attitudes – aren't you? Anyway, if you do try to force matters, you will find that each individual seed in a batch (let alone each species) has its own built-in dormancy clock and each will react differently to the treatment, just to keep you on your toes. You will need to wait until at least 10 per cent of a batch have germinated and then just have to hope that the rest of them are nearly ready as well so that you can sow them all together, unless you are prepared to monitor individual seeds over a long period until they decide to sprout.

STORAGE METHODS
Autumn-gathered seed can be planted on site immediately, to grow if it can at the mercy of every passing predator and competitor. Bury acorns about 5cm deep, beech about 2.5cm deep, and only lightly cover most other seeds in soil as deep as the seed is thick. Put them into bare soil, tread it down firmly and then try to fool the birds by disguising the patch somehow. Sow plenty of seeds at each station because most are bound to be found and eaten by mice and voles; thin them out later once the plants are well established, and transplant the thinnings to other sites. Seeds of oak and beech can be sown when they drop from the tree, and ash seeds should be sown while they are still green (they become sulkily dormant if allowed to ripen). In natural regeneration, losses in the wild are huge, but the predators are instrumental in dispersing seed over a wide area.

Autumn-sown seed tends to sit brooding and you are much more in control if you opt for sowing in spring – it will give you more peace of mind to know that the seed is safely stored rather than at the mercy of winter-hungry creatures, and then you can sow it in optimum conditions in spring when (with luck) it will germinate and grow away quickly while the predators are busily feeding elsewhere. In the interests of your own management efficiency, aim to sow all your seeds at more or less the same time, regardless of species, and choose storage methods that allow you to take charge of germination.

Seeds are living organisms: they respire. It is therefore important to retain sufficient moisture within them to perpetuate their viability. However, a seed is as viable as it ever will be at the moment you pick it and no amount of skilful treatment and storage thereafter will *increase* that viability. All you can do is try to reduce the rate of loss of viability, which often means avoiding a loss of moisture within the seed.

The main winter-storage methods are:

- Stratification: cold, moist storage out of doors.
- Refrigeration: cold, dry storage in a refrigerator.
- Bagging: cold, dry, well-aired storage in bags.

Seeds with no dormancy factor at all germinate as soon as they are in a warm, moist environment and therefore need to be stored dry if you want to delay germination until spring – typical examples are acorns and field maple.

The deep-dormancy species are generally best left to their own devices to germinate when they will, and the most common method of storage is by stratification.

Stratification

This is the overwintering of seed in moist, sharp sand out of doors so that the elements can do their work. Use very sharp grit sand or floor grit – not builder's sand, which retains moisture too well, and not something from an aggregate company which has dug the stuff out of the sea bed so that it is full of salt.

Seeds always have some kind of protection. They may be enclosed in fleshy fruit or in pea-like pods, or in cones or nuts, or are winged. Each type requires a different method of extraction before being stored: fleshy fruits should be macerated, pods crushed through a sieve, and cones can be heated gently on or near a radiator until the seed can be tapped out.

To macerate fleshy fruits, simply put them in a plastic bag and tread on it (take your shoes off!) or thump the bag against a wall or roll it with a milk bottle. Many of the deep-dormancy seeds can then be mixed up with the sharp sand complete with the bashed fruit: there is no need for carefully extracting each seed from the flesh and skin, which will rot down during the long wait for germination. There are exceptions, as described in the species notes on pages 70–72.

Be consistent in the proportions of seed to sand, and record them so that, when planting time eventually comes, you have a good idea of the density for sowing. Aim for approximately two thirds sand to one third seed. Mix the whole lot well enough to ensure that the sand is in contact with the seeds.

That was the easy part. The big problem now is to keep hungry predators away from the seed – and you will need all your guile to deter them, especially as the mixture is going to be stored out of doors. In principle you want to contain the mixture, retain adequate moisture but drain out the excess, and above all to put up a barrier against mice and to a lesser extent birds. Depending on the quantities involved, you could use flower pots – preferably the type designed for container beds, which have little slots at the side that are better for drainage than the standard pot holes. Put sharp stones in the base of the pot to help drainage further, then put some large angular stones (about 5cm in diameter) on top of the mixture to give the mice a hard time. Better still, use a catering-size tin from a restaurant, or an old oil drum if you need a larger container, and punch drainage holes in the base. Alternatively you could use an old-fashioned bushel-sized apple box covered with very small-mesh wire netting to keep the mice out: you must always use square mesh to deter mice rather than hexagonal chicken wire, because a hungry mouse can squeeze through even 1cm hexagonals, which are supple enough in structure to accommodate it, and then the mouse gorges on your seed, fattens up and gets stuck half-way through the mesh when trying to escape! Even if you double chicken wire, mice still manage to undulate their way in if the lure is attractive enough.

Put your stratification container well out in the open, *not* in a sheltered place because that creates the risk of some seeds germinating in February, when your seed-bed will not be ready and will be too cold and damp so that the seedlings will die or be eaten by winter-ravenous birds. Sycamore manages to germinate in the first week of February almost without fail, however carefully you store it.

Refrigeration
Virtually any kind of seed can be stored in well-sealed polythene bags in a domestic refrigerator as long as the seed is clean (with no bits of fruit attached) and dry before being bagged. It is essential that the bag is properly sealed, or the seed will dry out and become useless. The ideal temperature for most species is 0–4°C.

Bagging
This method is often used for storing dry seeds like alder, hazel,

acorn, beech and birch in a cool, dry, airy building with no extremes of temperature. The seeds will tolerate a little frost but should not be subjected to massive frosting.

Small seeds can be bagged in large brown envelopes which are then lightly sealed (not all the way round); larger seeds can be put in hessian or canvas bags. The biggest problem, of course, is keeping the mice away. Never stack your bag in a corner; the mice will work in secretly from the back without you noticing them, and in the spring all you will have is a bag of empty nut shells. You could try dangling the bags in mid-air by hanging them on long strings attached to the rafters, but even that will not pose a problem for a determined, acrobatic mouse.

Alternatively, forget about bags or envelopes and dry-store a small quantity of seeds in a mouseproof tin. A large tin with plenty of airspace within it is preferable to a small tin punched with lots of airholes.

Seeds stored in bags will need to absorb moisture before being sown so that they can plump up. Let them start imbibing from about mid-February: very small seeds like birch can be stratified in moist sand at that point and put outside for four or five weeks.

STORAGE OF DIFFERENT SPECIES
Alder   This is a non-coniferous conifer! Put alder cones into a plastic carrier bag and bash it against the wall, or put them near a radiator for a day or two to extract the seed. The seeds are very small and should be stored dry, not stratified. They germinate quickly on damp mud.

Apple   Hook out the seed when the apple is a nice, rusty brown (which, in the way that nature defines it, means the apple is ripe). Clean off and dry the seed, then store by refrigeration.

Beech   Wait until the mast has curled back of its own accord, unless you have the teeth and dexterity of a squirrel. There should be three or four seeds in each mast. Choose the fat, plump ones: press them between your thumb and finger, and discard any that cave in. Test their viability in water – good ones sink, poor ones float. Beech seeds are liable to lose a great deal of their potential during dormancy if incorrectly stored: test again before sowing. Sow in spring fairly deep to avoid mice and game birds, and then protect the shoots from pigeons, which love them.

Birch   Store dry. Birch can be quite difficult to germinate. You might try burning straw over the seeds to encourage germination: birch is the kind of plant that quickly colonises burnt land.

Box   Easily propagated from cuttings rather than seed.

Butcher's Broom   This interesting, spiny-leaved shrub has male and female forms: you need a female plant for seed production, so plant both. If it does seed, it does so prolifically and self-seeds readily on site, germinating in its first spring. However, unless you want to introduce genetic variation, it is much easier to propagate by division of the clumps: you can get scores of plant clones that way.

Guelder Rose   A very thin fruit with a large seed quite easy to separate, but it smells like a tomcat! Typically of native shrubs, the seedlings are fairly weak.

Hawthorn   Crush the berries in a plastic bag and stratify. You cannot rush hawthorn: just leave it outside to find its own moisture and wait for it to germinate, probably in the second spring.

Holly   Treat as hawthorn. After eighteen months, germination should be imminent: sow the seed in small containers, as the seedlings will be rather small and slow to grow.

Hypericum   Crush the berries with a wooden pestle, stone or milkbottle, grinding them in a tray, box or saucer or through a sieve. The seed is very tiny.

Juniper   A rare species, but it should not be. Typical eighteen-month dormancy: after its long sleep it comes up like a weed – excellent potential germination rate.

Lime   Germination is very poor and erratic even after the eighteen-month dormancy; try propagating by cuttings instead.

Maple   Field maple has an erratic dormancy factor – it could be anything from fifteen to twenty-four months before it germinates. There is no need to de-wing the seed before storing, unless that would make sowing easier. Norway maple and sycamore will germinate in their first spring.

Nut-bearing Species   In general, store nuts dry, either by bagging or refrigeration. To test for viability, cut samples in half and look for a fat, white embryo. The ones that are good to eat were the viable ones!

Pine   Store the seed dry in an envelope or in a refrigerator; sow in spring.

Small Woods and Hedgerows

Privet Crush and stratify, then sow in spring. It tends to damp off in the seed-bed, so sow it quite densely.

Rosaceae All the *Rosaceae* species respond to art better than to science: each reacts differently but all can be macerated and then stratified. The family includes the *Sorbus* species (rowan, whitebeam, wild service), *Prunus* species (cherry, blackthorn), pears, crabs, roses and brambles. You do need to extract the seeds physically from the fruit or you will have dormancy problems. Cut a rose hip in half and scrape out the seeds – but remember that they used to make itching powder from hips. Stratify in sand in small containers. Some can be sown in the first spring but others will not germinate until the second spring.

Sloe Determinedly dormant! Store it for two years and then there will be virtually 100 per cent germination. Just separate the seed from the fruit – there is no need for total extraction – put the fruit in a plastic bag without any holes in it and tread with stockinged feet or break up by hitting with a piece of wood. Stratify in sand. The fruit, of course, can be turned into sloe gin or wine.

Spindle A lovely shrub which has beautiful autumn foliage, lurid pink and orange fruit and a wealth of folklore and provides a sure resting place for blackfly. Its very hard seed can take plenty of rough treatment: crush by rubbing with a flat board on a handle to expose the white seed from its orange coat. You will probably only achieve 40–50 per cent germination: store in a refrigerator or stratify and it should come up in the first spring. It is a typical native species: not very vigorous.

Wild service tree Seeds affected by parasitic grubs have a pinched look at the top, and anything from 60–100 per cent will be infected. Stratify or refrigerate viable seed; sow in first spring.

Yew The seed in a yew berry is highly poisonous and can be lethal, but the flesh that surrounds it is not poisonous at all. Pick the seed out carefully if you want to propagate it, which needs considerable patience, and then cook and eat the very sweet, sticky red fruit if you are quite sure there is no trace of the hard seed left in it!

Wild flowers Primrose seed is easy to store and sow but, like all wild flowers, it needs soil of *low* fertility. Bluebells set tons of seed if they set any at all, but there is a three-year wait for germination. These flowers are as much a part of the woodland as any of the shrubs and trees, so why not try growing some?

SOWING

Sow all your tree and shrub seeds at the same time in spring, regardless of the species. The problem will be to determine when exactly it *is* spring. It used to come in March in southern England but now it is more often April. Ignore the calendar: use your intuition and observation instead.

You want at least four factors to come together at the same moment: viable seed ready to germinate, adequate soil warmth, the right amount of moisture and adequate oxygen. Only when all four are right will the seed germinate and continue to grow. In addition, the embryo in the seed must no longer be inhibited by any dormancy factor or it will not be able to germinate however ideal its environment. That environment is important: you can begin to germinate a seed on a barren concrete slab, but it will soon give up.

Disease is the seedling's enemy. In the case of native species you should give the seed a sterile bed while it germinates, if you can – and that is pretty difficult. Commercial nurseries use a rather potent granular substance which is put on cultivated soil in autumn, while the ground is still warm and moist, and is then sealed under polythene until spring. It kills *everything* in the bed, including earthworms. In the spring the sheeting is removed and some experimental grass seed is scattered on the soil: if it germinates, the bed is ready to be sown.

The soil in a seed-bed should ideally be free-draining, with a pH of 6.0 to 6.5 and only moderate fertility: superphosphates can be incorporated, but nitrogen should be quite low. Use a balanced, slow-release fertiliser if necessary, and if the soil is heavy open it up with peat and sand. A southerly aspect helps but the site needs to be protected from strong winds and should not be in a frost pocket.

Raised Beds

A raised bed is excellent for seedlings: you will not tread on it and it is well drained and well defined. However, seedlings on the outer edges tend to become rather 'bony' in dry months and develop thick, thongy root systems, though the rest of the seedlings will do well. Raised beds are suitable for most of the species discussed in this chapter except perhaps for those with very small seed like birch.

Raise the soil to at least 15cm with a slightly convex surface to shed excess water, and make the bed no more than 1m wide so that you can easily reach the centre from either side; the length can be whatever you need. Incorporate fertiliser, if necessary, as you make the bed and then firm everything to avoid loose pockets of soil. Rake the top to a fine tilth.

Make a drill rake from some two-by-one timber, with prongs

10cm apart to make three drills at a time. Draw the drills across the width of bed so that they drain to each side. Regardless of species, take out all the drills to the same depth: the difference will lie in the depth of cover you put on top of the seeds rather than in the depth of the drill. It is much too fiddly to take out different drill depths if you are dealing with a large number of seeds and species.

It is usually worth trying to leave the seed in its winter container as late as possible – right up to the moment when the radicle *just* starts to break through, but not a day later. A 1cm radicle is already too long and will probably give you a crooked plant, and if it is something like horse chestnut it will probably strangle itself. But if you sow too early in the season, the seed will simply lie dormant and be the victim of vermin and cold March winds.

You can sow all your seeds at the same density if they are roughly of the same size. Stratified seed can be sown complete with its sand and debris: you know how much sand is in the pot and the proportion of sand to seed, so you can judge how much seed you are sowing. Large seeds like acorns can, of course, be sown individually (perhaps 250 acorns per square metre, or 120 horse chestnuts, or 400 maple).

Work from the side of the bed and sow half a drill at a time (the sand will show where you stopped in the middle), putting the seed on the base of the drill and not up its sides. Label the rows as you sow and before you forget what is in them; you will find it difficult to differentiate between many of the seedlings when they appear. Cover the seed with very coarse *grit*, not soil: use 6–9mm clean, washed, lime-free white grit (13mm for small species like hawthorn, birch and viburnum) to a depth of at least 25mm. The seedlings are quite capable of pushing their way through, and the grit will deter birds and mice partly because it is angular to walk on and partly because they will feel exposed to birds of prey. For added protection you could use 8-gauge galvanised wire hoops covered with small-gauge taut wire mesh. The major pests will be mice, game birds, pigeons and slugs.

The grit will also suppress weeds and retain soil moisture so that, with luck, there will be no need to irrigate before, say, July. The aim is to encourage the *downward* growth of the radicle, and if you irrigate you will encourage rooting closer to the surface instead, which means that the seedlings will be unable to cope with a summer drought. If you have to irrigate before July, put on as little water as possible, but when you irrigate after that – flood it!

Containers
Smaller seeds (such as birch, broom, rhododendron, hypericum, larch and cypress) often do better in containers like pots, seed trays,

cell trays or concertina paper pots. Concertinas can also be used for acorns, and one of the best acorn growers is the cardboard tube from the centre of a toilet roll: germinate the acorn in compost inside the tube and then plant it out in the tube, which will gradually disintegrate into the soil.

Concertina systems were originally devised in Japan and are popular in Scandinavia. The containers arrive folded flat and open out concertina-wise into hexagonal paper tubes held together with a soluble glue so that the entire tube can be planted out with the seedling, just like the acorn in the toilet-roll tube. The open sheet of tubes is clipped into a plastic tray and seeds are sown individually into compost in each tube.

Special plants like *Daphne mezereum*, birch (difficult) and hypericum can be sown in trays in a 50/50 mixture of peat and sharp sand with a slow-release fertiliser. Fill the tray with the mixture, scrape off the excess and firm the medium with a flat piece of wood. Sow a maximum of 200 seeds per tray. Cup your hand so that its 'life line' forms a channel to dispense the seed and sow zigzag fashion. Cover fine seed with sand passed through a fine sieve. Cover the tray with glass and a sheet of newspaper until the seed germinates, then remove the covering. Put in a sheltered, wind-free place outside; thin the seedlings to forty per tray, or prick them out, or pot up in clumps. Always beware of pot-bound plants: they will never grow out of their root-ball when they are finally planted on site and it is therefore essential to pot them on as soon as they reach the limit of their container.

Thinning

Do not try to thin your seedlings until you can assess the success of germination positively and accurately. Then you can thin to perhaps one seedling in every 5cm of drill-length. Thin with great care, perhaps using a small table fork; otherwise it is easy to expose the roots of neighbouring seedlings.

Some tree seedlings, especially birch and alder, will probably surprise you with their vigour and will make a large seedling in their first season. Others can reach anything from 10 to 40cm in height in their first season, depending on species.

UNDERCUTTING

By late September or early October in the seedling's first year, a tree's taproot needs to be severed or it will fail to thrive when it is eventually planted out. It needs to develop fibrous laterals. Use a small fork to dig down and *wrench* the plant to break the taproot, even if you intend to leave it in the bed to continue growing for another season. It is slow but essential work. Commercial growers use cutters that slice right along the whole bed in one operation. Your tree is now a 1u0 (see page 54). You can leave the plants in the seed-bed for another year after undercutting, and then undercut again after those twelve months so that you have 2u0.

Alternatively, you can transplant your seedlings. Lift them in October (commercial growers use mechanical vibrating fingers for this) and line them out in another raised bed of similar dimensions in a three-row system: put them in rows 30cm apart, with 30cm between each plant in the row so that they are equidistant in all directions for even growth. At this stage your plant is a 1 + 0. You still need to undercut annually to encourage fibre and avoid thick, thongy roots: use a strong, steel-shafted spade (a heavy one is the lightest to use because it does the work for you) to dig into the bed and wrench the taproot.

Some species, like alder, can leave the nursery and go out to their final home in the environment after only two years as long as their stem girth is big enough, and no species should really still be in the nursery by the time it is four years old. The younger you plant out an oak, the more successful it will be – give it, say, a year in the seed-bed and a year in the transplant line (1 + 1) – but for most species two years in the nursery is the minimum, three the norm and four the maximum. All lifting and transplanting should be during the last week of October or first week of November (in southern England) and this timing is especially critical for birch.

When the tree or shrub is at last in its permanent environment cut it back to ground level (unless it is beech, which is unable to throw up a bud like other plants). It needs to establish a good root system and the top growth can come later. If you are planting with conservation in mind, a multiple-stemmed plant will be of greater benefit later on, but you can always choose a good leader instead and bring it on as a single stem if necessary. Feed the plant well after you decapitate it.

CUTTINGS

Some species grow so slowly from seed that you might do better to give up the whole idea and instead propagate them vegetatively to save a year or more. A holly seedling, for example, might be only 25cm high after two years. A yew is even slower and will just about struggle to 5cm as a one-year seedling, but in two years you could grow a yew plant nine times as tall from semi-ripe cuttings. Yew cuttings root easily and really take off!

Cuttings should always be taken from the current season's growth. Softwood cuttings should be taken from May or June until September; semi-ripe cuttings in August/September; and hardwood cuttings in November. Any good gardening book will explain the procedures but the main points to bear in mind are that absolute sterility is essential: your hands, your knife blade and the surface on which you cut (for example, a glazed white tile) need to be scrupulously clean, and the cut should be made cleanly too. There is usually no need to use hormone rooting powder: it gives you a false sense of security and also has a very short shelf-life. Even if you keep it in the refrigerator, you do not know how long it was in the shop before you bought it. Simply make a small wound to expose the cambium – perhaps a cut 1cm long just above the bottom bud.

Particularly good subjects for cuttings are elder, willow and poplar. Willows root very well from 25–30cm hardwood cuttings and with most species your success rate will be 95 per cent (perhaps rather less for goat willow): you can simply push the cuttings straight into the ground outside and they will root. Poplars are equally simple from hardwood cuttings. Alder will root from hardwood cuttings, and hazel might, but aspen will not and is best propagated from its suckers. Birch will root from a softwood cutting but is quite difficult to manage afterwards.

Lift rooted cuttings in October: plant them out within a year so that there is no need to undercut them.

NATURAL REGENERATION

Any native or thoroughly naturalised broadleaf can regenerate in its own environment with a little help from you and this can be a wonderful way of rejuvenating tired woodland.

If the best of the existing trees on a site are prolific seed-bearers as well as exhibiting qualities you seek (for instance, good straight stems, lack of deformity, plenty of vigour, freedom from disease) and if they are pollinated from equally good trees, you are on to winners without even trying, but you can still help by encouraging the seedlings to grow well. As soon as you spot a heavy seed crop developing of its own accord, open up some breathing space: create a gap in the canopy when the crop is ripening or when the resulting seedlings have already made progress, but not before or you will simply make an ideal habitat for competitive brambles and grasses. You could be even more far-sighted and plan to thin your woodland so that the good producers always have a chance to develop bigger seed-bearing crowns, but that is a very long-term strategy.

To encourage the new seedlings, let in the light and scratch up the ground so that it is receptive when the seeds fall. (If you work a horse, use it to drag a heavy log with some rough branch-stumps on it as a harrow over the ground, for example.) If you are seeking a grant, make sure that the regeneration area is large enough to qualify.

Fend off browsing predators as you would for any newly planted crop: fence out livestock, pop a tree shelter over every seedling you notice, and be on guard (even if you cannot do much about it) against mice and voles gobbling up fallen seed and new seedlings in a flush year. Look after the young plants for at least three years, keeping their surroundings weed-free and keeping the crop clean.

Your abundant seed-producer might also spread its bounty further afield, either by means of the seeds' own airborne wings or hairs, or carried by careless birds and buried by forgetful rodents, and will regenerate merrily in areas of disturbed soil or in ungrazed or lightly grazed grass. What fun! Let it start a new wood somewhere and, if you discover where that is, protect the colonisers and help them to thrive.

VI

COPPICE MANAGEMENT

If you cut almost any broadleaf tree down to a stump, it will defy your wanton execution by sending up a host of vigorous new shoots almost before your chainsaw has recovered its breath. This simple fact is the basis of coppicing, which was once a major woodland industry and which is again attracting the interest of those who manage smaller woodland packages. In the context of this book, and in terms of both productivity and wildlife conservation, coppicing crops of small-dimension produce are far more important than the long-term production of valuable timber trees. Small-scale woodland is not the same as large-scale forestry for pulp, boards and planking: instead, it is mainly for producing timber which will be useful on the holding – fencing, firewood, rough building materials, strong supports – with perhaps some interesting crafted goods as a more or less lucrative sideline. The working up of many of these items is described in Chapter VII, while the essence of this chapter is the general management of coppice. The basic principles can be applied to most of the common coppice crops.

In broad terms, coppice is harvested rotationally. Small areas, of a size easily handled by one or two people, are effectively clear-felled and then left to regenerate from the stumps before being harvested again a few years later. The length of the interval depends on the species and on the size of 'pole' required (a pole being anything up to 12m long and at least 7.5cm in diameter – smaller stems are known as rods) and also on the age of the plantation in its early stages. Incidentally, perhaps because of the generation to which they belong, most coppice workers continue to think in imperial measurements, not metric, so that to them a pole is up to 40ft long and at least 3in in diameter.

Newly planted trees must be allowed to become thoroughly established before the first cut is taken, in order to build up a reserve of root strength to withstand the stress of continual cropping later over a very long productive life. On average, each stump will probably be harvested perhaps half a dozen times in a century.

Coppicing is generally seen as a low-input, low-output system as long as the only produce required of it is for home use or for a small,

Table 18
COPPICE CROPS

Main markets for coppice produce today: pulpwood; turnery; fencing; firewood
Shorter rotations (up to twelve years) suitable for osier wands, faggots, wattle, pea-sticks, bean-poles, spars, walking-sticks, rural crafts, home firewood, energy crops
Medium rotations (say, twelve to fifteen years) for fencing, cleaving, firewood, small turnery
Longer rotations (fifteen to thirty years or more) for large turnery, large cleft products, firewood, pulpwood

SPECIES DETAILS

Alder Suitable on sites with high water-table. Rotation ten to twenty years for turnery (brush heads, chair legs), clogs, boardwalks, riverbank protection, firewood, pulpwood, charcoal.
Ash Very fussy about where it grows: likes moist, fertile loams in favoured areas only (if it is not already growing well locally, do not even try). Rotation ten to twenty-five years for turnery, scythe and tool handles, general turnery, rakes, barrel hoops, fence poles, hurdles, baskets, gates, firewood; more than twenty-five years for specialist sports equipment, pulpwood, ship-building.
Birch Thrives on acid, sandy heathland. Rotation two to five years for brushwood (besoms, horse-jumps, but not very good for pea-sticks); fifteen to twenty-five years for firewood, charcoal, pulpwood, rustic poles, rustic furniture, turnery (brush heads, spools, cotton reels).
Eucalypts Prefer well-drained, fertile, lowland soils. Experiment with foliage for florists, firewood, etc. In right place, could grow very fast.
Hazel Will grow well on wide range of soils. Rotation six to ten years for great variety of rural products – thatching-spars, hedging-rods, clothes-line props, walking-sticks, barrel hoops, wattle fencing, sheep-hurdles, pea-sticks and bean-poles, sheep-cribs, rustic garden use, showjumping poles, firewood. Density: possibly 1500–2000 stools per hectare.
Hornbeam Likes acid soils with moderate clay content. Rotation fifteen to thirty-five years for firewood, pulpwood, charcoal, turnery, carving.
Limes Prefer acid soils, often loess-rich over boulder clay. Rotation twenty to twenty-five years for turnery.
Maples Will grow almost anywhere but especially on calcareous clays and loams. Rotation ten to twenty-five years or more for firewood, turnery, fencing poles, pulpwood.
Nothofagus (southern beech) *N. procera* grows in the west, *N. obliqua* in the east. Still in the experimental stages for all products.

Table 18 cont'd

Oak Grows well on moderately acid loams to clay loams. Rotation eighteen to thirty-five years for fencing (cleft and sawn), turnery, hurdles, spelk basketry, charcoal, firewood, tanning bark. Could plant at a density of 200–500 or 600–800 per hectare.

Sweet chestnut Likes soils ranging from acid loamy sands to clay with flint in warmer and sunnier regions in southern England. Prime coppice species. Rotation ten to twenty years (average twelve to sixteen) for fencing (stakes, posts, poles and rails – round or cleft – and paling spiles), hop-poles, trugs, ladder rungs, or on short rotation (two to five years) for walking-sticks. Plant at a density of 800–1000 per hectare.

Sycamore Will grow happily on wide range of soils – tends to spring up like a weed where it is not wanted. Rotation ten to twenty years for turnery, fencing, firewood, pulpwood.

Willows Prefer damp areas. Special crops produced for very local areas (for example, osiers in Somerset). Mainly very short rotations (even annually) for basketry; also hurdles, trugs, riverbank protection. Can plant as many as 55,000 per hectare for annual cropping.

Mixed species short rotation Locally suitable species may be grown on short rotation (seven to ten years) for rural crafts, fuel, walking-sticks, etc. Plant at a density of 2000 per hectare.

regular income. It is laborious work in that some aspects of it are not readily mechanised. Although the actual felling and length-cutting of the poles is easily enough done with chainsaws, many stages in working up the product can be done only by skilled craftsmen using hand-tools – and they are a dying race. Those who need coppice products for their own use would be well advised to scour the countryside for an ageing coppicer willing to let them learn the crafts.

Although the term 'coppice' is generally applied to woodland which is the result of vegetative regeneration from stumps cut fairly close to ground level, the trees do not have to be in woodland: you could coppice, say, an overgrown hedgerow or carefully thicken up a shelter belt using coppicing techniques. If a tree is cut at about head height, it will still throw up a crop of shoots but the term for this is pollarding and the original point of the higher cut was to produce harvestable shoots out of reach of browsing livestock and wildlife. A stool cut at about 0.6m might just be clear of rabbits but you need a height of 1.5–1.8m to be out of reach of fallow deer and cattle. Pollards can be harvested like coppice but it is usually harder work!

MANAGING ESTABLISHED COPPICE
Traditional coppice has a very long history stretching back literally

Small Woods and Hedgerows

thousands of years and has been a major influence on the formation of British broadleaf woodland. If you look closely at your wooded area, you are quite likely to find evidence of past coppice management. The main systems were either pure coppice of one species (such as hazel or sweet chestnut), mixed coppice of more than one species (for instance hazel, ash and oak), or coppice with standards – that is, a random or deliberate scattering of larger-diameter timber trees with coppice stools as the understorey (for example, oak with hazel). Quite often a coppice stump may have been managed to produce a single straight 'high forest' stem, known as stored coppice, rather than a regular crop of poles. Some coppice stools might be hundreds of years old and yet are still capable of producing a good crop, given the chance.

Old coppice can be a very rich environment for native flora and fauna, and even commercially productive coppice has a considerable conservation value. The cropping of small areas at spaced intervals provides a great variety of habitats in the woodland, ranging from the full sunlight of a freshly felled area that brings out the flowers and butterflies to the dense shade and privacy of the mature stands before their poles are felled. Yet even then the canopy does not remain dense long enough to expunge all life beneath it, so that flowers and ground vegetation will be ready to spring back into life after the crop has been taken. If the coppice includes a mixture of species and some standards as well, there is an extra dimension to the woodland and the conservation benefits are that much greater. The provision of grassland access rides further enhances the environment, and most coppices have the added bonus of being visually attractive in the landscape and useful for those interested in shooting.

The essence of coppice is that the area falls naturally into small units so that the disturbance of felling is limited to the 'coupe' or 'cant'. These patches are generally anything from about 0.1–1.2ha, which is a reasonable size for one or two people to work in a single winter, though today the more commercial enterprises would establish cants of perhaps 1–2ha or as much as 4ha at the most. If the area is too big, the work seems overwhelming and there is also the risk that surrounding stands might be too suddenly exposed to the elements. The simplest method of calculating the optimum cant size is to divide the total area by the number of years of the rotation for the crop, so that you have a constant annual yield, and then plan to work adjacent sites so that wildlife can simply move next door when it is disturbed.

NEGLECTED COPPICE

Take a good, long look at your neglected coppice if you want to manage it actively again. Examine it closely, but also from a distance. Never forget that it is part of the general landscape as well as part of your holding, and bear in mind the principle that coppice is worked piece by piece, so that although the harvested area will look suddenly and radically different, the visual effect overall is much less glaring than clear-felling a mature crop of timber.

In your site assessment, identify what species are present, how old and vigorous the stools are and how they are spaced, and then find out how long it is since the wood was actively coppiced. The longer the neglect, the more cautious you need to be, but if it has been worked within living memory you can rejuvenate it (hazel less readily after thirty years of neglect) and encourage those old stools to start producing their poles again with the help of some judicious enrichment where stools have died. The gaps can be used for introducing large new standard trees, big enough not to be swamped, or new coppice plants. The enrichment does not have to be from planting anew: it is often possible to bend down a stem from a neighbouring stool and peg it in place to root as a new layered plant (see Figure 2). If a gap in the coppice is larger than about 6m square, it is worth filling it. Like any new plants, these enrichments need to be protected from browsers until they are well established, and there is a case for creating a laid hedge around the wood if there are suitable plants already in place along farmland boundaries.

If standards are part of the woodland, you need to ensure (for the sake of the coppice) that their crowns never meet or cover more than perhaps 30–40 per cent of the ground area: the coppice stools need light. Aim for perhaps fifty standards per hectare at the most. Henry VIII set the level for standards in coppice when he introduced a statute specifying a dozen to the acre (30 per hectare). As with any neglected woodland, aim to grow on the best timber trees and remove the worst: leave good, straight stems of oak and similar species to mature.

From the point of view of wildlife, tackle the most derelict areas first, as that is where you can do the greatest good. You will probably need to coppice the understorey first so that you can assess any standard trees. Deal with a small area at a time, and start in the middle of the jungle or otherwise you risk damaging new growth when you drag the crop out through areas closer to the road. Plan well ahead and proceed gradually. Open up your access and extraction routes before you start working. Think about the order in which areas need to be cut and what you are going to do with those long-standing poles that might now be pretty hefty trees but not as valuable for sawmill timber as genuine standards, and how you are going to get them out and away. In the initial stages you will be

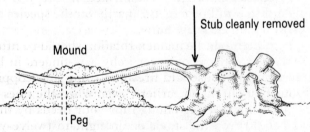

Figure 2: Layering a new coppice plant

Line of partial cut

(i) Partially cut through selected stem.

Stub

Pit

Peg

(ii) Bend the stem down to lie horizontally and secure it with pegs underground in a well-dug pit as a rooting medium.

Stub cleanly removed

Mound

Peg

(iii) If the stem cannot be persuaded into a pit without being torn, peg it and then mound the soil over it instead. Cleanly cut off the sharp, protruding stub. The earthed stem should root itself in due course and form a new coppice plant.

using a lot of labour for little in the way of financial returns as the products will be low-grade until the rotation gets into its swing.

Do try to leave some standards of different ages and sizes for variety but be aware that the sudden removal of all those neighbouring growths will expose remaining trees to the elements. Are they well enough built to take it? Be as methodical in felling standards as in coppicing: at each coppice crop take the oldest standards and replace them. In a typical coppice-with-standards system, an oak would outlive five or six coppice rotations (its own harvest would be at 100–130 years old) and an ash three to five rotations (it would be felled at 60–100 years old).

When neglected coppice is first opened up, there will be a huge surge of life as the light rushes in, but not necessarily the kind of life you want. Brambles, for example, will enjoy the enriched soil more than the many woodland plants that prefer fewer nutrients in their growing medium – but at least the brambles might protect the stool shoots from browsing deer!

NEW COPPICE

When establishing a new coppice, give it the protection of a shelter belt of uncut trees and shrubs, especially if the site borders on arable land: the belt will also protect the coppice from drifting herbicides. You can coppice the belt later when the adjacent coppice crop has grown up.

If you want a new coppice to have a long productive life, go easy with it in its youth. Your aim is to let new plants establish a really vigorous rootstock to sustain subsequent continual cropping. Let the maiden trees become thoroughly established before you take your first crop. When this will be depends partly on the species and the site, and partly on your ultimate aims.

For commercial production, the maiden rotation should be fifteen to twenty years, though some people get itchy saw-fingers in half the time. If you want only household firewood from your coppice, you could take your first cut much earlier – even when the trees are five or six years old if they are big enough for your needs by then, and thereafter you could crop the stools on an eight-to-twelve-year rotation.

The first flush of shoots after the maiden stem has been removed will not be quite as productive as subsequent crops, though there may well be from 50 to 150 shoots from a single stump in the first year. Growth improves after the second crop, and the shoots generally thin themselves so that you are left with perhaps ten or fifteen after twenty years. Some people believe in artificially thinning out the shoots to perhaps five or ten per stool during their second year of growth so that all the tree's energies are concentrated in the fewer poles rather than spread over the many, but it is not really necessary. As the poles grow, the more vigorous will soon shade out the rest which will therefore die off in any case.

To create a new coppice plantation, follow normal woodland planting practices by controlling competitive weeds before and after planting, and protecting the very young trees from browsers. Plant 2 + 1s or 2 + 2s in a square grid (not staggered) and use plants about 0.5–1m tall.

ACCESS AND EXTRACTION ROUTES

These vital corridors serve several purposes. They let you get *in* for a start. When you have cut your coppice, it all looks open and accessible, but in no time at all it will be an almost impenetrable jungle and inspecting your wood, or enjoying it, will be a struggle. Access routes also let you get *out*: it is almost impossible to take out a crop through coppice of more than a year's growth unless you have planned a ride of reasonable width if there is wood to be harvested beyond the copse. You will also need access for vehicles to take away your harvest without mucking up land unnecessarily and getting stuck. That also applies to horses, working or otherwise, and to ramblers – give them an identifiable route for your sake and theirs.

Good access makes a standing crop much more attractive to a potential buyer, who will be happiest with a roadside site with ample space for stacking, loading and turning large vehicles on surfaces hard enough to avoid time-wasting.

Grass rides, on the other hand, can be miniature nature reserves. They give wildlife the favoured 'woodland edge' habitat so beloved by butterflies, flowers, songbirds, pheasants and bees – but not if they are long, straight wind-tunnels. Include a draught-deflecting kink near the ride's woodland entrance or leave some well-placed shrubbery as a wind baffle. Wider grass rides are as good as glades for wildlife.

THE COPPICE HARVEST

In theory you can cut any time between August and April, but in practice cut your poles in winter from October to March. For a start there will be less of a problem with leaf-heavy crowns and the undergrowth will have died down, allowing easier access. There will be less disturbance to wildlife and less damage to ground flora. The crop is also at its full growth for the season and the new crop will have a whole summer ahead of it to get growing, beat the competition and become frost-hardy. The disadvantage is that the ground might be wet, but it might be frosty instead, with a good firm top, and once you start burning the brush you will have the warmth of the fire as well as the warmth of your labour.

There are two very different attitudes to coppice harvesting. The more commercially efficient is to avoid double-handling the crop at any stage: get the fire going and fell the poles towards it, trimming off the lop-and-top and cutting each pole to length as you go, splitting it where it lies, then picking up a trailer-load to shift the poles to the sawbench for pointing, sorting and loading. However, a craftsman producing, say, chestnut palings handles all the material several times and takes pleasure in a 'tidy job' at each stage. He will probably cut his poles to length and stack them in groups over the site, then come back in the summer to drag or cart them to his camp on a barrow, sorting them in lengths varying by 15cm (all will be between 1 and 2m). Then he will hand-peel, split and snub them before bundling and neatly stacking them ready for collection. That is work for craftsmen who value art above time.

At felling remove any interfering whippy stems and then work methodically, spiralling around the stool towards the middle poles (if there are any). Cut as close to the stool as possible: you want to encourage regrowth from the stool rather than from pole-stumps. Slope the cut surface downwards away from the centre of the stool so that rainwater is not encouraged to collect in its heart and cause rot. Tackle each pole separately: do not try to undercut the whole group in one by slicing right through the main stool! Above all, cut cleanly and leave the stool clean and tidy, free from splits, splinters and sawdust. The traditional implements are axe and billhook but, in spite of what the purists say, the slightly rougher cut of the chainsaw does not seem to cause any harm to the plant in the long run. If you are harvesting the maiden stem, cut it as close to ground level as possible: an ideal stool height is about 7.5–15cm.

The stools are precious repositories for future crops: take every precaution to avoid tearing or damaging their bark. Watch out for stones which might be hidden in the stool and will do your tools no good at all, and look out for staples or fence wire in older stems along the edge of the coppice.

Burn lop-and-top as you go, but make sure that your fires are well away from the stools because a scorched stool will probably die. There was a time when the brushwood would have been used rather than wasted on the coppice bonfire – twiggery from some species would have been bundled up as stove faggots for bread ovens, for example. The characteristic chips that result from pointing a stake can provide very useful kindling for home fires and wood-burning stoves if they are allowed to dry out: they can easily be bagged up for delivery to the house if they are not needed for strewing on boggy tracks to help get the crop out of the wood. Unless you are a very careful cleaver, make sure that the site is cleared before the spring, removing all poles and worked-up produce, in order to avoid damaging the regrowth once it starts.

If all this sounds like too much work and time, you could get someone else to harvest your crop. Many people sell a standing crop to a local cutter or put up larger areas for sale by tender or by auction, but check whether the crop will be removed immediately or will be worked up on site by a semi-resident craftsman. ('I hadn't expected a *factory*!' cried one outraged retired general, though the term factory is hardly appropriate for a solitary cleaver plying his hand-tools.) If you are faced with a long-neglected coppice which you want to restore for conservation purposes more than anything else, you might get help from a task force through the Manpower Services Commission or a similar employment scheme, or from a group of British Trust for Conservation Volunteers, but in both cases they are likely to be learning the job as they work and will probably take quite a long time to complete it.

STACKING

Sort out your poles into those good enough for fencing or working up in some way and those good enough only for firewood, charcoal or pulp because of irregularities, twisted growth and so on. The latter group are stacked as cordwood.

A cord is a locally standard unit of wood by volume, and the volume (traditionally measured imperially) varies from perhaps 117 to 144 cubic feet, depending on where you live. A typical cord has a volume of 128 cubic feet and is stacked in a heap measuring 8 × 4 × 4ft. Traditionally cords are still measured imperially, but the metrically equivalent stack would be 2.4 × 1.2 × 1.2m. As logs are by nature rounded and irregular, clearly the actual volume of timber in the cord is nominal: a lot of the stack will be air, and the looser it is stacked, the less its market value. If you are selling by weight rather than volume, sell it quickly before it loses moisture!

Cordwood is generally stacked between end-stop poles and rests at base on a couple of poles along the longer sides of the stack and between the corner poles to allow the passage of air under the logs, which are piled on top of these horizontal supports at right angles to them.

Poles for conversion into end products which have no bark should be peeled at the time of felling: the bark will come off much more easily while it is still green and the sap is still soft, and peeled poles are less attractive to damaging insects and fungi while the wood is in store.

SWEET CHESTNUT COPPICE

Today sweet chestnut is the major commercial coppice crop, but only in south-east England where it finds adequate warmth and sunshine, and an average rainfall of 500–850mm a year. It is also known as the Spanish chestnut: it does not grow wild any further north than southern Europe. It is not a true native species in this country but was no doubt brought over by the Romans who cultivated the trees for their nuts as much as anything else. For centuries chestnuts remained an important part of the winter diet in rural areas of Italy and Spain where they were ground into flour which was baked in cakes. In Britain today the nuts are sold roasted by street vendors and are used in large quantities to stuff festive turkeys at Christmas, but they do not grow as large or ripen so easily here as in Mediterranean countries and are usually imported.

Sweet chestnut has one major fault in the eyes of the forester: it tends to twist as it grows so that the trunk is often spiral rather than straight. It is also prone to 'ring shake', which means that the wood splits along an annual ring and you cannot detect the problem until the tree has been felled. However, these problems have less chance to develop if the plant is coppiced rather than grown on for saw timber, and it is as coppice that the chestnut has proved its worth.

In 1982 some 12,500ha of sweet chestnut coppice were being worked in Kent, the major chestnut county, with another 4,750ha in Sussex and a total throughout England of 19,000ha (there were none at all in Wales or Scotland). The main outlets are for fencing materials – stakes, posts, rails and that special chestnut product, split staves for wired paling fences. Every southern farm should have room for a chestnut coppice to meet its own needs.

The ideal soil has a pH of 4.0–4.5, which is quite acid, and growth is poorer on poorly drained soils, but the crop is often grown on a site simply because it is unsuitable for any other species. The usual rotation is ten to twenty years (on average twelve to sixteen years) and the period is determined by the demands of the market rather than the optimum productive stage of crop development. The important factors in judging a commercial crop are the number of *straight* stems and the internode length; the volume per unit area of ground is a secondary and indirect consideration.

The majority of southern England's chestnut was planted in the mid-nineteenth century and has already been worked for perhaps as many as nine rotations. It might therefore be expected that stool mortality and site exhaustion would have resulted by now in lower productivity, but this is not yet evident. Experiments to improve productivity have had mixed results but in general it seems that liming depresses stem diameter increment, though the latter can sometimes be improved by the application of phosphate fertiliser if leaf analysis suggests a deficit. The Forestry Commission has shown that both volume and weight per hectare increase exponentially with the age of the crop, with a rapidly rising rate after about twenty years of growth. FC Bulletin 64 is packed with formulae and figures relating to the growth and assessment of sweet chestnut for those with a serious interest in the crop.

HAZEL COPPICE

Hazel used to be the other major coppice crop, grown for firewood, nuts, wattle for fences and wall-daub, sheep-hurdles, thatching-spars, clothes-pegs, pea-sticks, bean-poles and so on, but even in the last thirty years the area of worked hazel coppice has shrunk from 60,000ha to a mere 3,000ha. However, there is still a substantial area of unworked, overgrown hazel coppice either in pure or mixed stands or, commonly, under oak standards.

The ideal hazel rotation is seven to nine years, producing shoots 4–5m long. Unlike sweet chestnut, hazel coppice growth declines rapidly after fifteen years. The art of cleaving and weaving hazel rods for wattle fencing is dying but not yet dead, and the lightweight panels are becoming more popular again for gardens.

WILLOW

Osier wands are the product of willows coppiced on a very short rotation but today nearly all the osier production is limited to little more than 150ha, mainly on the wet alluvial soils of the Somerset Levels, particularly around the village of Stoke St Gregory, where they take their osiers seriously. They set the plants at 16,000 to the acre (you could stock as high as 55,000 sets per hectare, harrowing the ground beforehand and then pushing in sets 30cm long and spaced at 30×60cm intervals) and harvest in the third year from November to March. A well-managed osier bed could remain productive for at least seventy to eighty years. Harvesting is by hand with a very sharp hook, cutting as close to the ground as possible (which is back-breaking work). In some places the crop is cut annually at 2–3m tall.

Short rotation willows can also be coppiced as 'energy' crops. Several other species are used in this system, which is described in more detail under 'Fuel' in Chapter VII. It involves close-planting vigorous coppice species and harvesting them mechanically on cycles of one to five years. The whole crop, twigs and all, is put through a chipping machine to produce fuel and it might also be possible to use the foliage for fodder.

VII

COPPICE PRODUCE

There is considerable scope for imaginative woodland production from coppicing for your own use, or for sale as raw material, or for working up into saleable products.

FUEL

Wood has always been used as fuel all over the world, and it is only in the last two or three centuries that it has been increasingly displaced from Britain's hearths by coal, gas and electricity. A small-holder could heat the whole house with wood using a system of log-burning stoves and open fires, but there are other possibilities (forgetting straw briquettes and straw-bale burners for the time being). It might be worth combining with other small-scale pro-ducers to set up a fuel centre selling a variety of wood-based fuels, and the stoves in which to burn them as well.

Firewood

Even the smallest patch of woodland can supply you with firewood for home use, and a managed coppice of mixed species would be better still. If you then take the trouble to cut logs to a manageable size, splitting them if necessary, and let the wood season for a year, you can sell your logs to produce a small, steady income. The points to bear in mind are these:

- Coppice could produce perhaps 5 tonnes per hectare of green wood per annum.

- Wood is a poor conductor of heat, and will burn better if the logs are less than 10cm thick. The most useful diameter of growing timber for firewood is 5–20cm, and the larger pieces need to be split for the fire.

- For use in wood-burning stoves, green logs should be seasoned to less than 20 per cent of their original moisture content, and this is likely to take at least a year from felling. Damp or green wood leaves dangerous tar deposits and burns inefficiently.

- 2 tonnes of green wood are the equivalent of 1 tonne of air-dried

Table 19
COPPICE PRODUCTS

HOW TO SELL

Coppice products may be sold as:
(a) Standing crop to a contractor.
(b) Cut, unsorted poles, ready for lorry loading, to a merchant (for firewood, pulpwood, etc.).
(c) Sorted poles, straight and fairly free of knots, to special outlets (sawmills for turnery and planking, sports equipment, tool handles, rake heads, brush heads) or to water authorities for river piles (oak, alder, sweet chestnut).
(d) Purpose-cut, fairly straight, small poles for fencing stakes, bean-poles, thatcher's wood, etc.
(e) Worked-up produce, especially fencing, also firewood logs (cut to length, split and seasoned).
(f) Craft products.

MAIN PRODUCE

Fencing Posts, stakes, rails, paling, wattle, hurdles, panels, rustic poles, hop-poles, clothes-props, gates
Fuel Firewood, charcoal, energy chips, biogas
Brushwood Besoms, jumps, faggots, pea-sticks
Special outlets Tool handles, sports equipment, rakes, mauls, stools, rustic furniture, bird tables, roundwood furniture, roundwood building materials, roof shingles, clogs, tent pegs, thatching-spars, clothes-pegs, sculpture, carving, whistles, walking-sticks
By-products Bark (tanning, gallops, horticulture), chips (heat heaps, horticulture, surfacing), sawdust, wood ash, leaf compost, pollen, seeds and seedlings, wines and beers, ornamental foliage, fruit and nuts, syrups and resins, sugars and starch, protein, cellulose, lignin
Basketry Osier baskets, trugs, spelk baskets, fruit punnets, duck nesting baskets, eel and fish traps, lobster creels, wicker furniture, egg baskets, bird cages, poultry baskets

DIRECT SALES

Garden centres	Thatchers
Allotment societies	Craft workshops
Hop-growers	Hunts, race-courses, stables
Farmers	Water authorities
Fencing contractors	Conservation groups
Nurseries	Members of the public

Table 20
FIREWOOD

SUITABILITY OF VARIOUS SPECIES

Alder, poplar, willow Not recommended – they either spit or smoulder, and give off little heat; more suitable for charcoal
Apple and other fruit trees Good if available; pleasant smell
Ash The best firewood, even when green; burns rather fast in stoves
Beech Excellent
Birch Very good for heat but might burn too fast
Cedars Spark like other conifers but reasonable; said to burn better after being struck by lightning!
Elm Difficult to split logs; tends to smoulder but plenty of heat in heartwood for stoves; sapwood lacks heat and makes a lot of ash
Douglas fir Not worth trying – sparky; low heat value
Hawthorn Good, lasting
Holly Very good, even when green
Hornbeam Good, especially for stoves
Horse chestnut As fierce-burning as ash in stoves
Larches Sparky; heat value a little less than elm
Lime Reasonable
Monkey puzzle Very resinous and fiery – fun on a bonfire
Oak Intense heat and good burning if old and dry – gives more heat than ash and as much as beech
Pines Very explosive; a lot of flame for little heat
Spruces Sparky; very low heat value
Sweet chestnut Treat with caution – can vary from sulky to dangerously sparky to a very reasonable log
Sycamore Reasonable
Yew Explosive on an open fire unless seasoned for at least two years.

SELLING FIREWOOD

Normally sold by the solid cubic metre.
Standard logs 1m³ solid occupies about 1.8m³ of stacking space (55 per cent wood, 45 per cent air)
Conifer lengths 1m³ solid occupies about 1.53m³ of stacking space in compact stack (65 per cent wood, 35 per cent air)
Broadleaf lengths 1m³ solid occupies about 1.8m³ of stacking space (range 1.6–2.4m³)
A standard log is 18–30cm long; it should be split if more than 15cm in diameter
Roundwood is any length of timber of any diameter, including sawmill offcuts longer than 30cm
Seasoning It is understood that the user will season firewood unless ordered 'summer dry' (that is, felled before 31 March, stacked in sun before 1 May)

wood. Wood is at its heaviest when green: it will be easier to transport if it is stacked on site to air-dry first, or is turned into charcoal, which is 20 per cent lighter than air-dried wood and a great deal more efficient as a fuel. Removal of the bark speeds the air-drying process, and so does splitting.

• As the sole source of house heating, 7 or 8 tonnes of air-dried wood are needed for an average three-bedroomed house per annum. This could be achieved by working a 3ha coppice on a fifteen-year rotation, cutting 0.2ha each year. It is possible to start harvesting a firewood crop seven to ten years after planting a new coppice. Lop-and-top from trees felled for timber often yields plenty of good firewood logs too.

• 7 tonnes of air-dried wood take up about 9 cubic metres of stacking space.

• Fast-growing species produce large yields of low-density wood which burns fast and often spits – for example, willow and conifers. Slow-growing species produce firewood of a higher density and better quality – for instance, ash, hornbeam, lime, oak and sweet chestnut (though chestnut can be too sparky for an open fire). Four conifer logs usually supply the same heat as three broadleaf logs. The heavier the dry log, the more heat it will produce.

• To air-dry wood, stack in 1m lengths (as described for cordwood in Chapter VI) with plenty of air movement around and between the logs. Leave them in the open, exposed to wind and sun, for the whole spring and summer after winter felling, then reduce to fire-log size in autumn and store for further air-drying under a sunny log port (a lean-to with a roof, but open-sided for ventilation) or indoors for house-drying a few weeks before use. The more moisture that remains in the logs, the more energy is wasted on the fire by converting the water into steam instead of being given out as heat.

• Sell firewood by the solid cubic metre. 1 cubic metre makes a tight stack $2 \times 1 \times 0.9$m, and the same volume of wood weighs about 1 tonne fresh-felled. Small-diameter wood can be bound in bundles and cross-stacked for storage.

• To split an awkward log such as field elm, work from the edges with the axe or wedges in line with the circumference rather than along the log's radius.

Energy Crops

The Centre for Agricultural Strategy suggests the idea of 'energy forestry', which is growing trees specifically for fuel and feeding them into a machine to produce chips. There are basically two systems: short-rotation coppice (say three to five years) or a longer-rotation single-stem plantation which is clear-felled after twelve to twenty years and then replanted. The entire plant is fed into the chipper so that none of it is wasted on the bonfire, though it might be an idea to use the foliage as animal fodder. Trials are still under way with species like alder, southern beech, birch, eucalyptus, poplar and willow to find out which are the most productive.

For either system, the site needs to be suited to mechanised planting and harvesting for greatest efficiency, and there must be good access roads. The crop is taken to a chipper at the edge of the plantation. This machine costs a pretty penny to buy, so if you are well organised co-operate with lots of other small producers to purchase one or find a good chipper contractor.

Table 21
ENERGY CROPS

SHORT-ROTATION COPPICE

Willow, poplar; possibly alder, eucalypts, other broadleaves.
Sheltered lowland site; fertile, moist soils.
Spacing 1 × 1m to 1 × 0.5m; density 10,000–20,000 per hectare.
Plant cuttings, by hand or mechanically.
Fertilise for rapid growth (nitrogen).
Harvest every three to five years: chainsaws, bush saws, tractor-mounted harvester to bundle stems.
Replant after twenty to thirty years.
Yield: 10–15 tonnes dry matter per hectare per annum.

LONGER-ROTATION SINGLE-STEM PLANTATION

Poplar, alder, birch, eucalypts, sycamore, spruce, larch, pine.
Lowland or upland, valley sides, hillsides, but not too exposed, waterlogged or steep.
Spacing 2 × 1m to 1 × 1m; density, 5,000–10,000 per hectare.
Plant bare-root transplants by hand.
No fertiliser necessary.
Harvest at twelve to twenty years: chainsaws and skidders, feller-bunchers and forwarders. Then replant.
Yield: 8–12 tonnes dry matter per hectare per annum.

Charcoal
The energy in 1kg of charcoal is twice that for the same weight of wood, yet the charcoal is half the volume and its price could be ten

times higher. It is easy to store, easy to ignite, easy to control while it burns, and it burns with virtually no smoke and with a higher temperature than wood. Its sulphur and phosphorus contents are very low and it will not put tarry deposits inside the chimney.

Wood becomes charcoal when it is burned in controlled conditions with a limited air supply which prevents its complete combustion. The process is known as carbonisation, or charcoal burning, and it used to be a major local industry in coppiced woodlands, where the itinerant charcoal burner would set up camp in the wood and live in a tent of poles and sods next to the charcoal pit. The product was needed in large quantities as fuel for smelting, and in earlier times it was essential for the furnaces of the glass, iron and brick industries – industries which thus did much to shape English woodlands.

Today the charcoal burner is more likely to have a portable steel kiln than to dig an earth pit but he is still itinerant and something of a loner, spending endless hours in the woods while the kilns burn and ranging over a very wide area. There are probably less than a dozen portable kilns in England whose operators are members of the National Association of Charcoal Manufacturers, and most of the charcoal used in Britain today is imported. However, in Cumbria the New Woodmanship Trust (a charity which develops uses for trees) is supporting a local charcoal enterprise to meet the demand for barbecue fuel, and there could be scope for similar enterprises in other parts of the country where coppice crops are available. But the competition from imported charcoal is fierce, especially as it is often produced in countries where labour comes cheaply. The charcoal burner also needs a cheap source of raw material, like sawmill offcuts.

The main uses for charcoal, apart from domestic barbecues and grills in catering establishments, are in smelting top-quality steel and refining non-ferrous metals, and in soil improvement and animal feeds. Charcoal also has the ability to absorb gases and is therefore used in gas containers, medicines and light-buoys. 'Activated' charcoal removes colour from liquids and is used to refine chemical solutions; it is found in batteries and water filtration systems. Most charcoal is sold in lumps; it is also available in granules or as a powder, the latter sometimes bound into briquettes.

Charcoal and coppicing go hand in hand. The main species of trees used in charcoal production are oak, birch and hazel, but in practice any kind of wood can be carbonised: the species will, however, affect the properties of the charcoal. The greatest demand at present is for big chunks of hard charcoal with a low ash content and good mechanical properties, and fine, even-grained hardwoods are more suitable for this market, particularly (and in order of

(TOP) Open grown oak in a hedgerow.
(ABOVE) Trunk growing around fencing wire: this tree has been ruined as timber.

(LEFT) Epicormic growth on an oak. (BELOW) The Forestor 'baby' bandmill being used to saw a log into planks. (*Forestor*)

OPPOSITE PAGE (ABOVE) Pigs are excellent ground-cleaners in woodland renovation. (BELOW LEFT) Deer fencing to protect Christmas trees. (BELOW RIGHT) Typical tree shelter, looking like a field drainpipe.

(TOP LEFT) Old chestnut stool with good regrowth.
(TOP RIGHT) Woodman's barrow.
(ABOVE) Woodman's camp: freshly cut poles waiting to be worked.

(OPPOSITE) Basket-maker with duck nesting basket. (*Anna Oakford*)

(ABOVE AND LEFT) Cutter-cleaver Fred Goodall of Astolat peeling a chestnut pole in preparation for cleaving into palings, and George May making a wattle fencing pane (*C. P. Betteridge of Astolat*)

OPPOSITE PAGE
(ABOVE) Pointed stakes: note the blunted tips.
(BELOW) Woodman's cradle.

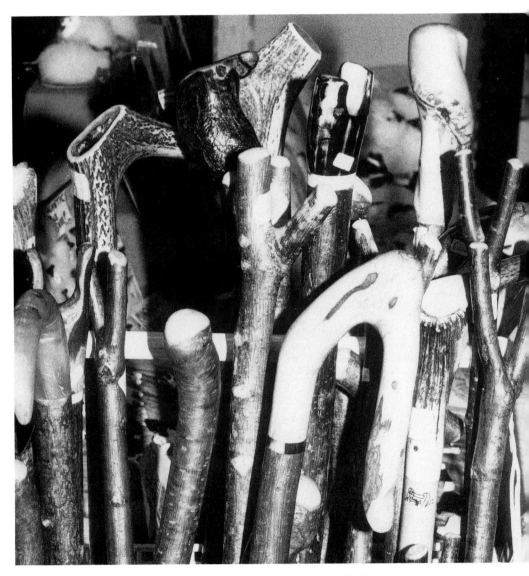

A selection of walking sticks. (*Anna Oakford*)

preference) beech, birch, hornbeam, oak, ash and elm. Conifers make easily ignited charcoal for domestic barbecues but it will burn away rather quickly.

Despite its coppice history, charcoal today is more often made from timber waste than from coppice crops: it is a productive outlet for slabwood (the outside sections that are wasted when a stem is squared up for planking) and waste wood from furniture and allied manufacturing industries. However, for portable kilns coppiced wood might be preferable: the ideal material is perhaps 0.5–2m long and 3–20cm in diameter. Bigger material would need to be split before being loaded into the kiln. Slabwood naturally includes quite a high proportion of thick bark, especially from a mature stem of oak, and this will increase the ash content of the charcoal substantially, reducing its quality. (Bark charcoal has an ash content about four times greater than that of wood charcoal.)

Seasoned wood produces better results than green: ideally it should have a moisture content of 20 per cent or less, which probably means that the wood weighs half as much as it did when felled. To produce 1 tonne of charcoal, you need about 8 tonnes of green wood or only 4 tonnes of thoroughly seasoned, air-dried wood.

Charcoal quality also depends on the method of production. Fast carbonisation at low temperatures produces an easily ignited charcoal with a high percentage of volatiles and a fixed carbon content of 60–80 per cent and this is the type generally used for domestic purposes. Slow carbonisation at higher temperatures is less volatile, with an 80–90 per cent carbon content, and is preferred for industrial use.

The general method of making charcoal is to heat wood under controlled conditions, ensuring that there is never enough air for total combustion, which would leave you with nothing but ashes and smoke! There are several stages in the process:

• Drive off the moisture in the wood by raising its temperature: stack the wood (this is an art) with a central flue, fire it from the centre and let the steam escape without admitting so much air that the whole lot goes up in flames. At this stage, part of the wood in a kiln is used to produce enough heat to begin the carbonisation process.

• Increase the temperature to more than 270°C to release the wood's volatile gases and liquids. The gases then produce enough heat to continue the process, and temperatures will increase to 400–600°C, depending on the type of kiln.

• Watch for the smoke becoming thin and turning blue or transparent instead of grey: most of the volatiles have now been

released, the wood is charcoal, and carbonisation must be
terminated to prevent the charcoal being burnt to ashes. Exclude
all air; cool the charcoal for a long while until there is no danger of
self-combustion when it is eventually exposed to air.

The traditional method of making charcoal is in a kiln – originally
an earth kiln based on a levelled hearth with an earth or ash floor
and a central stake around which is built a chimney of split logs
surrounded by carefully stacked layers of round logs which build up
into a flattish dome. The wood is then covered with sods, straw,
bracken and other handy materials to retain the heat and exclude
air. In due course the stake is removed to create a flue through the
middle of the heap, into which hot charcoal and kindling are dropped
to start the fire. The flue is then sealed with turf and the heap very
slowly burns for several days or even weeks. Any weak points in the
earthen jacket must quickly be sealed to prevent an influx of fresh
air. Small mounds carbonise the wood much faster than larger ones:
it is possible to produce charcoal in a day in a mound holding perhaps
0.5 cubic metre of wood for household use. More typically the base
of the mound is perhaps 5m in diameter and holds anything from
15–60 cubic metres of wood. In some places the kiln is a pit rather
than a mound, and these are on average from 1 to 3 cubic metres in
capacity, though they can be ten times as big. A pit 1.2m deep, 2.5m
wide and 10m long would hold about 25 cubic metres of stacked
wood but needs a system of air intakes and smoke outlets, and careful
management: the yields are often rather low.

The advantages of pits and mounds are that there are no capital
costs involved and they can be built right on site next to the wood
supply, but they do need very skilled attention over many days.
Portable steel kilns work on similar principles and are generally
easier to control: they can be set up anywhere, even at a sawmill to
take advantage of slabwood and offcuts, but of course there is the
initial cost of the equipment to be considered. A typical portable
kiln is a circular drum with a diameter of at least 2m and its own
lid, chimney and airflow controls. A cheap home-made kiln can be
created from an old oil drum (say, 200-litre size) and this is a popular
kiln for converting coconut shells into charcoal in the South Pacific.
With a few elaborations, an oil drum can produce 15–25kg of charcoal
from small pieces of wood and brush, and one person could operate
perhaps five single drums to produce 2.5 tonnes of charcoal a month.
But a proper portable batch kiln, with interlocking steel sections,
can deal more quickly and efficiently with a greater volume of wood –
and it will cost you a four-figure sum to buy a new one.

The merit of earth kilns and portable kilns is that there is no need to transport heavy wood to the kiln: the kiln comes to the wood. However, fixed kilns require less labour on site in that the loading and unloading can be mechanised, and they have their place in areas where the transport of the wood is no problem. The types include a traditional beehive – made of mud in villages in developing countries, or of brick or concrete and built in batches for larger operations – and of course they last for several years. On an industrial scale, kilns are replaced by continuous vertical metal retorts, perhaps 30m high, which can also extract and utilise the volatile by-products such as wood tar (Stockholm tar), acetic acid, naphtha and pyroligneous oils.

Apart from their advantages of scale, scope and automation, the retorts also overcome the problems of smell and smoke emission which are drawbacks in other kiln systems and which would make you most unpopular if you chose to set up your kiln in a built-up area.

Briquettes are made from the 'fines' which must be screened and ground, mixed with a binder like starch, clay or dung, then formed or compacted (by hand or with a press) and dried. They are denser than normal charcoal and less easy to ignite.

FENCING

The simplest livestock fencing, if your hedges are inadequate, is a couple of strands of barbed wire stapled to stakes between more substantial straining posts at the corners sustained by struts. These three types of support are the bread and butter of many a coppice – reasonably quick to grow, simple to work up and always in demand. They need no more than cutting to length and pointing, and a thicker stake can be split down its length to make two. The minimum top diameter of a typical round stake 1.6–1.7m long is 7.5cm, and of a split one 10cm at the face.

The main requirement is that the coppice poles should have grown straight, with no twists in the grain or distortions in the length. Depending on where you live, these posts are generally of sweet chestnut coppiced on a fifteen-year rotation, or oak thinnings, or softwoods like Lawson cypress, western red cedar, larch and pine.

The two hardwoods contain chemicals which inhibit rot, and their unusually durable heartwood lasts for several years in the ground without being treated with preservatives. Of course, if the ground is permanently wet, the posts will rot that much sooner. The pale outer layer of sapwood of even these durable species, however, is not resistant to decay but is able to absorb preservatives if necessary, though oak resolutely rejects the indignity of being impregnated with any kind of preservative and sweet chestnut is almost as obdurate. In any case both species have only a very thin layer of sapwood.

Many softwoods can be used for fencing as long as they are thoroughly treated – and that means ensuring that the preservative penetrates as far into the pole as possible so that the heartwood of less durable species is protected. Some would claim that untreated sweet chestnut or oak can last for perhaps ten to fifteen years in reasonable ground; others swear by 'tanalised' or 'celcurised' timber which, as its slightly greenish tinge betrays, has been pressure-treated with copper chrome arsenate (CCA) and is claimed to last for twenty-five years. However, these CCA treatments have been widely in general use for perhaps only twenty years.

In post-and-rail fences the barbed wire gives way to long, cleft poles which are simply nailed to the stakes. More sophisticated is the cleft post-and-rail fence, typically of Sussex oak, in which triangular cleft rails are shaped at either end to fit into mortices cut into cleft or sawn posts: there is no need for nails to keep the rails securely in place. A good oak log can be cleft into four or six rails.

Cleft posts and rails are more durable than sawn ones in that the splitting is along the grain of the wood so that the cells remain largely intact and able to shed water, whereas in sawn timber many cells are damaged and the wood is therefore much more likely to absorb water. Cleft wood is also much stronger, but you will need sawn timber to make your own gates and stiles. Oak is the traditional sawn wood for gates, though today most are made of pressure-treated softwoods or imported hardwoods. Designs for and methods of hanging gates are described in detail in the British Trust for Conservation Volunteers' *Fencing* handbook, including kissing gates, hunting gates, deer gates, rambler gates, water gates and several different stiles. If you have the timber and the equipment to make sawn-timber gates, remember that wood, though traditional, is a heavy material and many farmers prefer the lightness of tubular metal.

Peeling

For agricultural fencing the bark is generally left on the posts (to the delight of cattle and horses, which rather enjoy stripping it off!), but timber must be peeled before it can be treated with preservatives and is also peeled for palings and other uses. Peeling can be laborious but is worth the effort as bark tends to harbour destructive insects and water and thus makes the wood more prone to fungal infection. Bark is easiest to remove immediately after felling, on the spot, especially in spring and summer. The traditional tools are a peeling iron or spade for larger diameters or, for much coppice work, a rinder or draw-knife (see Figure 3). You will need a peeling brake

Figure 3: Basic tools

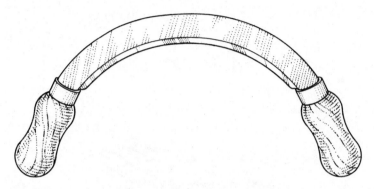

(i) Rinder or draw-knife:
     This one is typically handmade: the blade is part of an old
     fag-hook. Other types have straight blades.

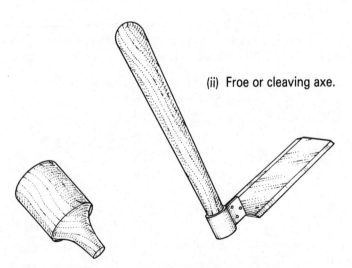

(ii) Froe or cleaving axe.

(iii) Maul or froe-club:
      A disposable billet of wood for driving in the froe during
      cleaving.

Figure 4: Cleaver-cutter's devices

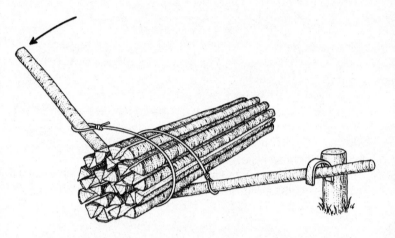

(i) Woodman's grip:
    To tighten the bundle, put one pole under the hook on the
    right and create a tourniquet by applying leverage on the
    other pole.

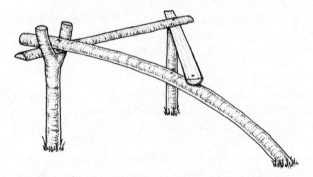

(ii) Cleaving brake:
    Simple version using a long, naturally curved pole and two
    split lengths, nailed or lashed together in a tilted triangle with
    two uprights. The cleaving length can be braced under one
    side of the triangle and over a second side.

to act as a vice for the pole while you pull the blade towards you, a job which will certainly warm you up in cold weather.

Bark has its uses, though it is usually discarded. There was a time when the bark of oak and sweet chestnut was in great demand for leather tanneries, but these industries now use imported chemicals rather than tannin direct from British bark.

Cleaving

You will also need a brake for cleaving. The cleaving brake is a triangular arrangement (see Figure 4) which braces the pole while you split it with a cleaving iron or froe and mallet: a skilful job. Larger poles are split with wedges and a sledge hammer. The cleaving of chestnut paling by an expert with a break adze is a joy to watch, and a really experienced cleaver can get as many as twenty-five pales from a single pale-length in the twinkling of an eye, working to a spider-web pattern, though more practically he would cleave out up to eight pales from each length and go on to produce four or five hundred a day. Even more magical is the art of the hurdle-maker cleaving a long, whippy hazel rod no thicker than a thumb.

Pointing

The point of a stake is made with four sloped cuts, leaving a small square tip rather than a sharp point which would snap at its first bite into the ground. The simplest, quickest method is to use a chainsaw if you are competent enough not to take your feet off, but you can also use a billhook or side axe. However, today's coppices sing to the sound of the sawbench, where a diesel-driven circular saw or hydrapointer with two angled blades shaves stake points as quickly as an electric pencil sharpener.

Bundling

Spiles for wired chestnut paling fences need to be bundled for easy handling. They are sorted according to length as you work (in 15cm steps between 1 and 2m) and then 'cradled' on curved pail handles between posts to form bundles of twenty-five. Take a piece of chain, cable or rope about twice as long as the circumference of the bundle and attach a stake at either end, each perhaps a metre long and at least as thick as a tool handle. Straddle the bundle in its cradle and put the cable of your 'grip' or press rope around the bundle, then tighten it by pressing down on the stakes so that the cable holds the material firmly together while you bind it with wire or withies. (See Figure 4.)

Chestnut Paling

Wired paling fences used to be produced in great quantities, and in

Small Woods and Hedgerows

Kent, Surrey and Sussex you can still see the long sheds that house the wiring machinery. The fencing is wonderfully stockproof and also good protection against weather and intruders: it is used in gardens, around woods and plantations, as a snow baffle beside vulnerable roads, and to keep intruders or snoopers away from building sites, roadworks and army land. It can be rolled up and moved to a new site, though it is nothing like as handy as electric fencing for temporary livestock defences. It is also heavier and a great deal more expensive, which is probably why its manufacture is now almost entirely restricted to Kent. But it is a versatile design: it can be any height from around 1 to 2m and the palings can be set very close or quite widely; and, of course, the wider apart, the fewer pales and therefore the lower the cost.

The basic process of construction is to set the pales between two or three double lines of wire (top, middle and bottom), twisting the wire between each spile with the help of a windlass before inserting the next one. The wire is twisted in alternate directions: clockwise after one spile, then anti-clockwise after the next – or you would end up in a right old tangle. The twists must not be so tight that the wire snaps, and any tendency of the spiles to slip from their loops can be deterred with staples. The fence can be made up *in situ*, driving each spile into the ground a little as you go along, but most fences are made up at the yard in runs of 10m long. Each spile is snubbed at the top to shed rainwater and avoid snagging clothes, and the run is generally set between stakes about 3m apart, with the palings clear of the ground to reduce the chance of decay. Today most paling is machine-wired and is made of sweet chestnut, as it is such a durable wood, but you could try ash, hazel or perhaps field maple.

Hurdles

Wattle (woven) hurdles are generally made from hazel, coppiced on perhaps a seven-year rotation, while sheep-hurdles and gate-hurdles might be made from willow on a similar rotation, or ash or chestnut using smaller poles from traditional rotations, or a combination of more than one type of wood.

Wattle used to have many applications: it can still be found under the mud plaster of wattle-and-daub timber-framed houses built in medieval times, for example, with plenty of horse-hair mixed into the mud. Wattle was also used to control sand dunes and to protect pond and river embankments, and some people still use willow wattle to surround islands in newly dug ponds (the willow soon sprouts to create a living mat which roots into the island and weaves itself into a protective barrier). However, it is hazel which has always been the backbone of wattle work, and it was the demand for wattle that has left us a legacy of hazel coppice today, now sadly often neglected.

Wattle is light to carry and easy to erect as a temporary fence. It is still in use, though more often as 'rustic' panelling sold by garden centres than as agricultural fencing. The hazel rods need to be worked as they are harvested in winter, while they remain pliable, and the normal coppice practice was to fell the crop in 3-acre (1.2ha) cants, separating the rods according to their suitability for firewood, thatching-spars, bean-poles and hurdle-making. For hurdles, longer rods about 2.5cm in diameter and shorter ones up to twice as thick are used.

The basic essentials for making a wattle hurdle are a slightly curved, heavy wooden base mould about 2.1m long with ten equally spaced holes in it into which the uprights (known as sails) are inserted upside-down. The two end stakes, known as shores, are about 30cm longer than the eight central sails and are pointed for driving into the ground when the fence is erected. They are roundwood (and sometimes of ash for extra strength), whereas the sails are riven with a billhook. The weaving rods are a mixture of round and cleft: the round rods are used where extra strength is needed – for example, at the top and bottom of the panel, and along a stretch about a third of the way down from the top if the panel is given a square gap so that it can be transported on a pole. The cleft rods are split with a billhook with great skill: unlike when making chestnut paling, the cleaver does not use a cleaving-brake but simply holds the rod in one hand and opens and lengthens the cleft by twisting the hook held in the other.

The weaving is equally skilful, and a craftsman makes a very tidy wattle from whichever side it is viewed: one face will show the bark and the other will be clean except for the roundwood, and the overlaps between each length are as neat as good knitting. Like woven cloth, each row is pressed snugly against the preceding one with the aid of the back of the billhook as the work proceeds.

Gate hurdles are more open affairs and make very useful sheep enclosures, as those who have watched television's *One Man and his Dog* will recognise. The skill in making gate hurdles is to make good mortices in the two end-uprights (or heads) to take five rails or bars, which each have tapered ends to fit snugly into the mortices. A central upright and two diagonals are then nailed across the bars as braces.

CREATIVE OUTLETS

There is still a local market for those horticultural essentials, bean-poles and pea-sticks, which have always been useful coppice products, especially from hazel grown on a three-to-four-year cycle or cut selectively each year by the removal of about a third of the stems. For relatively short pea-sticks, coppice every other year. In the first year prune shoots down by half or two thirds of their length to encourage them to branch for pea-sticks; for bean-poles you need long, straight rods and should let them grow for perhaps three years before cutting. You can use the brushy top of the bean-pole as pea-sticks. However, hazel is normally managed for the most valuable outlet, which is wattle, with thatching spars next in importance, and bean-poles and pea-sticks are mere by-products of longer rotation crops.

If you are working a coppice, there are plenty of more exciting potential products, particularly if you are prepared to learn how to work up the products yourself or can co-operate with craftsmen locally, or perhaps set up a small crafts industry in a converted barn. The biggest problem is likely to be marketing the goods, many of which were once considered essential but are now more often sold to tourists and gift shops.

John Makepeace's centre for woodland industry in Dorset is probably the major one for research into possible uses of woodland produce – here they are especially interested in finding practical uses for roundwood which is too small for the sawmill but which they believe could be used in building and certainly in furniture-making. All over the country there are craftsmen producing fine furniture in competition with the bigger factories but the majority of them are more interested in larger and more high-quality trees than your coppice can produce. For example, in my own valley Robin Carter makes beautiful tables and other furniture from English hardwoods and, with remarkable foresight or luck, he had purchased a mobile bandsaw mill the day before the October storm in 1987. His machine is hydraulically driven with the aid of a Land Rover and for many months after the storm he was kept busy slicing through some of the finest windblown trees in Sussex, including beautiful yews more than two centuries old in Petworth Park. He will make up the timber into furniture and also treen such as goblets, platters and bowls.

Woods for turnery, carving and similar artistic uses need to be very special but there are several sculptors in the country working with less promising materials. For example, South East Arts funded resident artist Michael Fairfax, whose work included an imaginative piece entitled 'The Trees Rattle Too', created from cleft chestnut and cleft sycamore. In North Wales another environmental sculptor, David Nash, uses hedge-laying methods to train ash trees into the interesting shapes that form the basis of his sculptures.

'Artistic' pieces can also be practical. My local 'Forest Crafts' workshop produces very original rustic Wendy houses and tree houses for children and all sorts of bird tables, nesting boxes and a possibly unique high-level rabbit hutch for the resident bunny who sits safely on his platform 2m above ground watching the world go by and mocking the local dogs. The father and son who produce all these unusual items have vivid imaginations (their playground equipment includes galleons, forts and haywains) and are in love with wood: they can see potential in every misshapen old tree or stump and also make full use of local coppices and small woodlands. There is also a two-man sawmill in the valley where the waiting timber stems lie like sleeping giants, offering a perch to the resident peacocks.

In other parts of the country there are still craftsmen who can produce useful hand-made wooden items like rakes, forks, milking stools, tool handles, thatching-spars, clothes-pegs, hay cribs, roofing shingles, ladders, barrels, butter churns, trugs and spelk baskets, or larger items like wheelbarrows, cartwheels and wagons. The main outlets are through rural-life museums and garden centres, which might also sell hand-made wooden toys, rustic furniture, plant troughs, carved decoy ducks, wickerwork ... there is *so much* that can be made from wood. There is not room here to do justice to the intricacies of these crafts but some good books on craftwork are listed in the Bibliography.

WALKING-STICKS AND CROOKS
Making walking-sticks and crooks is a craft so intimately bound up with coppice management that it does merit a more detailed look in this book as an enterprise for smallholders. A plantation for producing suitable material for walking-sticks can be worked on a very short rotation, giving you good returns quickly even from new planting. You can plant intensively and can probably take a first crop within four or five years, which is much earlier than for other coppice products. Then you can either supply a manufacturer or work up the sticks yourself, bundle them into the car boot and sell them. There is plenty of scope for variety in the woods used, the manner of shaping the sticks and the type and material of the handles. If you live in southern England, pay a visit to Cooper & Sons at Wormley, near Godalming in Surrey, which is one of the few major walking-stick factories in the country.

The traditional, simple walking-cane with a curved handle is still produced in huge numbers by Coopers for supplying to hospital patients recovering from, say, hip operations. Hospital sticks must be of sweet chestnut but canes are also made from ash and hazel, and these three are the traditional woods for many kinds of walking-

Small Woods and Hedgerows

stick. However, almost any wood can be used, according to personal preference – cherry, holly, blackthorn and hawthorn, for example. In effect, if a countryman sees a stick of the right shape growing in the hedgerow, he will cut it as a walking-stick whatever the species – and he will cut it when he sees it, whatever the season, before someone else takes it.

To be more methodical about walking-stick production, you would probably do best by planting a mixed coppice, especially of the typical quick-growers like ash, hazel and sweet chestnut. You can plant very closely indeed, which means you can make the most of a small patch of land: experiment with a spacing of about 0.5m between plants. Take your first crop after four or five years if you want to establish a good enough root system for continued cropping, and thereafter coppice the rods on a three-year rotation if they grow well enough to give you butts of 2.5cm in diameter.

The rods can be grown straight and clean for mass production of curve-handled sticks (the curve is created by steaming the wood and bending it round a form) or you can be much more imaginative and produce corkscrew sticks, thumb sticks, cross-head sticks, knob-head sticks and all manner of 'natural' sticks which you have deliberately fashioned during their growth. Many of these involve pruning, layering or partial uprooting; one of the simplest desirable distortions, however, is the corkscrew look of a stick which has been chosen as a climbing post by woodbine (honeysuckle) – the bane of the forester but definitely to be encouraged in a walking-stick plantation if you want sticks with character.

For simple curved canes, a crop of straight rods is harvested between autumn and spring (when it is easier to see what you are cutting). If the bark is not to be a feature of the stick, it is easier to peel soon after cutting. A green stick can to some extent be straightened if it is hung up with a weight on the end while it seasons – and careful seasoning is important: do not subject the sticks to heat or very dry conditions or the wood will develop shakes and cracks. Let them hang individually in an open shed so that the air can circulate around each one, or lay them horizontally on open racks, but do not keep them in bundles.

To form a curved handle on a straight rod, put it in a 'bath' of moist sand heated from below so that it steams. Leave it in the sandbed until it becomes pliable enough to be bent gently over a round former – and wear gloves, because the stick will be hot and needs to be handled while it is still warm. A simple former includes a jig to secure the stick while you work. Be very gentle: if the wood is not yet pliant enough, or if you bend it too quickly, it will split. You need to give it a tighter curve than you want eventually, then bind it to keep the shape until it has 'set'. When you release the binding, the curve will spring open to some extent and be the shape you want – if you have judged it right. Trim it up, polish it to a fine finish, pop a ferrule on the tip, bundle a score or more into your car and visit the local fete or agricultural show.

Of course, a stick or crook does not have to be wooden from top to toe and you can give your imagination free rein with handles made of bone, horn, metal, ivory, glass or resin. Crooks need careful thought: their main purpose is not to give the shepherd something to lean on or flourish but to help control livestock by hooking them around the leg, neck or chest. They are commonly used for working with sheep (though today many shepherds use light aluminium crooks rather than wooden ones) but there are also goose or swan hooks which should be designed to catch the bird gently by the neck – not by the legs, which are easily damaged. If you are ever involved in animal rescue work, you will find all sorts of uses for both shepherd's crooks and swan hooks.

If your imagination really runs riot, you can start carving your sticks or their handles, or moulding handles in resin, or painting them, or specialising in gadget sticks concealing whisky flasks, swords, snuff, scent and so on; or, as described by baculumary Peter Philp, how about a handle which becomes a wind-shielded briar pipe, or contains a dog-whistle, or holds a bird-watcher's spy glass or a tool kit? No doubt you can think of something original that will become a valuable antique in its time.

BRUSHWOOD

Birch produces a good volume of twiggery which some consider fit for no more than the site bonfire but which others, in the tradition of those who work the land, turn to good advantage. Everything has a use, be it the pig's squeal or the birch's brush. The main outlets are brushwood jumps (for use on race-courses, at hunter trials and point-to-points and in show-jumping) and besoms. In times past brushwood was bundled tightly into fuel faggots for the stove, and perhaps this is another idea which could be resuscitated for wood-burning stoves, or incorporated into an energy-crop production cycle. Birch can be coppiced for brush on a rotation as short as every three years, though four or five would be better.

Besoms still find quite a good market, and if you also grow ash, hazel or sweet chestnut coppice for the broom handles, you could consider a small besom-making enterprise and set yourself up as a broom-squire. Like any other squire, you will need a horse – a broom-horse, to be precise, which is a wooden bench on which you sit astride to control a wire clamp with your feet while you bind the twigs. If you have hazel and willow to hand as well, you could use the more traditional withy binding. You need good, hard hands for dealing with birch brush (in some areas besoms are made of heather or, of course, broom) and the material is ideal for gardens and rough surfaces in yards. However, it will rot if left out of doors, and that means your contract to supply brushwood fencing to the local race-course is an annual affair that could run and run.

BY-PRODUCTS

Not long ago a local FWAG adviser sent out a leaflet from a company willing to accept large quantities of branchy material from 7.5 to 10cm in diameter and smaller, who actually wanted to tackle poor-quality underwood, open up overgrown rides, clear windblown trees and unsaleable thinnings, as long as the minimum area of woodland was around a hectare.

This company had found uses for material that many woodland owners believe to be useless, and there is a growing trend to utilise the whole biomass of a tree, from its topmost leaf and twig right down to its nethermost rootlet. The technology exists and it is only a matter of time before it can be used economically on a more general scale in the countryside. Wood is a source of stored energy: a growing tree accumulates all that powerful sunshine and builds up a great store of potentially useful chemicals as well as the more obvious woody tissues that humans have always exploited. There is talk of extracting and using all the sugars, starches, proteins and other nutrients, and of harnessing the alcohols − not just maple syrup, birch wine and spruce beer but alcohols for industry and sources of energy. In the meantime the chipping machines are hard at work converting the cumbersome biomass of trees into a more manageable material which can then be utilised in so many different ways by so many different industries from paper mills and chipboard factories to race-courses, horticulture, playground construction and urban landscaping.

Bark

In 1973 an article entitled *Bark: a Potentially Useful By-product*, by J. R. Aaron of the Forestry Commission's harvesting and marketing division, appeared in the Institute of Wood Science's *Journal*. It stated that about 10 per cent of the fresh weight or volume of all coniferous roundwood grown in Britain is bark, most of which was incinerated or dumped, at some expense. However, as Aaron pointed out, 'if uses are developed, a waste material becomes a useful by-product and the cost of disposal can often be turned to a net income'.

Since time immemorial, except in our own age, people have made use of every material they could find: nothing has been wasted. This is particularly true of organic matter. If it could not be eaten, it could be used as a tool or as shelter or raiment or ornament. There is a use for everything, which we tend to forget today. One of the earliest examples of this is that the skin of an animal whose flesh has been used as food can be preserved for many years after the animal's death and can be treated so that it is tough enough to endure rough treatment but also soft enough to be pleasant to wear. And from almost the beginning of this discovery, humans have used tree bark to tan leather.

Oak bark was our own country's main source of tannin for animal hide, but sweet chestnut in fact contains a higher percentage of tannin in its bark (15.2 per cent of its dry weight, as opposed to 13 per cent in the case of oak) and some softwood barks are richer still (Japanese larch 16.5 per cent, western hemlock 16.7 per cent and sitka spruce 17.5 per cent); and the black wattle, which is now the major source of tannin extracts imported by Britain, has more than 30 per cent. Local bark is rarely used now in the leather industry, partly because harvesting is labour-intensive and partly because the easiest time to strip off bark is in a brief few weeks in May and June when the cambium is actively dividing and the bark is relatively loose – especially in the case of oak. Bark peeling is not a process easily mechanised without rupturing the tissues and releasing enzymes that render the tannins insoluble.

There are other substances in bark which could be extracted – for example, dihydroquercetin, which has medicinal properties, and a wax in species like Douglas fir which is almost as good as beeswax for polishes. The problem with these and other bark extracts like furfural is largely one of scale.

From a commercial point of view, there is much greater potential in using the bark itself, in bulk, than extractives, and the main uses are in horticulture – pulverised bark is used in composts and mulches and as a soil improver. It also makes a very good substance for plunge beds: it is naturally resistant to decay, remains clean to handle for a long time, retains its bulk for years, is relatively free-draining as a medium, is generally free from weed seeds, makes pests feel unwelcome, keeps the plunged roots warm, and as a bonus its dark colour and texture look good in contrast with plant foliage.

Bark is also used in the equestrian world. Coarsely pulverised it becomes an excellent ground cover in the arena and in chips it makes a very good surface for training gallops. It can be used as a surface for play areas, too, and on footpaths to dry up muddy patches and give a pleasant walking surface. It is a resistant and long-lasting material; after all, its main purpose on the tree is to protect the tissues from drying out or from being attacked by fungi and insects, and these properties should be valued. Another interesting quality is the ability of bark to absorb ammonia and other noxious gases, which makes it a deep-litter medium that renders a cow-house a little less smelly than if the animals were bedded on straw, though there are the disadvantages that bark is not as absorbent of fluids as straw and it can also be dishearteningly dark on the floor. Fresh straw brightens the place up.

Bark is also good insulation, both for sound and for warmth, and there are several schemes to develop bark building blocks and boards. It absorbs oil, too, and there is an important potential use for it in the control of oil pollution by means of bark booms. There are also possibilities for developing bark as fuel, but its major drawbacks in this respect are that it produces a large amount of ash – four times as much as its own wood would produce – and it cannot be made smokeless. Even so, there was a move to make bark briquettes for domestic fuel but the idea was dropped when the horticultural market proved far more lucrative.

Birch bark has its own peculiar properties, the best-known of which must be as kindling for camp fires. In Russia they used to distill a fragrant oil from birch, and glass engravers used pyrobetulin extracted from the bark, but perhaps the most attractive use was that by Scandinavian farmers applying birch bark as a durable, waterproof covering to their wooden houses – and very pretty it looked, too.

What about cork? The cork oak, *Quercus suber*, grows throughout the Iberian peninsula and around the Mediterranean except on limestone or chalky soils, and it will grow in the climate of southern and eastern England – or even in the Midlands and perhaps in the north of England, though it could hardly be said to thrive. Still, the idea of growing your own cork for your home-made wine is quite a pleasant one!

Wood Chips

There are chips and chips: they come in all sizes and shapes and meet a wide range of purposes, especially in the manufacture of pulp and boards. Smaller chips, wood shavings and sawdust can be used for animal bedding and poultry litter, and chips of various sizes can replace bark for horticultural mulches, gallop surfaces and pathways. An increasingly important outlet for wood chips is, of course, for fuel, as described under 'Energy Crops' (see page 95), and there is a very minor outlet in making sawdust briquettes for burning, preferably laced with coal dust.

Table 22
EDIBLE PRODUCE

Ash Keys (pickled)
Barberry Fruit (jellies, not raw)
Beech Nuts (especially for salad oil), young leaves
Bilberry Fruit (fresh with sugar or cooked; jelly, jam)
Blackberry Fruit
Blackthorn Sloes (not raw; jelly, sloe gin)
Broom Young shoots (mild diuretic and heart tonic), flower buds
    (salads, pickles)
Cherry Fruit of gean (can be sweet or bitter); bird cherry very bitter
Crab apple Fruit (not raw; jelly, cider, verjuice, etc.)
Cranberry Fruit (cooked, sauce)
Elder Flowers (flavouring, tea, wine, fresh food, cosmetics), fruit
    (cooked or as sauce)
Guelder rose Fruit (*must* be cooked – raw makes you sick)
Hawthorn Young leaf shoots (nutty and delicious raw), flowers
    (liqueur), fruit (raw or jelly)
Hazel Nuts
Juniper 'Berries' (rich in oil, used to flavour gin, etc.)
Lime Young leaves of common lime (raw), flowers (tea)
Medlar Fruit (raw if bletted; baked; jelly)
Oak Acorns (roasted as coffee substitute in dire need)
Pear Fruit of wild pear as astringent jelly
Pine Kernels
Wild rose Petals (flavouring for many dishes); hips (very high vitamin
    C content – rose hip syrup)
Rowan Fruit (jelly)
Sea buckthorn Fruit (rich in vitamin C)
Wild service tree Fruit (bletted)
Sweet chestnut Nuts (especially roasted, or chestnut purée)
Walnut Nuts (high in calories, rich in vitamin C when green)
Whitebeam Fruit (bletted)
Yew Fruit (but *seed* is highly poisonous)

Muka

In his most interesting book, *Towards Holistic Agriculture*, R. W.
Widdowson describes a Latvian method of making the most of
woodland waste. Muka is a dried, ground-up mixture of pine
needles, petioles, deciduous leaves and small twigs (6mm maximum
diameter) which is used mainly as a feed for livestock, forming up
to 5 per cent of the diet – at which level some types of muka
(depending on the species of tree) seem to improve the animals'
health, growth, productivity and reproductive capacity. Widdowson
suggests that more than 7 per cent of the weight of a tree is yielded

Small Woods and Hedgerows

as dry muka, and that a typical conifer plantation at felling for timber could produce perhaps 40 tonnes of muka per hectare; a traditional broadleaf coppice perhaps 5 tonnes of muka per hectare per annum; and a crop of willow or poplar grown specifically for muka production and harvested annually possibly more than 12 tonnes of muka per hectare at each harvest. But before you rush to put your garden trimmings through the mincer, read Widdowson's book for more about the effects of different foliage on different animals.

Fruit and Nuts
With all the emphasis on the woody produce of trees, it is easy to forget that many of them also produce fruits – edible fruits – especially the hedgerow trees and shrubs. The harvest in woodland tends to be nuts rather than fleshy fruits, and nuts are a rich source of protein and fats. Apparently a hazel nut has 50 per cent more protein than the same weight of egg, and 450g of walnuts can provide more than the average adult's daily dietary requirement of calories. Perhaps you could set aside some of your coppice for nut production, harvesting judiciously so that wildlife can still feast.

Fungi
There is a species of wood fungus known as shii-take which is said to be the industry of the future for smallholders in Japan, Taiwan, the United States and several European countries, though no doubt the claim is something of an exaggeration. However, it is already being produced by one or two enterprising people in Britain and it could be worth considering. It goes well with your steak; its protein content is at least 20 per cent, its fat content and calories are low; it is a useful source of vitamin B, vitamin D and certain trace minerals; and it is said to lower the blood pressure, reduce blood cholesterol levels, and possibly even act as an anti-cancer agent.

To produce shii-take, save some small-diameter (up to 15cm) hardwood logs about 1m long and free from rot when you are felling an area of woodland. Species with dark, thick bark are probably best and oak seems to be best of all, but try sweet chestnut or beech by way of experiment too and talk to Seale-Hayne Agricultural College in Devon about their own attempts to grow the fungi. (The two lecturers particularly involved in the scheme are Dr Bill Slee, a land-use specialist, and Dr Alastair Campbell, a microbiologist.) Drill some holes in the logs and inoculate them with shii-take spawn (in sawdust or in impregnated wooden dowels) then simply leave them outside to incubate and fruit perhaps eighteen months later, probably after a spell of cold weather.

Another wood fungus, this one not grown for food, is *Fomes fomentarius*, the dried flesh of which is known as amadou. It used to be thinly sliced and used as tinder after being boiled in saltpetre and dried. Until recently it was also widely used by anglers to dry flies; it is a handy styptic to reduce bleeding too, and if you wipe your spectacles with amadou they will not get spotty in the rain! Long ago in Germany they made all sorts of things with amadou, such as oven aprons, picture frames and tobacco pouches.

Foliage

Your woodland and hedgerows could produce seasonal foliage like holly, ivy and mistletoe, either sold fresh or made up into wreaths and other decorations, perhaps as a sideline to Christmas tree production. Mistletoe is fussy about its host, and if you decide to try to establish a plant you need to know where your seed berries have come from. A lot of Christmas mistletoe is imported from the Continent these days, and it seems that French mistletoes do not take kindly to English trees! There are in fact sixty or seventy species of mistletoe, each with a preferred host tree (the plant is a parasite), and you will be more successful in propagation if you attempt it on the same species of tree on which the parent plant was living.

Probably the most common host tree in this country is apple but you will also find self-seeded mistletoe on poplar, lime, maple, hawthorn, rowan, sorbus, and occasionally on horse chestnut, Scots pine and cedar (though on the whole it avoids conifers). It very rarely grows on oak, so no wonder the Druids endowed the 'golden bough' with magical properties!

Mistletoe is a benevolent parasite, unless it grows so well that it weighs down the tree's branches. It takes some time to become well enough established to be cropped. To propagate, imitate nature – the plant is 'sown' by birds pushing the berries into bark crevices, and your best course is to press ripe berries into notches or under bark flaps on the underside of a branch near its base in May. The berries usually stick in place with the help of their own viscid pulp, which sets like glue. Some people try ripening the seed first by leaving mature berries on cropped shoots and hanging them in a cool, even temperature of 4–7°C until April or May. When the berry germinates on the tree, its radicle very slowly penetrates the bark and grows gradually under it. To harvest, cut just above the junction with older growth where there is a bud which will produce new growth later. Only the female plant is berry-bearing, and it will not usually produce fruit until it is perhaps seven years old.

Foliage for florists can be taken from the more attractive conifers and from various eucalypts, and these special crops are discussed in Chapter VIII.

VIII

SPECIAL TREE CROPS

There are some species which can give quick returns within a few years of being planted without being coppiced, and some are suitable for small-scale enterprises – but you need to be sure of your markets and to do some thorough market research before you start planting. You must also aim for quality, which means more concentrated management in the short term than is required for long-term timber trees.

CHRISTMAS TREES

Fashions in Christmas trees come and go, and for the most part the fashion for artificial trees seems to be waning, with greater interest being shown in more unusual species than the standard Norway spruce (*Picea abies*). For example, in Denmark they prefer the decorative bluish-grey noble fir, and perhaps there is also a place for the delicate, drooping western hemlock.

You need to keep your finger on the pulse of fashion: your trees are likely to be in the ground for perhaps seven to nine years and the market might change in the meantime. Try to establish your outlets well in advance of the crop's maturity, and then consolidate your good contacts by supplying top-quality trees of the sizes required, year after year. That means planting with a view to rotational cropping. It is a highly competitive market and plenty of other people are trying to enter it, so you need to establish and maintain an excellent reputation for reliable delivery, and at the same time you need to find your own special niche either in the manner of marketing or in the type of tree you produce.

At present the most popular sizes are 1.2–1.8m high, but who knows what people will want in the twenty-first century? Think of it from the householder's point of view rather than the grower's or retailer's. Christmas comes but once a year but the needles can linger in the carpet for weeks, and the earlier a tree is cut and subjected to dry conditions indoors, the sooner it will shed. Think also of the demand for something 'different' and consider the possibility of planting species that look more delicate, or are more open in growth (which the Americans prefer) or more compact for small rooms, or with more horizontal branches for easier decorating, or with colour-ful foliage. Nor do you necessarily have to harvest whole trees: if you are felling or thinning some more mature conifers, you can make use of their tops.

Of course, some species are easier to grow in various environments and this must sway your choice to a certain extent if you want to make economical sense of the whole venture. To take the traditional Norway spruce as an example, the species is nearly always raised artificially in nursery beds: it does self-seed but is not native to Britain, though it grows wild over much of northern and central Europe and was introduced to this country more than four centuries ago. Its seed is tiny, and so is its seedling, which in an ideal situation might reach a height of 8cm in its first year. It is usually kept in a seed-bed for two years and then moved to a transplant-bed for another year or two before being planted out, and it is important to encourage a good rooting system in the nursery because on a plan-tation scale the little trees will be planted under a lifted or overturned turf with their roots spread out near the surface (if the roots were planted more deeply, the trees would make no progress). At first, growth will be slow, though as a timber tree the spruce grows upwards rapidly in due course and yields a lot of timber.

If they are to be Christmas trees, the young trees are planted out at 0.6–1.8m apart and are thinned in their fourth year in the plan-tation if necessary. As the shape of the trees is so important to their market value, it is essential to stay on top of the weed growth and keep the trees clean and bushy. Some people even prune their trees to control spindly side shoots or leggy leaders, but spare a thought for the displaced tree-top fairy! Tell the rabbits to go elsewhere for several years and watch out for little pests like aphids and red spider. When the trees are ready for harvesting, your first decision is whether to cut them or sell them with roots attached, which many customers prefer but which obviously involves more labour.

Harvesting time will be chaos as it must all be concentrated into the six-week run-up to Christmas during November and early December, and as well as harvesting the trees you need to be racing around the area keeping all your outlets happy and supplied in good time. The adrenalin will be flowing! And then, suddenly, everything stops and is peaceful again for ten months, while you and your competitors gear yourselves up for next year. The 4,000ha Yattendon estate in Berkshire, for example, is probably the biggest Christmas tree producer in the country: it devotes some 300ha to about two million trees and sells 150,000 each Christmas (the country's total sales are perhaps 4.25 million); and all of these are quality trees, many being exported to Germany and even to the Persian Gulf and

Small Woods and Hedgerows

the Far East. Yattendon is searching the world for new species that will eventually displace the needle-shedding Norway spruce, and most of their trees are now the luxuriant Caucasian fir (*Abies nordmanniana*) but they also grow Scots pine, blue Colorado spruce, Serbian spruce, noble fir and the white fir from New Mexico. Another of your major competitors will be the Forestry Commission, and in the Scottish highlands FC helicopters lift trees from inaccessible areas and drop them by the roadside at a rate of one tree every three seconds. Beat that!

Most people sell directly or indirectly to retail outlets but a few sell direct to the consumer, sometimes on a 'pick-your-own' basis if the site is suitably accessible. That will save you the worry and cost of harvesting and transporting the trees, but are you prepared to accept the general public on your land? And if they do come along to browse amongst the trees and choose what they like, will you trust them to cut or dig up their choice or will you undertake that yourself? Think about some of the drawbacks like parking, dogs, litter and unintentional vandalism (as well as the possibility of theft on a minor or major scale – your whole crop could vanish overnight if there are professionals in the area), but think also of the advantages: once you have encouraged people to visit the site, you can sell them other items like hand-made Christmas decorations – wreaths, garlands, table centrepieces, gilded and glittered cones or bright dried flowers for hanging on the tree, a tub or holder for the tree itself (some people sell their trees set into a log, for example, but this inhibits watering – and cut trees do need to be watered) and perhaps gifts to go under the tree as well as Christmas fare if your enterprise includes turkeys, preserves, cakes and home-made fudge. As a refinement, you could sell tree-bags to catch the needles that are bound to fall sooner or later, and of course (birds permitting) you can offer berried holly and mistletoe as well – especially as mistletoe is becoming increasingly rare because so many farmers and foresters think it looks untidy in the tree and can cause the development of spriggy 'witch's broom' growths on the branches. And there is another idea, which many people will abhor: you could hire out fully decorated trees!

If you want to join the Christmas tree market, you need as much marketing flair as expertise in growing the trees, and it would be worth talking to the British Christmas Tree Growers' Association if you have commercial ambitions.

WILLOWS

The coppicing of willows as basketry osiers or as energy crops has already been discussed. In general willows are easy to propagate and quick to grow or to regenerate after coppicing and pollarding, and they are also able to grow in situations which would be too damp for most trees apart from alders. Coppiced willow might grow as much as 2.5cm a day, and can yield more than 37 tonnes of green wood per hectare per annum when harvested on a four-year rotation. Willows are not fussy about soil but do best on the typically deep loams of the Somerset Levels, and you do need to select a species and strain suitable to local conditions and of known provenance.

Energy-crop willow can be used as stove firewood, if coppiced on a four- or five-year rotation, or can be fed to the chipper as described earlier, or can be distilled to produce fuel gases, chemical liquors and a residual charcoal. A longer rotation of, say, ten-year coppicing grows poles large enough for pulp mills.

Salix viminalis, the common osier, seems to thrive in British conditions and cuttings can simply be planted into grassland about 75cm apart (30cm for basket-making osiers). Use year-old shoots about 20–30cm long and push them into the ground in March or early April to a depth of perhaps 15cm; keep the grass mown to give them a fair start; establish a stool by cutting back growth in the first and second years and think about coppicing in the third or fourth year if the product is of the size you need.

Willow is very much a local crop. Osiers for basketwork and hurdles, for example, tend to be grown in Somerset and East Anglia, though in 1986 some enterprising people in Nottinghamshire gained a Venturecash award (sponsored by NatWest Bank, in conjunction with the National Farmers Union and the National Federation of Young Farmers Clubs) for their basket-willow harvesting machine.

Much more specialised is the growing of cricket-bat willow, *Salix alba* var. *caerulea*, thought to be a hybrid between the white willow, *S. alba*, and the crack willow, *S. fragilis* (the one that propagates itself by shedding its brittle twigs). The cricket-bat willow uniquely combines the properties of lightweight, white wood with the ability to recover rather than fracture after a severe blow – hence its use for making cricket bats; it is also used to make artificial limbs. The centres of production of the tree are generally governed by the location of cricket-bat manufacturers, and that basically means East Anglia. The very small handful of major merchants includes Edgar Watts Ltd of Bungay, Suffolk, and C. N. Wright of Little Leighs, near Colchester, who might be prepared to travel some distance for a minimum of four or five really good trees, which means at least 2.4m of clean, straight, knot-free stem and a girth of at least 1.6m. The merchants buy the standing crop and will also sometimes offer to supply transplants and advise on management as well.

The species is usually sterile and must be propagated from cuttings which are usually large, unrooted shoots as much as 3.6m long cut from the stools of mother trees grown by the hundred in set-beds. These 'sets' are planted in free-draining soils by well-oxygenated water, preferably flowing – for example, on sites along waterways or in areas with a high water-table – at intervals of 10–12m. The side-shoots are pruned off twice a year for three years after planting so that the tree has at least 2.2m of clean stem. In the right conditions the willows grow fast enough to be harvested in twelve to fifteen years, but because they are vegetatively propagated they can be the victim of diseases associated with genetic uniformity, the most serious of which for the species is watermark disease, a bacterial problem which stains the wood reddish-brown, turning to dark brown or black when a cut surface is exposed to the air. The disease can be detected in standing trees by means of a pulsed electrical current, though quite often there are no obvious symptoms until the tree is felled. Sometimes, however, leaves on some parts of the tree will wilt and become a reddish-brown without falling, and the infected shoots die back in the following year. If the leaves become prematurely yellow and brown instead, it could be a case of honey fungus. Watermark disease is notifiable and the county council can enforce the felling of infected trees and their destruction by fire on the premises in an effort to control its spread locally. These measures have kept the disease to low levels in Britain, and in the interests of other growers as well as yourself you should keep in contact with your local inspector of willows. (What a lovely title!)

POPLARS

One of the advantages of cricket-bat willows is that their wide spacing provides scope for multiple use of the land. The same is true of poplars: once they are well grown, you can graze livestock among them, for example. You can also obtain grant aid for growing approved poplar cultivars for timber.

Poplars in general are grown only in lowland situations, and the black poplar hybrids in particular are restricted to eastern and southern England. They are propagated from cuttings about 25cm long, pushed straight into a cultivated plantation site or rooted in a nursery bed for a year or two and then pit-planted on site. Unlike willows, poplars give up easily if the competition is too great, so each planting station must be kept clear of weeds (the usual 1m diameter for each plant should be a large enough area). They also compete intensely with each other, and are therefore planted widely spaced and are not thinned. Certain types (*Populus trichocarpa* and its hybrids) can be more closely grown at 2–4m apart for cropping on a short twelve-to-fifteen-year rotation as pulpwood, for which the diameter of the tree should be less than 30cm, and they will produce perhaps 150–270 cubic metres per hectare, which is a considerable rate of production. For better-quality trees for veneer, packaging and pallet-making, the diameter needs to be more than 30cm, side-shoots should be pruned annually at first to give a clean 5–6m stem, and the spacing can be up to 8m apart which is the limit for grant aid. Sets planted on fertile agricultural land, preferably well watered (the reason why you see them so often in waterside meadows) and at least 6m apart, will grow fast and be ready to fell after thirty years with a girth which could be as much as 2m round.

In the wild, poplars grow only in damp places – on marshy ground or beside streams – and indeed the seed has no 'shelf life' and needs to find a moist bed of bare mud within days of ripening. The seedlings grow very fast in the right conditions, but commercially poplars are generally struck from cuttings.

The traditional uses for poplar rely on its combination of remarkable lightness (though it is very heavy when it is green), its pale cream or white colour, its resistance to splitting and its supple toughness. Above all it is used for matches, matchboxes and fruit baskets like strawberry punnets, all cut from veneers (thin sheets of wood cut from a round log by turning it on a lathe). However, the home-grown poplar market for matchwood has completely collapsed in the last ten or twenty years and all our matchwood poplar is now imported.

Poplar was also once used as a light base for wheelbarrows and carts, though it needs to be treated with preservatives for outdoor use. As firewood, it is even more sulky than elm.

EUCALYPTUS
Like kangaroos and dingos, eucalypts are found naturally only in Australia and Tasmania. However, those which grow in Australia's temperate areas are relatively frost-hardy and can be grown in Britain. There are perhaps five hundred species altogether, many of them interfertile so that there is considerable scope for manipulative or unintentional crossing. Many species have been tried in Britain, especially in Victorian times; and in milder parts of the country like the south-western peninsula and western Wales or Scotland, where the Gulf Stream has its influence, collections of more than twenty species have been established. The main problem for British eucalypts is extreme cold in winter, especially if accompanied by persistent, very cold and desiccating winds and following a mild spell. Milder weather encourages growth, and the new leaves are susceptible to cold. However, at least five species are very hardy, the best-known of which must be the cider gum, *Eucalyptus gunnii*, from

Table 23

EUCALYPTS

VERY HARDY

Jounama snow gum (*Eucalyptus debeuzevillei*)
Cider gum (*E. gunnii*) – most widely planted eucalypt in Britain
Small-leaved gum (*E. parvifolia*) – hardiest of all
Spinning gum (*E. perriniana*)

MODERATELY HARDY

Black gum (*E. aggregata*)
Mountain gum (*E. dalyrympleana*)
Alpine ash (*E. delegatensis*)
Smithton peppermint (*E. nitida*)
Snow gum (*E. pauciflora*)
Black Sally (*E. stellulata*)
Tasmanian Alpine yellow gum (*E. subcrenulata*)
Urn gum (*E. urnigera*)

HARDY

Alpine cider gum (*E. archeri*)
Tasmanian snow gum (*E. coccifera*)
Tingiringi gum (*E. glaucescens*)
Varnished gum (*E. vernicosa*)

LESS HARDY

Heart-leaved silver gum (*E. cordata*)
White Ash (*E. fraxinoides*)
Tasmanian blue gum (*E. globulus*)
Tasmanian yellow gum (*E. johnstonii*)
Shining gum (*E. nitens*)
Narrow-leaved mountain gum (*E. pulverulenta*)
Manna gum (*E. viminalis*)

the highlands of central Tasmania, though the hardiest of all is *E. niphophila*, the Alpine snow gum.

Some of the eucalypts grow very fast indeed, which is one reason that *E. gunnii* is so widely planted in this country, but the much faster *E. nitens*, or shining gum, which makes good timber and firewood, is unfortunately one of the less hardy species and is unhappy at −6°C and probably dead at −10°C.

Not enough is really known about the timber qualities of British-grown eucalypts: it could be that our climate would affect the potential of trees which are extensively used for the production of saw timber in Australia, for example. However, you can get firewood as good as ash from the shining gum and the Tasmanian snow gum (*E. coccifera*), though the cider gum is as wet and sulky as elm unless you dry it out for at least a year. The eucalypts have considerable potential as fast-growing coppice crops, if you are prepared to take the risk of finding a use and a market for their poles. On the other hand, they are already valued as decorative trees and their ornamental young foliage is much appreciated by florists (prune the stems hard each year for fresh growth, or take juvenile foliage for the first three or four years after planting); and their flowers, at least in tropical and sub-tropical countries, are excellent bee pasturage if you are a honey producer. It is the foliage market which at present looks the most promising, though, and you can treat foliage plants as coppice: cut them back severely, or even down to the stool, in February or early March for a burst of pretty new foliage and shoots in late spring.

When establishing a eucalypt plantation, avoid frost pockets or exposed, windy sites above all. They are not fussy about soil and do not need a fertile medium; they will respond to dressings of nitrogen but probably become top heavy in the crown, with the risk of falling flat on their faces. Be careful on clay: they will suck up the moisture and crack the soil when they are grown to anywhere near their full size.

Plant container-grown seedlings 15–25cm high in May on a cultivated, weed-free site, and keep at least the planting station thoroughly clean, especially of grass. Do not plant them under overhead shade. Stake them if they are already rather tall, or cut them back to half-height. If they are well-grown seedlings and not pot-bound at the time of planting, they should grow away quickly and be 0.5–1.5m tall by the end of the first year.

SEA BUCKTHORN

This very thorny, tall shrub grows quite happily under the onslaught of sea breezes, which means it makes a useful hedge. More important, its orange berries are rich in vitamins. In the USSR the fruit is quite widely used to make juice drinks, health wines and skin creams, and is much in demand. Harvesting is difficult: in Russia they cut off the shrub's branches, which are then chopped into 30cm berry-laden twigs for processing. However, they have developed a thornless variety, which makes handling less uncomfortable, and a prototype mechanical harvester has been developed in this country. The shrub is rare among woody plants in that it has nitrogen-fixing root nodules like a legume. The combination of this ability and the value of the fruit could make it the subject of an interesting enterprise for a seaside holding, and it looks attractive in the landscape too. But it is a very invasive shrub and should not be introduced into new areas, even as a hedge, unless it is already growing locally.

IX

HEDGEROWS

The hedgerows of lowland Britain have become symbolic of the increasingly marked boundaries between those who farm the land and those whose interests in the countryside are less utilitarian. The fact that hedges primarily existed to contain and shelter livestock and to delineate the extent of property has often been forgotten. Instead, many a farmer regards hedges as more of a necessary evil, requiring maintenance and taking up agricultural land, than a practical benefit to the holding; and many a non-farmer regards hedges as symbols of a vanishing landscape heritage (even if the local history of enclosure has been relatively brief) and as havens and highways for wildlife. The arguments continue but, although we have lost 190,000 miles of hedgerow in England and Wales in the last forty years, there are still more than 300,000 miles left and they cover an area of something like 436,000 acres – which is more than the total area of all the nature reserves in the British Isles.

Some of our really old hedgerows date back to Saxon times and others even beyond; in Cornwall there are pre-Roman examples. They tend to be along parish boundaries, old drove roads and watercourses, and were often simply left in place when forests were cleared, so they represent strips of ancient woodland. However, a great many of today's hedges were deliberately planted during the peak era for land enclosure from 1750 to 1860, and many of these are basically hawthorn, or perhaps blackthorn, hazel and tree species like oak and elm. Single-species hedges are typical of that period. Mixed-species hedgerows often have earlier origins, their planters having made full use of the plants they found in nearby woodland, or they have been enriched by gradual natural colonisation. The orthodox method of dating a hedge is to count how many different species of trees and shrubs it contains, but the hypothesis that the number of species in a 10m length of hedge indicates the number of centuries of its age is wide open to misinterpretation, and at Monks Wood Experimental Station they are investigating the whole question of hedge dating and hedge management in great detail. If you really want to date a hedge, look to historical maps and manuscripts as well as carrying out a field survey, but if you find plenty of forest plants like bluebells, wood anemone and dog's mercury in the hedgerow, it probably is very old and was originally woodland.

Hedges today can be managed for many different purposes – stock confinement and shelter, crop protection, wildlife corridors and habitats, cover for game, property boundaries, markers delineating soil types, barriers against trespassers, a source of hedgerow trees or fruit, an asset to the landscape – or ideally for a combination of all these. Even the most 'efficient' farmer can respect the wildlife conservation and landscape value of hedges, and even the most absentee of city-based landowners can appreciate the value of hedgerows as cover for game. However pressing the demands for financial returns from the land, it should always be borne in mind that hedgerows and shelter belts are often the only permanent stands of vegetation on an arable farm and as such represent the typical 'woodland edge' habitat favoured by so much wildlife and game, as well as representing vital wildlife corridors between other habitats. Like it or not, hedgerows do have an essential role to play in wildlife conservation and, as the guardians of our countryside that most farmers are proud to claim to be, they have a duty to posterity to protect the future of wildlife and of the landscape.

In 1983 FWAG produced an information leaflet setting out a hedgerow 'code of practice' to help the increasing number of farmers and landowners who wanted to retain and manage their hedges as an integral part of the agricultural countryside, whatever the motives. FWAG is in the almost unique position of combining good farming with wildlife conservation, in that most of its members are practical farmers with an interest in conservation rather than conservationists seeking to tell farmers how to manage the land. The leaflet sets out some sensible arguments for and against the retention and management of hedgerows, and then suggests management techniques to satisfy both the farmer and the conservationist. Many of the recommendations are of course concerned with hedge trimming, which is often a source of friction between farmers and other local people on several counts, including the hideous appearance of flailed hedges, the disruption to wildlife, the destruction of potential hedgerow trees and the probability of punctured tyres from thorns and debris on adjacent roads.

HEDGE-TRIMMING

A hedge 2m high is of greater value to wildlife and livestock than one of half the height. A bird trying to nest in a 1m-high hedge is vulnerable to ground predators and it will be much safer in a hedge more than 1.8m high, though this might be awkward to trim. However, an unmanaged hedge allowed to grow up unchecked soon

Table 24
HEDGEROWS

FOR	AGAINST
Landscape value.	Immovable, therefore inflexible
Fruit, nuts, timber.	
Wildlife corridor.	
Habitat for birds: song posts, food, nesting.	A few troublesome bird species – eat seeds, buds, crop foliage.
Habitat for game.	
Habitat for insects – pollination of fruit, legumes, rape and horticultural crops; biological control of field pests. May be killed by spray drift.	Some pest species, especially aphids, overwinter on certain hedge shrub species.
Habitat for other invertebrates; food for birds and animals.	
Shelter for stock.	Land under hedge unusable for stock or crops. Nearby crops shaded.
Shelter for crops.	
Aid soil water conservation.	
Mark boundaries between owners and soil types.	
Prevent trespass and give direction to footpath walkers.	Restrict machinery handling.
Habitat for insectivores (hedgehogs, shrews).	
Habitat for other predatory mammals (stoats, etc.) to control herbivores.	
Perennial flowers: food for insects; give pleasure.	
Windbreak.	Can cause windfunnelling: laid corn. Reduce air circulation.
Soil conservation.	
Barrier to spread of disease.	
Around smaller fields, give frost protection and reduce snow drift.	
Up to thirty species of tree and shrub grow in hedges. (May be killed by careless burning.)	A few poisonous species of shrub and ground plants.
At least sixty-five species of bird nest in hedges.	
1,500 species of insect make use of hedges.	

Table 24 cont'd

FOR	AGAINST
More than twenty species of mammal, reptile and amphibian make use of hedges.	Mammals include potentially crop-damaging herbivores – rabbit, hare, vole.
600 species of wild flower and other plants in hedges and verges.	A few difficult perennial weeds if bare ground created by cultivation or spray in hedge base.

becomes less valuable – gappy, draughty and probably shading too great an area of adjacent fields as well as possibly causing wind turbulence to the detriment of the crop. The aim of hedge trimming is not so much to produce a tidy wall, however satisfying that might be, as to keep the hedge thick and well populated. If the hedge is intended to contain livestock, it is essential that it is not allowed to become gappy: whereas cattle might only find their way through a hedge almost by accident when they lean into it to browse, sheep will be quick to spot and exploit the faintest hint of a gap and will be through it in no time. To keep sheep in their field a hedge needs to be at least 1m high; for cattle 1.2–1.4m, or rather more if the hedge is A-shaped.

There have been many theories about the shape into which a hedge should be trimmed, with the choice generally lying between an A, an inverted U or a straightforward short-top-and-sides rectangle. All would agree, however, that a hedge should never be cut wider at the top than at the base. Advantages of the A shape are that the trimmings are less likely to fall into the hedge and it is easier to leave promising hedgerow saplings intact to grow on; the hedge also receives maximum sunlight, and can shed a heavy fall of snow which would distort a flat-topped hedge.

Hedges should be managed in such a way that those wretched flail cutters need never be used. Flails are designed for heavy growth but not for the stronger stems of overgrown hedges, and all too often one sees the hideous, ragged results of an onslaught by flails that simply tear rather than cut woody stems which should have been sawn instead. If you cut any plant raggedly you leave it wide open to disease, and most of those massacred stems will die back. If you are dealing with an overgrown hedge, make judicious use of the saw to prune and shape before you climb into the tractor cab for a quick flail. But a flail, despite its chopping method, can do a neat job on lighter growth.

Small Woods and Hedgerows

Table 25
HEDGE PROFILES

RECTANGULAR

Most typically seen. Regrowth may be poorer because at least one side
likely to be severely shaded, and tight dense top inhibits growth in
centre.
Heavy snow can distort shape.
Simple to cut if sides and top equivalent to typical machine's cutting
surface (0.9m) but taller hedge needs five passes.

A-SHAPED

Needs to be taller for stock because tapers at top.
Most effective windbreak: allows wind to pass over with less turbulence
than flat-fronted hedges unless very tall.
Both surfaces receive maximum sunlight.
Snow can slip off.
Vulnerably thin at top.
Probably best for giving higher hedge for nesting birds (they need to
be at least 1.8m above ground).
Only two surfaces to cut but probably two passes for each face.
Risk of asymmetrical cutting.
Easier to allow saplings to develop as hedgerow trees.
Thicker hedge bottom.

CHAMFERED

Increases height at which shoots are cut, while preserving some of A-
shape's light-catching and snow-shedding advantages.
Five surfaces to cut.

ROUNDED

Greatest strength against snow.
Suited to hand-trimming or use of handheld power tools rather than
larger machines.

One reason for the popularity of flails is that they chew up the
removed growth and in theory leave it as a mulch, to the benefit of
the hedge, so that there is no need for the laborious business of
raking up all the cuttings and burning them. In practice flails often
spew thorny material all over the road, and anyway hedge-cutting
is traditionally one of those winter jobs designed to keep people in
work at a quiet time and to keep them warm by the bonfire!

Unworked birch coppice.

Christmas trees interplanted with young hardwoods in tree shelters. This shelter has split apart and exposed its tree. Note the stunted Christmas tree in the foreground – the victim of deer and rabbits.

OPPOSITE PAGE (ABOVE) Disastrous result of a flail used on hedge-growth too substantial for the machine. (*Anna Oakford*)
(BELOW) A neatly hand-trimmed field thorn hedge which is no longer sheep-proof and could benefit from being laid.

Hedge-layer at work in Norfolk. (*Anna Oakford*)

OPPOSITE PAGE
(ABOVE) A sturdy piece of hedge-laying involving thick old stems. (*Nigel Stone*)
(BELOW) Remains of an excellent hollow nesting tree which has been felled;
ironically, the logs are about to be converted into garden nest-boxes.

(LEFT) Orchard tree ring-barked by sheep. Note how the animals' teeth have scored the wood. (*Anna Oakford*)

(BELOW) Well spaced birches planted in pasture – a good example of a silvopastoral system.

(OPPOSITE) Coppiced osiers deliberately harvested as browsing for a goat. (*Anna Oakford*)

High-seat for deer observation.

Well-managed hedges will not be full of thick stems and can be trimmed regularly with a cutter-bar, which will make a much neater job than a flail but which cannot cope with thick stems. Cutter-bars are ideal for annual trimming, which keeps the hedge well under control and encourages it to grow densely, but there might be disadvantages to wildlife in that flowering and fruiting are inhibited. If possible, therefore, either trim your hedges in rotation over the holding as a whole so that each stretch is cut every two or three years rather than annually, or perhaps cut one side one year and the other the following year.

For shorter or more inaccessible lengths of hedge, you can make a wonderfully good job with hand-tools once you have had some practice. Use a slasher or a billhook, keeping the blade well honed for clean cuts, or a hand-held hedge-trimmer.

The timing of hedge-trimming matters more to wildlife than it does to the trimmer. Do not trim in late spring and summer or you will cause serious disturbance to nesting birds, and try not to trim until after the autumn berries have filled appropriate bellies. For minimum wildlife disturbance, trim in late winter but avoid times of heavy frost when the cambium in the shrubs could freeze, which does them no good. If you have to be ruthless with a hedge, however, bear in mind that it is probably offering winter protection to some wildlife, which should be given a chance to find other quarters if necessary. Many insects winter in hedges, for example, and while some of them may be undesirable aphids, others are harmless, beneficial, or a vital source of food for birds in the nesting season.

LAYING

Hedges which are trimmed annually will not in fact remain thick forever; indeed, they will gradually die out from the base and cease to be stockproof after perhaps twenty years of regular trimming, sometimes much earlier. To maintain its vigour and ability to confine livestock, the hedge must be periodically laid, and if laying is carried out regularly it can remain healthy and stockproof for a century or more.

The aim of laying is to encourage new growth from the base of existing stems, and it should form part of a deliberate long-term management policy. You cannot simply trim annually for a while and then suddenly lay the hedge one year: you must plan ahead and prepare the hedge for laying. If you are lucky enough to find an experienced hedge-layer, listen to his advice and do not press him to do the job then and there if he thinks the hedge is not ready for it.

In their inimitable and commendable fashion the BTCV have

produced a thorough and detailed handbook, *Hedging*, which explains the mysteries of hedge-laying, and the National Hedge-laying Society (NHLS) also publishes literature on the subject. NHLS is a young society which arose from a growing demand for skilled hedge-layers in different parts of the country; it was formed officially in 1978 to encourage the craft, to train youngsters and to encourage high standards in hedge-laying competitions. Its formation was a signal that the craft, which for a while had become something of a nostalgic hobby, was once again in demand from thoroughly practical farmers and land owners who had realised that their hedges were worth preserving.

In essence, the main stems of the hedge plants are cut through so that they are almost but not quite severed. They are still sustained by their cambium, so that they continue to live, but can now be bent at an angle without being broken. The idea behind this is that where old vertical stems allow an animal to pass between them, stems leaning diagonally do not. In addition the cut encourages new stems to shoot from the base of the plant, just like a coppice stool; and further stems are encouraged to sprout along the diagonal or nearly horizontal main stems in much the same way that the main stems of a climbing rose produce vertical growths from buds if the stems are trained into a more or less horizontal position. Thus the laid hedge has the double benefit of its diagonal main stems and a profuse crop of new vertical growth. The hedge has been rejuvenated. However, although in theory this could fool an escaping sheep, in practice the sheep would browse the delectable new growth before it had a chance to become woody, and hedge-layers either have to employ various tricks to deter the browsers or put in a temporary 'fence' until the hedge has ripened. Incidentally, while the hedge is thickening, any stems which have been pruned out as unwanted can be 'planted' into the base of the hedge – not to root but to act as a dead hedge, rotting away in due course, by which time the living hedge has taken over.

Hedge-laying is a very local art and each part of the country has its own favoured styles and tools for the job, but the basics of the original diagonal cut of the stem, the bending and securing of the new direction of growth are universal, and the basic tools are slashers, billhooks and axes or chainsaws. It is the weaving, binding and facing that give each area's hedges their different appearances.

The basic steps of hedge-laying are:

• Take a close look at the hedge; slash away any rubbish and weeds, repair any banks if necessary, remove all traces of old wire and general junk, and take out those invasive elders.

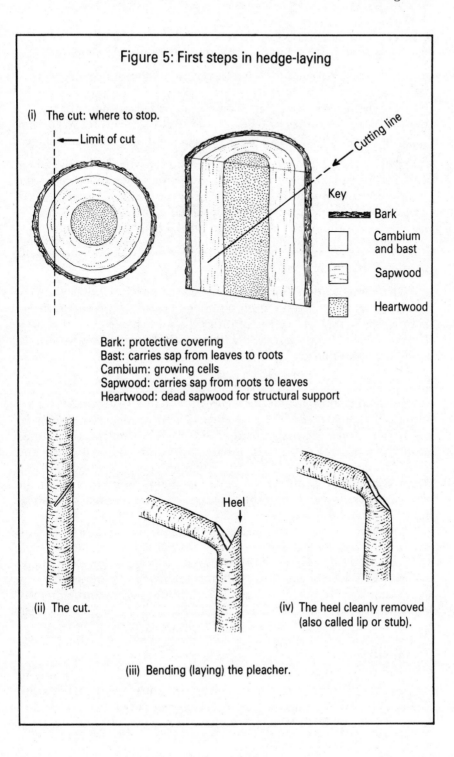

Figure 5: First steps in hedge-laying

(i) The cut: where to stop.

Limit of cut

Cutting line

Key

Bark

Cambium
and bast

Sapwood

Heartwood

Bark: protective covering
Bast: carries sap from leaves to roots
Cambium: growing cells
Sapwood: carries sap from roots to leaves
Heartwood: dead sapwood for structural support

Heel

(ii) The cut.

(iv) The heel cleanly removed
(also called lip or stub).

(iii) Bending (laying) the pleacher.

Small Woods and Hedgerows

- Select the main stems you want to retain (these are the pleachers) and remove all their side-shoots. Remove everything else.

- Cut cleanly into each pleacher at an angle of about 45 degrees, being careful to stop short of severing the stem: you must leave a thin lifeline of bark, bast, cambium and a little sapwood intact so that the plant continues to receive nutrients via its roots. Aim your cut to finish about 7.5cm above ground level in most circumstances.

- Very carefully bend the pleacher without twisting it on the sliver of lifeline or breaking it off. Take it no further down than horizontal ('sap never runs downhill') and probably nearer the diagonal, depending on the state of the hedge (usually an angle of 25–45 degrees above the horizontal). Trim off the protruding tongue.

- Drive stakes between the stems as you work, weaving the tips of the pleachers around the stakes.

- Twist some binders (long, thin withies of hazel, willow or ash) round the stakes to keep the pleachers where you want them, then trim the stake tops above the binding. In some places, the tips of the pleachers form the binding with no help from withies, or crook-ended stakes are used.

- Tidy up all your rubbish when you have finished the job.

Hedges are ready for laying when their stems at ground level are perhaps 5–10cm in diameter. If they are any thicker, it might be better to coppice the hedge instead. If the hedge has been trimmed annually, you need to leave it untrimmed for at least two years, and possibly as many as five, to let it grow high enough to be laid. Stop trimming when you notice the hedge is beginning to go thin at the base. It will also give potential hedgerow trees a chance to show themselves and develop as saplings.

The renewed interest in hedge-laying is growing quite fast and just in time to save a dying craft. Local agricultural training boards and colleges offer courses and the NHLS can give details of many societies which hold classes as well as organising competitions. It is also possible to obtain grant aid for planting, laying and generally renovating hedgerows in many situations – try MAFF, your local county council or the Countryside Commission.

HEDGEROW TREES

Hedgerows and very small spinneys or corner clumps are home to a surprisingly large percentage of our broadleaf trees in Britain – perhaps as much as 15 per cent. There are advantages and disadvantages with trees allowed to grow in hedgerows: they offer an extra storey of living space to wildlife, are features in what might otherwise be an almost two-dimensional landscape, provide shade for livestock and can be grown as a source of fruit (as in times gone by) if not of firewood or timber. However, their shade might be unwelcome over an arable crop, their presence might be resented by a hedge-trimmer in a hurry, and they are not usually of much value to a timber merchant in that they are likely to have short stems from growing in the open and, worse, have probably been used as fencing posts at some stage so that there are pieces of wire, staples and nails embedded in the wood. Quite often the reason the tree has been a fencing post is that its growth has suppressed the very hedge that surrounds it.

Yet many interesting species of tree do grow in hedgerows which would probably not be tolerated elsewhere on a farm and, however uneconomical they might be, it is worth encouraging them whenever possible. Look out for promising saplings (seedlings or suckers) in the hedge and flag them with something eye-catching like strips of plastic so that they can be saved from the hedge-trimmer. They will be of local provenance (which means they are well adapted to local conditions) and have not suffered the 'injury' of transplantation so abhorred by Oliver Rackham. And they are free gifts! With a little more care, you could also plant new trees in the hedge or, more easily, in the verges of established hedges, especially where two hedges meet, or in a corner where the trees will be of greater value to wildlife and less likely to be damaged by tractor-powered trimmers. Transplants will need protection from browsing predators too. Leave at least 8–10m between hedgerow trees, and make the distances irregular unless you are planting a municipal park.

The choice of species is considerable, depending on whether you want timber trees for posterity, a source of firewood, or trees and large shrubs which produce flowers and fruit and thereby enhance the landscape, feed wildlife and set you thinking about new cottage industries.

SHELTER BELTS

If you are planting shelter belts to protect crops, livestock, orchards or buildings, take the opportunity to provide a good wildlife habitat at the same time: plant a mixture of native hardwoods, with shrubs as well as trees. Shelter belts become quite dominant landscape features and should be visually pleasing as well as practical, and they therefore need careful siting and shaping. Although they are generally required to grow fast, try not to opt for that soul-destroying block of quick-growing Leyland cypress that is so often used as an instant screening hedge. The species is very effective as a windbreak but tends to look completely out of place in the countryside, however acceptable it might be in town. Shelter belts should blend with the landscape, not shout at it: they are, after all, woodlands.

Like hedges, shelter belts should be protected from agricultural activities (for example crop-spraying and stubble-burning) by means of a broad grass strip, and the same applies to corner spinneys. Any clump of trees and shrubs, whether shelter belt or spinney, should be linked to other wildlife habitats by safe 'corridors' of largely undisturbed cover, ideally hedgerows, rather than being in splendid isolation. Islands are often prisons or barren no-go areas for wildlife rather than havens.

HEDGE-PLANTING

It is quite simple to grow your own hedging plants in substantial numbers, as Chapter V shows, but most people buy nursery plants or in some cases forestry transplants. Do not aim for an instant hedge. Use small plants, perhaps three or four years old and certainly a lot less than 1m tall (say, 45–90cm and no more than 60cm in exposed or difficult situations). Look for really sturdy plants with a good root system rather than a luxuriant growth resulting from nursery pampering, making sure that they have been transplanted at least once in the nursery. A hedge should have a very long life ahead of it and it is worth giving it the best possible start. Plant in good weather conditions, in autumn for preference if you can keep the lagomorphs away.

Choose the site carefully (hedges are intended to be permanent features) and mark out the line of the proposed hedge with posts or a furrow, in a straight line or following a contour or boundary. Prepare the hedge-bed thoroughly to give the plants a really good root run with no soil pan or weed competition. If you are planting on the site of an old hedge, bring in fresh soil. The bed should be perhaps 60cm wide and 30cm deep on a flat site. If a ditch is required, dig it out after the bed has been prepared and spread the excavated soil thinly over and beyond the bed. However, if the hedge is to be planted on or into a bank because the site is wet or exposed, prepare the bed as described, then dig out the ditch (say, 90cm wide × 75cm deep), putting the excavated subsoil on top of the cultivated bed with the ditch's topsoil capping it as the rooting medium for top-of-bank plants, and pack the sides of the new bank with the ditch's turves, grass side out, to hold the bank in place. It is important that the hedge plants are set in top soil, not subsoil, and if you are planting into the side of a bank or at its foot, set the roots into the original cultivated bed under the excavated subsoil.

The plants can be set in single rows or, more effectively and more commonly, in staggered double rows which will usually give a much

Table 26

HEDGING PLANTS

HEDGES

For hedges, select species which are quick-growing, long-lived, hardy,
resistant to disease and insect attack, suitable for local soil conditions,
able to tolerate and responsive to regular cutting, stockproof and not
eaten by animals, cheap to establish, non-poisonous, and provide
good shelter from the base of the hedge to its top. Most hedges have
a high content of thorny species for obvious reasons; the major thorny
hedgerow plants are hawthorn (quickthorn) and blackthorn. Note
also that many hedging species provide fruit and flowers for wildlife.
The most useful species are:

Beech	Hornbeam
Blackthorn (fast and thorny)	Field maple
Dogwood	Plum, myrobalan (fast and thorny)
Gorse (can be gappy)	Sea buckthorn (coastal hedges, but
Hawthorn (fast and thorny;	do not introduce if not already
traditional 'quickthorn' or 'May')	present – very invasive)
Hazel	Spindle (host to bean aphids)
Holly (very slow-growing but	Willows (sallow on wet land)
evergreen and stockproof)	

HEDGES FOR LIVESTOCK

Avoid the following species:

(a) WEAK GROWTH

		(c) INVASIVE: CHOKES OTHER PLANTS
Ash	Privet	
Buckthorn	Sycamore	
Guelder rose	Tamarisk	Elder
Horse chestnut	Whitebeam	Honeysuckle
Holm oak	Willows	Wayfaring Tree

(b) POISONOUS

Box	Laburnum
Broom	Rhododendron
Cherry laurel	Yew
Cupressus	

PLANTING DISTANCES FOR HEDGING

Single rows	20–30cm between plants in the row
	10cm if to be trimmed but not laid
Double rows	Staggered rows 15–45cm apart
	25cm between plants in 15cm rows
	30cm between plants in 30cm rows

more solid and stockproof hedge. Double rows can be planted in a single trench 30cm wide, or in two slightly narrower parallel trenches set 15cm apart, or in one much wider trench twice the width of a single one.

Set each plant with individual care. This is not a situation for the forester's slit or notch planting: you are planting for the landscape of the future and, who knows, your hedge might still be there several centuries hence. Spread out the roots and work friable soil around them as you proceed; plant to the root collar so that it is set at the same depth as in the nursery; check that the plant is straight and then firm it in place with your feet. Treat each hedging plant as if it is to be a specimen tree or shrub, even if it is time-consuming and back-breaking work. If you are planting a double-row hedge, set one row at a time.

Like any young transplant, the new hedge will need protection from browsing livestock and wildlife until it is properly established and must also be kept free from competitive weeds both within the hedge and for perhaps 1m outwards from the line. The young plants need help in obtaining moisture until their roots are self-sufficient, and that means a combination of watering in dry weather and mulching to conserve moisture as you would for a woodland transplant. Inspect the hedge for failures each autumn and replant any gaps if necessary.

If you are planting a mixed hedge and want it to be stockproof, use a predominantly thorny species and interplant with other species in groups of three or four in both rows. Choose your mixture with care to avoid management problems later on: talk to an experienced local hedge-layer for advice.

When the plants are established, start cutting them back to encourage vigour. Typical thorn hedges (such as hawthorn and blackthorn) are generally cut back to 7.5–10cm soon after planting if they are strong – it is probably better to wait until the end of their first growing season. Do not be so ruthless with other broadleaf species, which should cut back by not more than a third of their height, and with evergreens restrict pruning to a trimming of the side-shoots until the plants reach their final hedge height. You can start topping stockproof hedges when they are about 1.4m high but let a shelter hedge's leaders grow to 1.5–1.8m before trimming for height, meanwhile keeping the sides clipped to promote density: it needs to be tall and narrow. However, consult local people about their methods of managing a newly planted hedge: customs vary, and generally for good reason based on experience of the local environment.

The Henry Doubleday Research Association at Braintree in Essex was asked for advice on planting traditional English hedgerow trees such as the wild service (for making spoons and wine-press screws), hornbeam (for windmill cogs), apple (for the mill's big gears) and spindle, that shrub with dawn-kissed berries and with wood as hard as iron (for making butcher's skewers and spare parts for spinning-wheels), on the basis that hedges were originally not only barriers against stock but also sources of useful wood for various purposes on the farms and in the villages. The association's director, Lawrence D. Hills, pointed out that specimen trees in a new hedge would need adequate space for all-round development and that the Tree Council recommended up to 22–23m between the trees, though perhaps a third of that would be adequate for less vigorous species, allowing for thinning as they mature. However, for a conventional stockproof hedge he recommended planting at 60–90cm apart in a double staggered row, a density which would encourage rapid growth. When the hedge had attained a height of 1.8–2.4m he suggested clipping it to shape, leaving specimen saplings every 4.5–6m to grow on above a maintained hedge which should for preference be traditionally laid. The distance between the trees depended to some extent on the intended final effect and on the growing habit of the species.

A very different hedge-planting technique has been developed by a sculptor-landscaper team in County Durham. Raf Fulcher and Elizabeth Tate are helping gardeners who want tall hedges quickly and cheaply, and they are exploiting the natural ability of the crack willow, *Sali fragilis*, which grows like a weed in water meadows and regenerates itself readily from broken twigs. The technique is to take straight, young stems from mature willows in June at least 2.5cm in diameter, trim them to 90cm long and remove all leaves and side-shoots, then plunge the bottom 20cm in silty garden pond water. The rods begin to show roots within a week and can be balled up within three weeks in soil and hessian when they are 5–7.5cm long and buds are beginning to sprout, then returned to the pond until autumn when they are transplanted at intervals of 45cm. Thus far, the same result could be achieved by sticking cuttings straight into the soil, but now comes the difference. Any buds pointing out of the hedge line are rubbed off as soon as they are noticed, so that all the side-shoots grow along the line, where they are woven like a living wattle fence so that they are a good screen in winter as well as in full leaf. It looks as if you could have a 2m hedge within two years of taking your cuttings, and no doubt other willows would respond to similar treatment. It is a genuine example of lateral thinking, too!

X

MULTIPLE LAND USE

Hedges and shelter belts are excellent examples of the integration of trees with landscape, farming and horticulture. Although for much of this book trees have been considered as a crop or feature in their own right, it has also been pointed out that they should be considered in the context of the whole environment whether they have been planted for commercial reasons or for amenity or wildlife conservation. Trees are versatile and should be integrated into the general scheme of things rather than considered in separate blocks.

In 1988 the AFRC Institute for Grassland and Animal Production suggested that the future patterns of grassland use in Britain would include intensive production from small areas, more extensive production from larger areas, and the management of grassland in association with conservation and timber production, with many farmers integrating all three systems on the same farm. In the third system, grassland would no longer be managed entirely for agricultural production; it would also be partly managed for amenity value, for the preservation of wildlife, for the conservation of the landscape, for the increase in opportunities for rural employment and leisure, and for silvopastoralism – that is to say, timber production closely linked with grazing of livestock. This polysyllabic word is one of several describing multiple land use: others are agroforestry, agrisilviculture, agrosilviculture and even agro-silvipastoralism – all of which broadly mean the combination of tree-growing (silviculture) with crop-growing (agriculture) and/or livestock management (pastoralism).

In 1981 the ecologist James Sholto Douglas described the whole business thus:

> Essentially, agri-silviculture, in its broadest sense, defines all plant culture and livestock keeping as parts of one whole biological cycle, looking upon each farm unit for the production of foodstuffs and other materials as a progressing entity in time and area. Translated into terms of field work and planning of development, this means that forestry or silviculture cannot properly stand alone and separated

from farming, horticulture and animal husbandry – nor these activities from tree growing – but all should wherever possible be integrated to a greater or lesser extent, to achieve maximum effect and safeguarding of the land, combined with the best output and results.

Integrated tree-growing does not have to be limited to agricultural crops and grassland livestock enterprises; it can also lend itself to horticulture, fruit-growing, leisure activities, rural industries, wildlife habitats, housing . . . the possibilities are endless.

AGROSILVICULTURE

It is possible to grow crops between trees, especially in the early years of a widely spaced plantation, though there is the risk that the young trees will be damaged during cultivations. In the New Zealand park system, the trees at maturity are perhaps 14–15m apart so that the canopy never closes and the site can grow crops for years, producing annual returns in the interim until the timber can be harvested and providing a pleasant landscape as well. When Bryant & May were still encouraging the British to grow poplars for match-wood twenty years ago, it was common practice to intercrop the wide rows with grain.

There are easier and less space-consuming ways of combining trees and crops. Robert Hart's book, *The Forest Garden*, offers some interesting ideas for small areas which could even be adapted for town gardens. Hart's aim was to grow a 'natural' forest of fruit and nut plants, vegetables and herbs, making full use of the multiple levels found in woodland – the uppermost canopy of the taller trees, an understorey of lower fruiting trees, a shrub layer, a herbaceous layer (herbs and vegetables in the case of the forest garden), a horizontal ground layer of sprawling plants in contrast to a vertical layer of climbers, and the underground layer of roots and tubers. This intensive layout also included fences and trellises for vines, soft fruit and fan-trained or espalier top fruit. Hart was inspired to create his multi-storey plantation by a scheme in the rain forests of southern China where there was a riot of self-perpetuating productive species like rubber trees, tea and coffee bushes, cacao, cassia, cardamom and cinnamon; and by other peasant systems all over the world, including the Mexican Indians' home *huertos* (orchards) where mangos, bananas, oranges, limes, zapote, mamey and coffee grew in glorious, unregimented profusion around the houses. Diversity is the essence of Hart's forest gardens, not just for the sake of a variety of produce but also to reduce labour to a minimum because the system is virtually self-perpetuating and looks after itself, rarely needing watering, weeding or fertilising, and resistant to pests and diseases partly because of the inclusion of aromatic plants but mainly because the system is the antithesis of monoculture and gives no toehold to the epidemics which so often plague single-species crops. Pests and pathogens reel back in bewilderment at the confusion of it all!

We specialise too much and at our peril, and we are so intent on obliterating the land under the monocultural blanket that in our haste we run the risk of destroying much of value. For example, I know of quite a substantial farm which, not so long ago, had been several minor farms and smallholdings. Today the landowner concentrates on grain and conifers, splashed with broad brush-strokes of gold and green over the canvas of his land. Yet here and there the land's history struggles to survive: pieces of cloudy blue glass and old horseshoes are turned up by the plough, bearing witness to the days of the working horse and, much further back, to the days when there were glassworks in the Weald alongside the ironworks, two ancient industries which relied heavily on charcoal from the wealden oak forests. And in forgotten corners of the grain baron's land you can still find individual fruit trees whose names have long since been forgotten but whose fruits taste like honey, however small or misshapen they may be. This was once an area of scattered cottage gardens, each with its home-grown apples, pears, crabs, cobs, walnuts, mulberries, medlars, quince, damsons, greengages and plums, and it had been a land where, within the century, the October air would have been rich with the scent of ripe fruit and potent ciders, each cottage having its own recipe and its own variety of apple so that there was an excuse for distant neighbours to visit each other and compare their brews, merrily no doubt.

Where are they now, the orchards of old? Ask Common Ground, a charity which seeks to encourage people to value and enjoy their own familiar surroundings and common cultural heritage. Recently Common Ground launched a project called Trees, Woods and the Green Man which embraces the practical, aesthetic, cultural and spiritual values of trees and woodland. Within that project is included an Orchards campaign to save old orchards before they have all been grubbed out or replaced by commercial orchards relying on nine dominant varieties of apple (there are *six thousand* varieties recorded in the National Apple Register of the UK, and in earlier times it was common to grow as many as a hundred or even two hundred different varieties in the same orchard). And, as a letter in *Farmers Weekly* pointed out two or three years ago, orchards produce food for bees, firewood and the pleasure of blossom as well as fruit, *and* can offer grazing for livestock.

TREES AND LIVESTOCK

On an agricultural holding, large or small, perhaps the happiest situation is to combine trees with other crops and with livestock enterprises. For example, trees being grown for mature timber can be widely enough spaced to allow livestock to graze beneath them in due course and the spacing can still be close enough to produce a long, clean stem or, at the other extreme, can be so wide that the 'woodland' becomes parkland. Cattle, sheep, goats, horses and deer will, of course, devastate young trees unless they are well protected, but as the trees become mature the animals will merely browse the foliage from the lowest branches, if they can reach them at all. Indeed, in some situations forest farming is designed to feed livestock as well as produce trees, in return for which the animals manure the ground and yield a wide range of produce – not just meat and milk but eggs too. It might come as a surprise that chickens and most other poultry are natural forest birds and will thrive in lightly wooded areas and orchards. Orchards are also ideal for bees: many an orchard grower will *pay* you to set up a hive to pollinate the fruit trees, and you will be rewarded with some wonderfully flavoured honey. Then there are the game species – pheasants and deer in particular – which are also essentially creatures of the forest, so that woodland can be associated with sport for those who enjoy it.

It has been shown theoretically that silvopastoral systems can be more profitable in economic terms than conventional forestry or grassland enterprises on the same-sized area, especially if broadleaf trees are planted at 50–400 per hectare for harvesting as valuable timber thirty to fifty years later. In the early stages, the grass will flourish (fertilised if necessary) but its productivity naturally declines as the trees grow larger, until in due course the site is a forestry enterprise rather than a livestock one, with the promise of a good return from mature timber and the added benefit of returns from livestock in the intervening years.

In 1981 the Forestry Commission produced an Arboriculture Research Note on the subject of winter shelter for agricultural stock, reviewing the limited amount of quantified knowledge about the effects of sheep and cattle on the short- and long-term growth of trees. The authors pointed out that the separation of livestock and woodland is relatively recent: in the past grazing animals were free to wander and feed where they might, and one thinks immediately of New Forest ponies, moorland sheep, the feral White Park cattle of Chillingham, emparked deer and the age-old practice of pannage for pigs, who found much of their food 'for free' on the forest floors. But those were times when the land was unenclosed and much less densely populated and valuable than it is today.

Small Woods and Hedgerows

Some of today's woodland grazing systems include allowing sheep to 'weed' young plantations by grazing them (with close supervision to ensure that they do not browse the trees rather than the weeds) and wintering young beef cattle or in-lamb ewes in fenced broadleaf woodland so that they can benefit from its shelter. These over-wintered animals, if given adequate fodder, water and mineral supplements, do seem to reach slaughter weight more quickly or have lower lambing mortalities than those exposed to all that the weather can throw at them.

One of the drawbacks to livestock in woodland is that they trample the area and graze the ground flora so that natural regeneration and the composition of the ground flora can be radically altered. Cattle also tend to push over young trees and, if their appetite is not satisfied or their fibre and mineral intake is unbalanced, they do start bark-stripping. They will begin with younger trees, coppice poles and thin-barked species, de-barking them from a height of perhaps 2m down to ground level, but in due course they will also strip mature trees. In addition certain areas are bound to be poached: livestock tend to congregate at feeding and watering points or in favourite areas so that the ground becomes trampled, compacted and puddled with urine and dung. Tree roots might therefore find themselves in waterlogged ground, or have the soil around them eroded so that the roots and buttresses are damaged by treading animals. There is, in fact, a detectable difference in the girth increment of trees near feed and water troughs, even if there is no obvious damage to the trees, but on the other hand there is a significant increase in the stem diameter of trees further from the troughs: these trees have not suffered from poaching but have benefited from the animals' manure.

The lesson seems to be one of moderation: do not use the same patch of woodland year after year for livestock but have a rotation system to give each site a chance to recover from poaching and stripping and to make the most of its manuring. However, there are other possibilities (not yet fully investigated) such as cultivating land between trees to provide fresh fodder for the livestock as well as shelter in winter. If you start on the scale of a house-cow and a couple of lambs in the orchard, you will begin to see where the problems might arise and can work out a better management scheme for woodland on a slightly larger scale.

Even pig pannage is making a minor comeback. In the Chilterns of southern Oxfordshire, organic farmer Julian Rose runs a mixture of enterprises including a dairy herd of Guernseys, two hundred free-range hens on grass and a small group of free-range pigs whose rootlings are carefully rotated around 5ha of land needing cultivating and manuring. But in autumn the pigs are given access to 2ha of woodland and, as Rose puts it, 'What a joy it is to see pigs so thoroughly contented on a diet of acorns, beech mast and roots!' And what a joy, too, to let pigs do the work of clearing unwanted undergrowth in a scrubby copse, leaving it as clean as a pig's whistle.

Goats and trees, however, do not mix well: the goats will love it but the trees will be stripped bare by their browsing and no tree seedling will be allowed to struggle to so much as ankle height. Photographer Anna Oakford's method of combining trees and goats is very sound: she has planted quick-growing osier cuttings as boundary hedges which grow several feet each summer. In winter they are pollarded and provide fodder branches which are cut and taken to the goats (and the sheep) rather than the goats helping themselves from the living plants. She then burns any uneaten thicker branches and uses the potash to fertilise fruit bushes.

In fact, *Salix caprea* is called goat willow precisely because the first known illustration of the species portrayed a goat browsing on it! (The 'willows of the brook' were also mentioned in the Bible – *Leviticus* 23:40 – as being suitable decoration for Palm Sunday, and the goat willow is very much a plant of the waterside or damp woodland.)

WORKING HORSES

Horses can be as destructive as cattle among trees but, conversely, *working* horses can be seriously considered as an alternative form of horsepower in the management of woodland. In 1988 the Shire Horse Society published *History with a Future*, a book based on comprehensive and technical investigations into the possibilities of 'harnessing the heavy horse for the twenty-first century' and it makes very interesting reading indeed. A section of the book is devoted to the use of horses in forestry and woodland work.

Very often one of the big problems faced by woodland managers is the inaccessibility of the site because of lack of hard access roads, the generally muddy conditions or slope of the site, or the density of growth. A horse can tread where no tractor dares rush in, and the animal's treading will do considerably less damage to the site than the tractor's. It is quite frequently the case that horses are the only effective source of power in woodland, especially on farms, and, claims the Shire Horse Society, that is one reason why so many of today's farm woodlands have become neglected. Farmers have forgotten the many virtues of the horse, such as the fact that it runs on a continually renewable fuel (food) rather than exhaustible and expensive fossil fuels, that it can reproduce itself (which even the most advanced tractor cannot), that it gives as much to the land (manure) as it takes from it, that it does not pollute the atmosphere and that, in skilled hands, it is a pleasurable working companion. In addition, there have been considerable advances in the design of horse-drawn implements so that horsework is increasingly versatile.

There are perhaps two potential drawbacks in using horses in place of tractors and other mechanised equipment. The first is that they do require skilled handling by someone who has a basic empathy with the animals and the second is that they might be under-employed, which means that they are not realising their full economic potential. Both these drawbacks can easily be overcome by someone setting themselves up as a horsework contractor, either on their own account or as part of a co-operative of smallholders and farmers. When you consider the cost of buying new tractors and the uncer-tainty about fuel prices, you should also consider the advantages of working horses which, in spite of their magnificent size, are really on a more appropriate scale for smaller holdings, where they can be put to work on so many tasks about the place.

A typical use for woodland horses on a small scale is where one or two valuable timber trees are ready for harvesting (or have been windblown) or where a neglected wood needs thinning. The site has probably not been planted with tractor access in mind and the only practical way you can get the timber out is with a horse, which will avoid the need to clear an access route that a tractor will churn into indelible ruts. In Sweden, a country where forestry is a major industry, 30,000 horses are regularly employed in woodland work, especially and most economically where small areas require clear-felling, or for thinning or extraction of firewood and windblows, and always where any forestry operation is on a difficult site. And in Italy pack-mule trains are used on steep slopes to ferry firewood in what is virtually an automatic system: the train is led by a mare (mules are the result of mating a mare to a jackass) followed by a string of ungelded mules, with hardly a human in sight except to load and unload their packs.

So, if you have an awkward site, or a site you do not want to damage (for example, an SSSI or nature reserve), or if you want to undertake selective thinning or extract a handful of mature timber trees, or if your coppice is on a hanger or your Christmas trees are half-way up a mountain, why not use a horse? If you already like horses, or know someone who likes working with them, the advan-tages and opportunities are considerable. Contact the British Horse Society (the address is in Appendix II) for up-to-date details of heavy-horse training schemes.

POULTRY

Poultry in woodland has considerable attractions for those with some imagination. Most of the pheasant family, including the domestic chicken, are birds of light woodland, where they can roost safely in trees and make their ground nests in the shadowy places they prefer, which is fine if you are letting them raise their own broods rather than stealing their eggs for eating or for sale. Turkeys and guineafowl are very much birds of the woodland and are decidedly at their happiest given free range in the 'forest', even if it is only an orchard. Orchards and poultry go well together as long as the fruit trees are not sprayed with chemicals harmful to the birds, and if you have guineafowl in your orchard they will see off marauding wild fruit-eaters in no uncertain terms – and that includes human thieves or vandals. Here again, moderation is the key: if an orchard is stocked with poultry for as long as two years without a break, the trees will begin to suffer from too much poultry manure. Geese are also suitable for orchards, as long as they are not allowed to browse on bark in hard weather.

GAME IN WOODLAND

Although it might seem contradictory, those who shoot game are also wildlife conservationists, intentionally or not. For example, I used to live in a cottage surrounded by the arable fields of a land-owner whose idea of a beautiful landscape was 'an endless rolling prairie of grain'. Fortunately, before he succeeded in grubbing out every hedge in sight, he became interested in the social and economic attractions of shooting and decided to employ a gamekeeper to set up a virgin shoot. The keeper's first act was to put a halt to hedge-grubbing: gamekeepers are well aware that pheasants are birds whose preferred habitat is the woodland edge, and that hedgerows are both an extension of that habitat and corridors between one patch of woodland and another. Without hedges and copses, a shoot would be a massive failure. It is exactly these hedgerow and light woodland habitats which favour so many forms of wildlife, whether on wing or on foot, and several of the woodland species are of great interest to sportsmen, especially pheasants, woodcock, capercaillie and black game, hedgerow partridge, deer, foxes and the many creatures that find themselves the target of rough shooting, such as rabbits, hares, squirrels, pigeons, magpies and jays. If a glade is converted into a well-placed pond, the woodland also attracts wild-fowl to the guns.

Pheasants and Partridge

Pheasants require cover, shelter, food, protection from predators and freedom from disturbance in the wood. Many of these needs can be met in light, mixed woodland with adequate ground vegetation, including an understorey of berry-bearing shrubs (pheasants have catholic tastes for berries and nuts). The birds dislike a draughty environment, and ground cover can provide a warmer 'floor', especially if the woodland's edges are protected with hedging and if rides are baffled so that they do not become wind tunnels. Some warm, sunny glades will be much appreciated not only by pheasants but also by wild flowers, butterflies and other wildlife. Try to ensure that the canopy of small woodlands is never closed to the extent that it shades out ground cover, and try to encourage regeneration of a good variety of broadleaf species in the wood. Bear in mind that pheasants like to spread out and feed in open fields immediately adjacent to woodland, and that they readily make use of hedgerows as nesting places and a source of food as well as highways to other choice habitats. Coppiced hazel along a big, wide grass ride through the woods gives two woodland edges protected from the wind (as long as the ride is baffled), and small areas of group felling will also be appreciated. Broadleafs are preferable to conifers for pheasants, or at least to solid blocks of conifers: a scattering of them in a mixed broadleaf wood or a nurse crop of medium height offers the birds sheltered roosting (evergreens provide winter protection and also make the birds less conspicuous on the branch).

Above all, offer the pheasants a *warm* wood with plenty of areas open to the sun so that they can feel its warmth on their backs while they dry out after a wet spell or thaw the frost off their tails, and so that shrubs and accompanying insects are encouraged as bird food. A very wide ride could be planted with game food or cover crops for good measure, to encourage the birds to stay within the wood rather than go wandering all over the countryside and invading your neighbour's farm crops. Discourage their wanderings with a good, thick-bottomed hedge 1–1.5m high around the wood's perimeter.

Sportsmen will want their birds to fly high and fast, and keepers will create good flushing areas where the birds can fly up cleanly, unimpeded by the canopy – perhaps patches of young coppice regrowth no more than 10m across and scattered here and there according to how the beats are laid out, or a roughly triangular shrubby patch carefully sited. Rides and the woodland edge will also be used as gun stations.

If you have partridge on the land, the wild birds will be encouraged to nest and raise their broods if there are several rough areas scattered over the holding away from the normal hunting routes of predators – odd field corners, for example, or rough banks and undisturbed pond margins. Like any young game birds, partridge chicks need plenty of insect food: the Game Conservancy at Fordingbridge in

Hampshire gives advice on the management of cereal crop spraying in the interests of the birds. The Game Conservancy is a registered charity, financed largely by its members' subscriptions, which undertakes research into all the problems faced by game, and by wildlife too. It publishes many advisory booklets on game management (including wildfowl) as well as providing its members with a consultancy service. (See Appendix II for the address.)

The income from sporting rents on coverts can be quite useful and also brings in regular returns from woodland which might otherwise provide income only at intervals of many years. The stocking rate is immensely variable according to the environment but on a good 'wild' shoot you might expect one bird shot for every 1.2–1.6ha, though a neighbouring shoot might achieve only one bird on 4–6ha. On the other hand, if birds are reared rather than wild, the sky's the limit, but, as with intensive farming of any kind, a reared-bird shoot could be damaging to the general environment and upset the ecological balance. The Game Conservancy claims that good woodland management for game can boost the income of an estate of 160ha by £2,000 a year, generating cash at about £12 per hectare from the lease of sporting rights. For a commercial enterprise, you need to have a lot more than a few hectares of woodland.

Wildfowl

A woodland pond can be attractive to wildfowl if it is carefully sited and its environment is taken into account. It will offer the birds the privacy they might seek but, although they like surrounding ground cover where they can feel hidden from predators, especially while nesting, they are wary of taller cover too near the water. If the pond is virtually hidden from their aerial view, the birds will probably ignore it (though moorhens will make it their home). A good pond is open to the south – it needs maximum sunlight for a rich pondlife on which the birds can feed; however, like someone out on a stormy day, it needs to be able to 'turn its back' to bad weather.

If you are digging out a new woodland pond, make its contours and shape as natural as possible and keep its banks gently shelved, especially to the south. Ducks like to waddle out of the water and preen themselves on the banks, but they do have short legs and look most undignified trying to clamber up too steep an embankment. The sunbathing banks should be grassy (and grass will not thrive unless the trees are cleared well back from the water's edge), and ideally there should be broadleaf shrubs rather than trees set a few paces back from all but the southern aspect. For conservation purposes, you can provide artificial nesting sites or simply offer adequate shrubbery where the ducks can find their own homes. Put your pond in a quiet, secluded spot undisturbed by humans and dogs in particular.

Make the pond quite shallow – no deeper than 60cm at the centre, and it could be as little as 30cm – shelving gently at the edges, with an adequate inflow/outflow system as appropriate. If you hope to encourage breeding, give the pond an irregular outline with several spits and inlets where drakes can establish their territories out of sight of each other, especially if there are reeds and rushes for extra cover.

Deer

Lowland deer like roe, fallow and muntjac are found naturally in woodland, and deer-stalking can both take advantage of their presence and exercise some control over the population to minimise their browsing and fraying damage. Like pheasant-shooting, deer-stalking can be a source of income for the woodland owner as well as a source of meat for the table, but it is more suited to larger woodland areas. You also need to learn plenty about deer management, both for the sake of stalking and for the sake of tree protection: culling cannot be haphazard if it is to be effective, and replanting in areas where deer are much in evidence needs to be carefully planned since the species of tree and the patterns in which new trees are planted have an effect on the likely degree of damage by the deer. For example, trees in the open are attacked more often than those protected by undergrowth as they emerge from their planting tubes, and male deer will fray tubes as well as trees: their ideal fraying tree is five to six years old and 2m tall, but they do tend to choose specific trees and return to fray them regularly, leaving most other trees alone for that purpose. However, if you cull a roe buck, for example, his subordinates will have to re-establish their pecking order and will do so by fraying, as a means of advertising their presence and demonstrating their aggressive ability, so the cull could result in a lot more damage to new trees! The FC's *Wildlife Ranger's Handbook* offers plenty of useful, practical information on deer management in forestry.

Like pheasants, a lowland deer's ideal environment is a patch of mixed woodland (deciduous and coniferous) with trees of various species and ages, next to areas of open farmland and punctuated with warm, sunny glades as well as patches of dense ground cover where it can lie up safely. However, deer management and pheasant shoots do not necessarily go well together. The culling season for female deer, for example, is November to February – right in the middle of the pheasant season, when the shoot will not welcome the disturbance caused by stalkers. Nor are the returns from deer-stalking as lucrative as those from pheasants.

Incidentally, the 1987 October storm proved to be something of a boon for deer in southern England in that they suddenly had access to a huge quantity of food (twigs and bark) and also superb ground cover in the form of fallen trees which gave them shelter from draughty winds as well as hiding them from view, and the deer were more than happy that windblown trees should remain where they lay. For those who take pleasure in the presence of deer in the woods and have no intention of shooting them, the storm did bring its bonus, though it made no difference to the roe doe which has been visiting my garden for the last three years to browse my roses, shrubs and vegetables (especially perpetual spinach). She still brings her young into the garden during the summer, and last spring she gave birth to her kid in the field outside my windows. Although I did not witness the actual birth, I had the great privilege of watching her clean up the newborn baby and give it its first suckle, and she then left it to lie up in a clump of docks within 50m of the house while she went about her normal business, returning at dusk to suckle it again before they both finally withdrew to the more natural cover of the surrounding woodland during the night. It is for magic moments like these that I thank my valley for being wooded!

Foxes

The valley also has its population of foxes and their nocturnal winter calls are as familiar as the cries of the tawny owls and the occasional shriek of the barn owls which have been reintroduced by a local breeding-and-release scheme. Fortunately for the foxes, the area is rarely hunted: it is far too wooded and difficult. However, fox-hunting as a sport does depend on areas of woodland adjacent to open country, and where hunting is considered more important than the other sports with which it would conflict, an ideal woodland is coppice on a short rotation of perhaps five to ten years, with easy access along open rides – and no barbed wire or chestnut paling.

GAMES IN THE WOODS

At the eighth World Forestry Congress in Jakarta in 1978, our own Forestry Commission considered its role in providing facilities for the 'recreational enjoyment' of its forests. The FC at that time managed 1.23 million hectares of land, including half the total area of woodland in Great Britain, and 60 per cent of that woodland was accessible to major urban and holiday centres. In a statement of its recreation policy, the FC declared that it welcomed the public on foot in all its forests – provided that such access did not conflict with the management and protection of the forest – but that motor vehicles for recreation were generally prohibited. Specialist activities by daily permit included fishing, shooting and deer-stalking, and the FC also permitted forest-compatible activities like pony-trekking, cycling, field archery, sailing and orienteering. Then there were the more informal activities such as picnics, forest walks and trails, camping and visiting arboreta, and the Commission provided tourist attractions like forest cabins, holiday houses and visitor centres.

You too could offer the public an opportunity for recreation in your woodland along similar lines, however limited the scale. Log cabins and caravan sites will need the permission of your local authority, of course, but there is certainly scope for nature trails, bird-watching hides, picnic places, wildlife information centres, bird hospitals, backpacking, orienteering and 'adventures', including children's treasure hunts, fitness trails and, if you must, war games and scrambling.

Trails

FWAG (and where would you be without your knowledgeable, kindly FWAG adviser?) can give plenty of help with establishing nature, woodland and farm trails which allow the public to see all sorts of wildlife as well as appreciating what farming and woodland management involve. FWAG suggests that the main reasons for setting up a farm trail are to improve the relationship between farmers and the public and to supplement traditional sources of income. Setting up the trail can be as simple as waymarking and publicising it, or it can be a much more elaborate business altogether with well-written guides, a choice of routes, a variety of aims (serious nature study or a pleasant amble, for example), information boards at points of interest, public car parks and toilets, a refreshment area, escorted tours by trailer or horse and cart, a chance to see craftsmen at work in the coppice or in the yard, somewhere to buy everything from bean-poles to hand-made gates and turnery, special viewpoints with a map of the vista, a woodcraft museum and souvenir shop – use your imagination and then come down to earth and see what you can really offer and whether you want the public on your land in the first place. For inspiration visit the John Eastwood farm conservation trail at the NAC, Stoneleigh, a $\frac{3}{4}$-mile route showing you new woodland planting, coppicing, pond care and agroforestry, with wildfowl decoys and a parish boundary hedge too.

A craft centre could be an interesting co-operative venture which might provide a useful outlet for the woodland produce of several smallholders, but to be successful it must be properly managed, attractively presented, easily accessible, well publicised and, preferably, combined with other public attractions such as a tea-shop, an energy centre supplying firewood and other fuel, and perhaps a produce shop as an outlet for all those home-made wines and preserves from your wild-berry and orchard-fruit harvests. Where else could you persuade people to taste bletted wild service chequers, chestnut soup, elderberry wine, bramble junket, rose hip cream, sloe cheese, may-bud pie, pickled ash keys, bird-cherry brandy, wild summer pudding, medlar comfits, roast quince, barberry mutton, whitebeam jelly, hazel meringue, nut nog, walnut fudge, beechleaf salad dressed with beechnut oil, acorn coffee, pine-and-honey toast? Why, you could start a gourmet restaurant!

NATURE CONSERVATION

Where would our wildlife be without woodlands and hedgerows? They are vital to many birds, mammals, insects and plants, and also offer additional niches to reptiles and amphibians. In conservation terms, the most valuable sites of all are ancient, semi-natural woodlands which have existed continuously for several centuries and are largely composed of native species growing as a result of natural regeneration (see Table 9, page 38). There are not many of those old woodlands left today.

The most valuable woodland features for wildlife depend on diversity, native vegetation, continuity and lack of disturbance. A good wildlife wood has a wide variety of tree species, shrubs and flowering plants, and the trees have a wide age range. The majority of the trees should be native deciduous species with glades and coppice areas to let in the light, which will encourage a diversity of ground flora and understorey. There should also be a diversity in the structure of the wood – plenty of different levels at which different species can find their niches high in the canopy, among the cover of shrubbery and ground plants, sunbathing in glades and rides, or along the woodland edge. The edge habitat is important to many creatures and you can increase the proportion of edge by varying the outline of the wood and extending it by means of hedgerows linking scattered clumps of trees, copses and spinneys and other woodlands. Edge habitats include the edges of rides and glades within the wood as well as its perimeter.

It is said that you will get a much greater variety of wild bird species, and a greater population density within the species, in smaller woodlands where the wood's circumference is a greater proportion of its area, as long as the area is large enough to offer seclusion and shelter to those creatures which seek it. In a detailed study of a score of small deciduous woods near Oxford, most of them covering less than 3ha (published in the British Trust for

Ornithology's *Bird Report* in November 1987, vol. 34), Hugh Ford found that there was a direct link between bird numbers and the density of understorey vegetation to a height of 1–2m above ground level. Understorey density tends to be greater at the lighter woodland edge than in the middle, and birds occur in greater densities at the wood's edge.

However, there is more to wildlife than birds. The true conservationist will also be concerned to offer habitats for mosses and lichens, fungi, beetles and bugs, flying insects, worms, snails – the diversity of nature is rich, and it demands an equal diversity of habitat to support it. Tidiness is anathema to wildlife: make a point of leaving deadwood on the ground for fungi and insects which will feed other life; leave a scattering of standing, dying trees, especially those with holes and hollows where creatures can hide, hibernate and nest; leave windtorn leafy branches lying where they fall to give an extra dimension of ground cover and some instant browsing for deer.

Table 27

CONSERVATION

VALUE OF WOODLAND HABITATS FOR WILDLIFE
(Based on *Nature Conservation and Agriculture, NCC*)

MOST IMPORTANT

Primary woodlands, especially near old pasture, marshes, ponds, unpolluted waterways

MODERATELY IMPORTANT	OF LITTLE VALUE
Broadleaf plantations	Conifer plantations with no
Hedges	ground cover
Neglected orchards	Commercial orchards and
Copses, corner plantings, etc.	horticultural crops
Recently planted conifer	
plantations	
Mature conifer plantations	

Note: Originally Britain was mostly forests and marshland, and its flora and fauna species were adapted to those habitats. Since Neolithic times human activities have affected the landscape to an increasing extent and for many centuries wildlife species have been in two groups – the original woodland and marsh survivors, and species adapted to living in the open habitats created by man.

Table 27 cont'd

APPROXIMATE NUMBER OF SPECIES OCCURRING IN EQUIVALENT HABITATS IN UNMODERNISED AND MODERNISED FARMLAND

	UNMODERNISED	MODERNISED	MODERNISED
	Hedges with hedgerow trees, semi-natural grass verges	Wire fences, semi-natural grass verges	Wire fences, sown grass
Mammals	20	6	5
Birds	37	9	6
Butterflies	17	8	0

AIMS IN WOODLAND MANAGEMENT FOR NATURE CONSERVATION

• **Diversity of species** of plants, trees and shrubs

• **Diversity of structure** – high canopy for birds, maximum woodland edge habitat, ground cover for animals and game, shrub layer, open sunny rides and glades, streams and damp patches, encouragement of natural regeneration

• **Wide age range** in trees, including deadwood for fungi, mosses, lichens, insects, nesting birds and roosting bats

• **Locally native** deciduous tree species of local provenance rather than conifers: they cast less shade, their litter is less acid, they support a greater diversity of species

• **Links** with other wildlife habitats – access under cover to other woodland (including copses, shelter belts, corner plantings, etc.) along hedgerow corridors; also to ponds, marshes, old pasture

• **Hedges** with range of species of trees and shrubs, and with banks, ditches and verges as sanctuary; dense and fairly tall hedges for nesting birds; thick continuous base as cover; trees for landscape value and as song-posts and 'vertical' habitats

• **Selective felling** and replanting, to ensure that the tree cover as a whole remains adequate at all times

• **Major changes avoided:** for example, clear-felling, major drainage schemes; all management of woodland *and surroundings* to be gradual and gentle

• **Chemicals** either not used at all or used with great caution, including on nearby farmland

• **Rare species,** if present, should have their interests specially considered: manage the environment to suit and encourage them (advice from NCC or FWAG)

Small Woods and Hedgerows

Many of the thousands of species of beetle found in this country spend much of their life in rotting or living wood, or under rotting bark, and they are the staff of life for woodpeckers and other birds. The woodpeckers busily exploit holes begun by the shading out of a lower branch on a standing tree and these holes will also be used by nuthatches, tits, redstarts, owls and other birds seeking a nesting place, especially in old oaks, dead elms and silver birches. Old hollow trees are important havens for many creatures, and one of the reasons all our bats are now protected species is that hollow trees used to be one of their main roosting choices but they have been deprived of these traditional quarters by clean-minded foresters. Woodman, spare that tree – and leave it standing!

Wetland and running water play an important role in woodland. Many woods are naturally graced with streams, and you should leave some good damp patches, boggy areas and natural ponds as well. Dragonflies might visit sunlit ponds, especially if there are also sunlit rides where they can hawk for their prey. However, the water that runs off conifer plantations on poor soils is so acid that it can kill water life, including fish, in woodland streams.

Many semi-natural woods have been coppiced in the past and this has helped to maintain the diversity of native tree and shrub species that is so favourable to wildlife. Coppicing also offers a choice of habitats because of the different stages of growth of different cants, and of course each harvest in the rotation lets the sunlight flood in to rejuvenate and enrich the ground flora. Forget about biomass coppicing (energy crops) if you are interested in wildlife conservation: the system is far too violent. Indeed, beware of any system of clear-felling, and if you are taking a mature crop of timber it is much kinder in ecological terms to aim for group-felling here and there than for a mighty sweep with the chainsaw like the scythe of Old Father Time. The NCC suggests that a single felling of up to 10–20 per cent of an area in any five-to-ten-year period is likely to be the 'safe' *maximum* in high-forest woods if nature conservation is deemed to be important, and that it is best to spread felling over as long a period as possible. A large felling, within the limits described above, could be dispersed over the area in a series of successive cuts here and there; with smaller fellings, try to cut successive blocks next to each other so that wildlife has a chance to move home. With coppicing, the clearing of adjacent stands in succession gives open-phase species the opportunity to move into each newly cleared area.

In the case of a neglected wood, a forester is likely to begin by harvesting the valuable timber – that is, the mature trees, but it is precisely these which offer the best wildlife habitats. If there is no timber of particular value in a neglected wood, start with the *younger* trees, preferably in areas of greatest uniformity, as these will be the areas of least interest for nature conservation.

The quite complex subject of broadleaf woodland operations in the interests of wildlife is covered in considerable and thoughtful detail by NCC publications such as its 1987 report, *Forestry Operations and Broadleaf Woodland Conservation*. FWAG and BTCV also produce useful publications on managing woodland for nature conservation, and your county council's countryside department or the county wildlife trust will be very helpful as well, both with advice and, perhaps, with grants or practical assistance. All these organisations are also concerned about hedgerow management for wildlife. In addition farmers and landowners can now take advantage of a series of management courses run jointly by the Agricultural Training Board and FWAG, with sponsorship from ICI Agrochemicals, which offer practical training for conservation as part of the whole farm plan: the courses cost only about £6 a day.

Reptiles and Amphibians

Reptiles and amphibians are usually regarded as creatures of sandy, sunny areas where they can find the warmth to survive. However, although they would shun the dank, cloistered depths of a conifer forest, there are plenty of areas in broadleaf or mixed woodlands where these cold-blooded creatures can feel at home, especially on south-facing slopes with open glades, edges and partially sunlit woodland ponds and streams. Dr Ian F. Spellerberg suggests that woodlands do have a part to play in the conservation of reptiles and amphibians, many of which are under threat in Britain. In particular woodland can offer two vital necessities to herpetofauna: food and warmth. Some of the animals feed mainly on insects, others on small mammals, and both types of food can usually be found in abundance in woodland. A woodland glade also traps the warmth of the sun, keeping off the cooling winds and storing the heat in the insulation of surrounding trees to maintain quite a stable microclimate compared to that of typical heathlands. It works both ways: during the memorable drought in the warm summer of 1976, reptiles and amphibians in some parts of the country fled to the woods for coolness and moisture.

Bats

All Britain's bats are now protected species – and they need to be. They are prime candidates for positive conservation in woodland, where the provision of roosting boxes can be a real life-saver. Bats are by nature tree-dwellers and cave-dwellers. Mature trees with old woodpecker holes, crevices under thick bark, hollow branches or thick ivy coats are ideal bat roosts, especially along woodland edges, near water or in parkland. But these natural tree sites are becoming increasingly rare, and windblows or fellings can be catastrophic for bat colonies which use them. You could provide artificial roosting boxes in the wood instead, to maintain a good population of insect-eating bats. People used to implore bats to stay in their woodlands and keep down the mosquitoes for them, and I know that a colony of three species of bats in my own roof does an excellent job of controlling the potentially huge numbers of flying insects in the woodside watermeadows around the house.

A bat roosting box can be fashioned from a log or made from sawn timber at least 2cm thick. Entrance is by means of a slit on the underside of the box, perhaps 10cm wide by 2cm deep. The wood inside the box needs to have a rough surface so that the bats can cling to it, and the preferred internal dimensions seem to be about 30–40cm tall by 10cm square, depending on the species for which it is intended. The location is more important than the design of bat boxes: they are more likely to be used in coniferous woodland, because there are few alternative roosting places, and should be positioned so that they are warmed by the sun for most of the day – for example, on the woodland edge, facing south or west. Put three or four boxes on different aspects of the same tree, at the same height, because bats do like to change quarters according to prevailing conditions. Place them quite high in the trees, and cluster them in groups in an area, then be very patient and give the bats time (possibly years) to find them and use them. The NCC offers good advice on the conservation of bats and will put you in touch with your local bat group.

Butterflies

Butterflies love sunshine and flowers, which go together. The Forestry Commission provides excellent advice on the management of woodland edges as butterfly habitats; and in the context, as usual, the 'edge' is not just the wood's perimeter but also the edges of the rides. The aim is to grade the edge in stature, from the tall trees of the main crop down to bare ground as a seed-bed for butterfly plants, with various stages of smaller trees, shrubs, scrambling and herbaceous plants and grasses in between. There is a detailed table calculating just how much sunshine (or at least shade-free area) you can hope to achieve with a combination of tree heights, ride widths and aspects at different times of day (FC Research Information Note 126: 'Enhancement of lowland forest ridesides and roadsides to benefit wild plants and butterflies', 1987). The ride edges can be shaped for the sake of visually pleasing variety and also to avoid the wind-tunnel effect: scallop the edges to form bays opposite each other for maximum light, and have different ranges of shrub species in each bay or a different stage in the succession from open ground to scrub. Each bay needs to be at least 7m long to provide adequate room for the greensward as well as a shrub belt, or at least 25m long within tree crops more than 20m tall. Open up glades by cutting off the corners where rides cross each other.

Cut back the shrubs every three to seven years and the grass swards every two to five years in October or later (you do not want to remove flowers before they have ripened their seed), and scrape out some bare seed-bed areas of perhaps 1–2 square metres with each cut to encourage natural regeneration. Read all you can about the favourite plants of different butterfly species both for feeding and for egg-laying, and manage your ground cover accordingly.

Consider the trees too if you would like to help one of our most rare and dramatic butterflies, the purple emperor, whose perfect habitat would contain forty or fifty mature goat willows in a breeding area of 25 × 50m (the larvae feed on sallow and willow). It would also have north-to-south rides crossing a metalled east-to-west road for maximum sunlight, and some good, big perching oaks 18–21m tall with a southerly aspect, above which the beautiful big butterflies could dance.

Then you can simply take pleasure in watching the insects and the flowers in the sunshine. After all, even the most commercially driven forester is a conservationist at heart and really uses his profession as an excuse to be out in the woods enjoying the seclusion, the scenery and the wildlife. It is that almost spiritual satisfaction that draws people to woodlands and makes all the management and work of rescuing these vanishing habitats so worthwhile. There is something hugely reassuring about the presence of trees.

APPENDIX I

GRANTS

The major sources of financial aid for planting, restoring or maintaining woodland and hedgerows are the Forestry Commission, the Ministry of Agriculture, Fisheries and Food (MAFF), and the Countryside Commission (usually through your local county council). Assistance might also be available, though not necessarily in the form of grants, from the Nature Conservancy Council, the Woodland Trust, the British Trust for Conservation Volunteers, or local councils (district, borough and parish). There is the possibility of tax relief too, but as this keeps changing you should consult the Forestry Commission and your tax adviser.

WOODLAND GRANT SCHEME (Forestry Commission)
The Forestry Commission's Woodland Grant Scheme (WGS) was introduced in April 1988 to encourage the continued expansion of private forestry in a way which achieves a reasonable balance with the needs of the environment. It succeeds the old Forestry Grant Scheme and the Broadleaved Woodland Grant Scheme and offers substantially increased grants for new planting and restocking. There is a single scale of grants for broadleaves, whether planted on their own or in mixture; there is also a supplement for planting on existing arable or improved grassland where a Farm Woodland Scheme annual payment (see below) is not being claimed. The grant band is determined by the total of the areas approved for planting or regeneration in each separate block or wood with a five-year-plan. At the time of writing the rates of grant for planting, restocking and natural regeneration were £615–1,005 per hectare for conifers and £975–1,575 per hectare for broadleaves, with the higher rates being paid for smaller areas (top band for 0.25–0.9ha, lowest rate for 10ha or more).

Applications may be made by the owner of the land, or by a tenant, provided that all parties concerned are joined in the application.

Grants are available for individual areas of *0.25ha and over* and it is not acceptable for individual areas of less than 0.25ha to be aggregated except where restocking is to be undertaken by planting very small groups of trees with the object of creating or infilling an uneven-aged wood (and then only with the FC's agreement).

The main aims of the scheme are:

(a) To encourage timber production.
(b) To provide jobs in and increase the economic potential of rural areas with declining agricultural employment and few alternative sources of economic activity.

(c) To provide an alternative to agricultural production and thereby assist in the reduction of agricultural surpluses.
(d) To enhance the landscape, to create new wildlife habitats and to provide for recreation and sporting uses in the longer term.
(e) To encourage the conservation and regeneration of existing forests and woodlands.

The production of utilisable timber must be an objective though not necessarily the principal one, and the scheme will encourage multiple-purpose woodland management. It might also apply to the rehabilitation of neglected woodland under twenty years of age which was not originally grant-aided. The planting of broadleaves on their own, or in mixture with conifers, will be encouraged where sites are suitable and will attract grant at a higher rate than that given for conifers alone. However, Scotland's native pinewood sites must be replaced or regenerated with native Scots pine.

Supplementary grants under this scheme were made available for replanting woodlands damaged by the storm of October 1987 and were set at £150 per hectare for conifers and £400 per hectare for broadleaves, available for five years.

The FC grant is paid in instalments (the first on completion of planting, the second five years later and the remainder five years after that) and full details of the scheme are available from the Commission. Once the FC has approved a grant for broadleaved planting under the WGS, farmers can then apply for *annual* payments under the government's Farm Woodland Scheme (MAFF) which is designed to cover the cashflow gap between planting and income from the first timber crop.

FARM WOODLAND SCHEME (MAFF)

Introduced in October 1988, this government scheme offered up to £22 million to applicants in its first two years. Payment levels are reviewed every five years. Initially planting grants and annual payments of up to £190 per hectare are available, depending on the area (for instance, disadvantaged or severely disadvantaged areas or lowland) and whether the trees are planted in unimproved grassland (including rough grazing), improved grassland (reseeded within the past ten years) or arable land.

Payments for oak and beech woodland last for forty years; for other broadleaves and mixed woodland containing more than 50 per cent broadleaves, thirty years; for other woodland, twenty years; and for traditional coppice, ten years. The limit for any single application is 40ha maximum, 3ha minimum per holding, and each planting must extend to 1ha.

MAFF also offers grant schemes for the provision and improvement of shelter belts to protect crops or livestock, or trees and hedges to shelter livestock.

Small Woods and Hedgerows

FARM DIVERSIFICATION GRANT SCHEME (MAFF)
The first part of the Farm Diversification Grant Scheme offered grants for capital investments with effect from January 1988; the second part, later in the same year, offered grants for enterprise feasibility studies and initial marketing costs. The grants are intended to assist existing agricultural businesses to develop alternative commercial uses for agricultural buildings or land and are designed to help farmers develop enterprises which are farm-based but non-agricultural. Activities relevant to this book include, for example:

- Processing of farm timber, including manufacture of, say, crafted furniture.
- Manufacture of craft items, including for example wood-carving and tourist souvenirs.
- Farm shops, including souvenirs, craft items, prepared food and other non-agricultural goods produced on the holding.
- Catering, from tea-bars to restaurants.
- Sport and recreation: for example, orienteering, but excluding field sports, horse-riding, any activity involving motor vehicles or firearms and air weapons. Recreation includes, for instance, nature trails, walks, picnic areas, public gardens and angling ponds, and will cover capital expenditure on provision and planting of trees and shrubs, regrading land and so on.
- Education and amenity facilities, including farm museums, craft workshops, nature trails and so on.

You must be able to show that the ancillary business is capable of being carried on as a profit-making enterprise or bringing about a lasting improvement in the economic situation of the agricultural business as a whole. To qualify, you must be active in agriculture or horticulture and have an established business, and you must invest a total of at least £750.

COUNTRYSIDE COMMISSION
The Countryside Commission usually channels its grants through county councils. Typical schemes include:

- Amenity tree planting grants on sites visible to the public from a road or footpath – native species only, and on sites of less than 0.25ha.

- Small-scale planting in woods of more than 0.25ha (or more than 275 trees).

- Other woodland work, for example restoring derelict coppices, opening up existing rides, creating new rides, possibly fencing. Grants for work in woodland management are based on net costs of work minus the retail value of wood and timber. The same applies to the restoration of shelter belts and wide hedges.

● Hedgerow management by laying, coppicing or replanting if the hedge is alongside a road, footpath or public right of way.

● Recommencement of pollarding for riverside willows or for trees like oak, ash and beech beside old tracks and on grazed commons.

● Replanting after the storm of October 1987.

NATURE CONSERVANCY COUNCIL
The Nature Conservancy Council (NCC) has limited funds, but will sometimes help with planting and managing small woods specifically for nature conservation. It will certainly need to be consulted over proposed work in national nature reserves or on sites of special scientific interest (SSSIs). It might be worth talking to the NCC if you want to start a nursery propagating native species of local provenance.

APPENDIX II

ORGANISATIONS

Agricultural Training Board
32–34 Beckenham Road, Beckenham, Kent.
Arboricultural Association
Ampfield House, Ampfield, Romsey, Hants SO51 9PA. Maintains register of consultants and tree surveyors who can advise and work on individual trees and amenity clumps.
Association of Professional Foresters
Brokerswood House, Brokerswood, Westbury, Wilts BA13 4EH.
Biological Records Centre
Monks Wood Experimental Station, Abbots Ripton, Cambs PE17 2LS.
British Association for Shooting and Conservation
Marford Mill, Rossett, Wrexham, Clwyd LL12 0HL.
British Deer Society
Church Farm, Lower Basildon, Reading, Berks RG8 9HH.
British Horse Society
National Equestrian Centre, Stoneleigh, Kenilworth, Warwicks CV8 2LR.
British Orienteering Federation
Riverdale, Dale Road North, Darley Dale, Matlock, Derby DE4 2JB.

Small Woods and Hedgerows

British Timber Merchants Association
Ridgeway House, 6 Ridgeway Road, Long Ashton, Bristol BS18 9EU.
British Trust for Conservation Volunteers
36 St Mary's Street, Wallingford, Oxon OX10 0EU.
British Trust for Ornithology
Beech Grove, Tring, Herts.
Coed Cymru
Ladywell House, Newton, Powys SY16 1RD.
Organisation set up to investigate and provide advice on existing farm woodlands in Wales. Project officers on the staff of nearly all the Welsh county councils.
Common Ground
45 Shelton Street, Covent Garden, London WC2H 9HJ.
Established in 1983 to promote the importance of our common cultural heritage – common plants and animals, familiar and local places, local distinctiveness, links with the past.
Countryside Commission
ENGLAND AND WALES:
John Dower House, Crescent Place, Cheltenham, Glos GL50 3RA.
SCOTLAND:
Battleby, Redgorton, Perth PH1 3EW.
Specialist advice on farm woods and recreation (local office in your telephone directory). Grant schemes for amenity tree planting, small woodland management schemes, etc.: apply through your local county council. Task Force Trees special unit set up in 1987 to cope with immediate effects of October storm. Working party examining feasibility of planting up to 40,000ha of mixed woodland in southern England and west Midlands, with possibility of multi-ownership. Main concern is for landscape conservation.
County Councils
See local telephone directory. Contact planning department – countryside officer – for advice on woodland planting and management for conservation; also for grants.
County Wildlife Trusts
See local telephone directory.
Dartington Amenity Research Trust
Shinners Bridge, Dartington, Totnes, Devon TQ9 6JE.
Research concerning greater educational and recreational use of woodlands. Pilot schemes for economic small woodland management based on co-operatives (Dartington Institute Research Study) – several schemes set up in other parts of the country (e.g. East Sussex, Gwent).
European Farm Development Group
Merrist Wood College of Agriculture and Horticulture, Worplesdon, Guildford, Surrey GU3 3PE.
Formed to provide free training in farm woodland management. Merrist

Wood College at Guildford, Brighton Polytechnic, and Holme Lacy College, Hereford, supported by many major national organisations including MAFF, FC and NCC, and working closely with European Commission. Principal objectives: to create new jobs, to provide opportunities for income-generating alternative enterprises leading to integrated rural development; to provide scope, with EC assistance, to regenerate some of the declining and/or threatened rural communities. Training on own land or in immediate vicinity for any farmer or landowner wishing to gain new craft and technological skills to run a woodland-based enterprise. Very limited number of places available, and no fee charged for the training programme (two days per month for three years).

Farming and Wildlife Trust

National Agricultural Centre, Stoneleigh, Kenilworth, Warwicks.

Charity launched in 1984 to promote and support the development of the Farming and Wildlife Advisory Groups (FWAGs) which have gradually built up, county by county, since 1969. FWAG advisers give guidance to farmers on maintaining, restoring and encouraging the best features of the countryside, bringing together farming and related countryside conservation interests by means of practical co-operation rather than confrontation. Have had considerable impact in the last twenty years – hedge-planting, farm ponds, effective woodland management, etc. Advisers are very knowledgeable and helpful, with deep understanding of local environment; on-farm consultation. Provides a forum for liaison between organisations and individuals involved in countryside management.

Forestry Commission

HEADQUARTERS:

231 Corstorphine Road, Edinburgh EH12 7AT.

RESEARCH STATIONS:

Alice Holt Lodge, Wrecclesham, Farnham, Surrey GU10 4LH.

Northern Research Station, Roslin, Midlothian EH25 9SY.

REGIONAL CONSERVANCY OFFICES AND LOCAL FOREST DISTRICT OFFICES:

see local telephone directory.

Established 1919. Charged with the general duty of promoting the interests of forestry, the development of afforestation, and the production and supply of timber and other forest products in Great Britain. Has a duty under the Countryside Acts to 'have regard to the desirability of conserving the natural beauty and amenity of the countryside', and is increasingly involved in protecting and enhancing the environment while still pursuing its main objective of wood production. Provides recreational facilities. Manages various grant schemes, e.g. the new Woodland Grant Scheme. Training Council and Safety Council at headquarters.

Game Conservancy Trust

Fordingbridge, Hants SP6 1EG.

Can give technical advice on all aspects of game conservation and shoot management. Offers useful publications on game birds, wildfowl and deer.

Home Timber Merchants Association
ENGLAND AND WALES:
Blackburn House, 1 Warwick Street, Leamington Spa, Warwicks CV32 5LW.
SCOTLAND:
16 Gordon Street, Glasgow G1 3QE.

Institute of Chartered Foresters
22 Walker Street, Edinburgh EH3 7HR.
Can supply list of professional forestry consultants who practise in all parts of Britain.

Institute of Terrestrial Ecology
66 Hills Road, Cambridge CB2 1LA.

Landscape Institute
12 Carlton House Terrace, London SW1Y 5AH.

Men of Trees
Crawley Down, Crawley, Sussex RH10 4HL.
International society for the planting and protection of trees, founded 1922.

MAFF, DAFS, DANI, WOAD, ADAS
See local telephone directory for regional offices.

National Agricultural Centre
Stoneleigh, Kenilworth, Warwicks.
Home of many agricultural organisations, site of the annual Royal Show. Interesting tree collection of about a hundred different species in the forestry area, grown to demonstrate growth rates, shapes, leaf types, etc. Also demonstrations highlighting the use of conifers for game cover, tree guards, amenity areas, biomass production (willow, poplar, eucalypts), FC weed-control trials, hedge management, hedgerow trees, etc. Well worth a visit for ideas.

National Farmers Union
Agriculture House, Knightsbridge, London SW1X 7NJ.

Nature Conservancy Council
ENGLAND AND WALES:
Northminster House, Peterborough, Cambs PE1 1UA.
SCOTLAND:
Hope Terrace, Edinburgh EH9 2AS.
Contact regional offices (see local telephone directory) for advice and grants in the interests of the conservation of nature and geological/physiographical features.

Oxford Forestry Institute
South Parks Road, Oxford OX1 3RB.

Parnham Trust
Hook Park, Beaminster, Dorset.
Set up to look at the better utilisation of small-size broadleaf timber, combining the growing and management of woodlands with the design and

manufacture of suitable products. School for wood craftsmen set up by furniture designer and craftsman John Makepeace in 1977, now with a worldwide reputation. Furniture school produces highest-quality furniture. Development of new building methods using small roundwood and finding outlet for small conifer thinnings in construction.

Project Silvanus
Poole House, 16 Poole Road, Bodmin, Cornwall PL31 2HB.
Named after the Roman god of farms and wildwood and devised by Dartington Trust to offer free advice on management of neglected woodlands so that they can contribute to the rural economy and retain their conservation and landscape value. Covers mainly Forest of Dean, Devon, Cornwall and Somerset. Sponsored by CC, MAFF, DoE, FC, RDC, NCC. Advice is free and covers all aspects of woodland management. Essentially a regional project, with emphasis on good market research.

Royal Forestry Society
ENGLAND, WALES AND NORTHERN IRELAND:
102 High Street, Tring, Herts HP23 4AH.
SCOTLAND:
11 Atholl Crescent, Edinburgh EH3 8HE.

Royal Institution of Chartered Surveyors
12 Great George Street, London SW1P 3AD.
Can provide list of chartered surveyors with specialist forestry experience.

Rural Development Commission
141 Castle Street, Salisbury, Wilts SP1 3TP.
Used to be CoSIRA (Council for Small Industries in Rural Areas).

Timber Growers United Kingdom Ltd
LONDON:
Agriculture House, Knightsbridge, London SW1X 7NJ.
EDINBURGH:
5 Dublin Street Lane South, Edinburgh EH1 3PX.
Will supply addresses of commercial advisers, managers and forestry workers. Advice on markets, etc.

Timber Research and Development Association Ltd
Hughenden Valley, High Wycombe, Bucks HP14 4ND.

Tree Council
35 Belgrave Square, London SW1X 8NQ.

Woodland Trust
Autumn Park, Dysart Road, Grantham, Lincs NG31 6LL.
Accepts donated woodlands and manages them. Operates a licensing scheme whereby the Trust plants and maintains an area of new trees for twenty-five years, after which the trees become the property of the landowner. Formed in 1972 to safeguard native British trees in broadleaf woods. Raises money to buy endangered woodlands, large and small.

APPENDIX III

RED TAPE

The restrictions given here are correct at the time of writing but can change: please check the current legislation with the FC or other relevant organisations.

FELLING

With certain exceptions, it is an offence to fell growing trees without first having obtained a licence from the Forestry Commission, whether you fell them on your own behalf or someone else's. If in doubt, consult your local FC office *before* you fell. The FC controls the felling of trees in Great Britain except for Northern Ireland and the inner London boroughs.

Exemptions

You do not need an FC felling licence in the following circumstances:

• The felling is in accordance with an approved plan of operations under one of the FC's grant schemes.
• The trees are in a garden, orchard, churchyard or public open space.
• The trees are all less than 8cm in diameter (measured at 1.3m from the ground); or, in the case of thinnings, less than 10cm in diameter; or, in the case of coppice or underwood, less than 15cm in diameter.
• The tree are interfering with permitted development or statutory works by public bodies.
• The trees are dead, dangerous, causing a nuisance, or are badly affected by Dutch elm disease.
• The felling is in compliance with an Act of Parliament.

You do not normally need an FC licence for topping or lopping as opposed to felling, and in any calendar quarter the occupier of the land may fell up to 5 cubic metres of wood without a licence provided that not more than 2 cubic metres are sold.

TREE PRESERVATION ORDERS

A Tree Preservation Order (TPO) will be made by the appropriate planning authority if it appears to them expedient to do so in the interest of amenity. The aim is to protect specified trees and woodland from wilful damage and destruction, and to prevent the felling, topping, lopping or uprooting of TPO trees without the consent of the authority. If the owner of such trees wishes to fell them, application should be made to the local authority or, if the proposed felling would normally require an FC licence, the application should be made in the first instance to the FC who will forward it to the local authority with comments.

SITE OF SPECIAL SCIENTIFIC INTEREST

Under the Wildlife and Countryside Act 1981, owners and occupiers of land within a Site of Special Scientific Interest (SSSI) intending to under-take any operations that appear likely to damage the scientific interest of the site must give notice to the Nature Conservancy Council in writing so that the NCC can assess the likely effects. If felling is involved, application must be made to the FC at the same time as notification is given to the NCC, and the two bodies will consult with each other. Note that *any* activity in an SSSI could possibly cause damage to the scientific interest, including replanting, and you should therefore notify the NCC of all such operations.

CONSERVATION AREAS

In general, if you propose to cut down, top, lop or uproot any tree in a Conservation Area, you must give six weeks' notice of your intentions to the relevant district council before the work is carried out. You would also need to follow normal procedures where relevant in the case of felling licences, TPOs and so on.

CHANGE OF USE OF LAND OR BUILDINGS

If you are considering setting up some kind of public enterprise, such as a woodland park, crafts centre or woodland restaurant, discuss your ideas in the early stages with your local authority's (normally the district council's) planning department to make sure that planning permission is not required. Talk to your parish council, too: its views are generally taken into account by the planning authorities.

WILDLIFE AND COUNTRYSIDE ACT 1981

The Wildlife and Countryside Act 1981 seeks to protect wildlife and its environment. In particular you need to be aware that, for example, all bats are considered to be endangered species and you may not disturb them or their roosts in any way. If in doubt, contact your local bat group or the NCC. Many other species are given special protection too: for example, you may not kill, injure or take any wild bird or take, damage or destroy a wild bird's nest while it is in use, or take or destroy the eggs – though there are exceptions in the case of game birds and pest species. It is also an offence to uproot wild plants, or even to pick any of the extremely rare plants listed in the Act's schedules, in which context it just might be difficult for you to propagate certain species.

REGISTERED SOURCES OF FORESTRY REPRODUCTIVE MATERIAL

EEC directives designed to control the quality (physical and genetic) and marketing of forest reproductive material have led to a set of British regulations applying to certain species – but only if they are marketed within the EEC for forestry purposes (that is, the production of wood). All other species are exempt. A quantity of seed capable of producing more than a thousand usable plants is subject to the full regulations, whether or not that seed is intended for forestry purposes. 'Forestry reproductive material' includes seed, cones, cuttings, plants and parts of plants (for example, clones from splitting a clump, roots, scions, layers). Those whose activities fall within the regulations must apply to be included in the British National Register of Basic Material (that is, plantations, stands, seed orchards and stool-beds) maintained by the Forestry Commission, so that the source can be inspected by a specialist. If the source has no undesirable characteristics and meets specified physical requirements, it may be registered as either 'Selected' or 'Tested'. Each registered source is allocated a consecutive Stand Number, by species, within the 'region of provenance' in which it is situated in Great Britain (there are four regions, numbered 10, 20, 30, 40). There are no restrictions on material collected (or plants grown from it) provided that it is for an owner's own use and not marketed. The regulations apply in full to the following species:

Abies alba (silver fir)
Fagus sylvatica (beech)
Larix decidua (European larch)
L. leptolepis (Japanese larch)
Picea abies (Norway spruce)
P. sitchensis (sitka spruce)
Pinus nigra (Austrian and Corsican pine)

P. sylvestris (Scots pine)
P. strobus (Weymouth pine)
Pseudotsuga taxifolia (Douglas fir)
Quercus borealis (red oak)
Q. sessiliflora (sessile oak)
Populus species (poplars)

APPENDIX IV

MEASUREMENTS

Roundwood is by its nature irregular in shape and it is not easy to measure its volume. Weight is not a good guide: a log weighs considerably more when it is green than when it is seasoned. For most fresh-felled timber, 1 tonne equals roughly 1 cubic metre; in time 1 tonne of seasoned wood could be equal to 1.2 to 2.0 cubic metres, according to species.

Appendix

The international unit of measurement for timber is the cubic metre.

APPROXIMATE VOLUME OF TREE RELATIVE TO DBH

DIAMETER AT BREAST HEIGHT (cm)	VOLUME* (cubic metres)	
	Conifer	*Broadleaf*
5	0.01	0.01
10	0.04	0.04
15	0.1	0.1
20	0.25	0.25
25	0.45	0.4
30	0.7	0.6
35	1.0	0.9
40	1.5	1.2
45	2.0	1.5
50	2.5	1.9

*These volumes could vary by up to 50 per cent according to tree shape.

HOPPUS MEASUREMENTS

The volume of a felled log is estimated by measuring its length in feet (L) and its circumference or girth (G) half-way along the log. Making the assumption that the log has a uniform taper, you can calculate its volume (V) thus:

$$V = L \times (G^2/4\pi) \times (\tfrac{1}{144})$$

However, the traditional British trade calculation is as follows:

$$V = L \times (G/4)^2 \times \tfrac{1}{144}$$

The first calculation is known as 'true measure', and the second as 'hoppus measure', which gives a volume of 110/127.3 times the true volume.

The apparently arbitrary hoppus came about because of the custom of measuring a log's 'quarter-girth': the girth at the half-way point was measured by means of a piece of string, which was then folded twice, giving a measurement of $G/4$ – that is, a quarter of the girth. To avoid having to work out the volume using π (a factor of 3.142), the quarter-girth was squared during calculations.

The volume of sawn timber is usually between 20 and 40 per cent less than the hoppus volume.

You can use specially marked quarter-girth tapes on which, for example, 4in. is marked as 1in., and 8in. as 2in. and so on. Or you can simply use metrication tables published by the Foresty Commission.

Girth measurement is the single parameter which sums the infinite number of diameters in an irregular cross-section.

Small Woods and Hedgerows

METRIC AND IMPERIAL CONVERSIONS

1mm = 0.039in.	1in. = 25.4mm
1cm = 0.39in. = 0.033ft	
1m = 39.37in. = 3.28ft	1ft = 0.305m
1m = 1.09yd	1yd = 0.91m
1cm diameter = 1.24in. girth	1in. girth = 0.81cm diameter
= 0.31in. quarter-girth	1ft girth = 9.7cm diameter

1m^2 = 1.196yd^2 1yd^2 = 0.84m^2
1ha = 2.47 acres   1 acre = 0.405ha

1m^3 = 35.31ft^3 1ft^3 = 0.028m^3
1m^3 = 1.31yd^3 1yd^3 = 0.77m^3
1m^3 = 27.74 hoppus ft   1h.ft = 0.036m^3
                                                    1ft^3 = 0.785h.ft
                                                    1h.ft = 1.27ft^3
                                                    1 Petrograd standard
                                                    = 4.67m^3

A standing volume of 1m^3/ha = 11.22h.ft/acre

1 tonne = 0.98 tons   1 ton = 1.10 tonnes

APPENDIX V

SPECIES NOTES

BROADLEAF TREES AND SHRUBS

Alder, common (*Alnus glutinosa*) Medium-sized waterside tree, often multi-stemmed; fast-growing, frost-hardy, wind-firm, needs light. Wide range of very moist soils, pH 4–7.5, base-rich preferred; avoid very acid peat. Wet sites but not stagnant water. Nitrogen-fixing root nodules. Very good for wildlife (timber beetles, woodpeckers, reed buntings, redpolls, siskins and other birds and insects). Light, pale wood is strong but easily worked for turnery. Original outlets were charcoal for gunpowder, tanning bark, clogs, broomheads, textile dyes. Useful for stabilising river banks. Related to birch.

Alder, grey (*Alnus incana*) Introduced species with broad, columnar growth. Vigorous on wide variety of soils.

Alder, Italian (*Alnus cordata*) Larger introduced alder – tall, conic, shapely, handsome, dense, adaptable and vigorous, with rapid growth.

Alder buckthorn (*Frangula alnus*) Shrub or small tree for fenland soils, damp peats and acid sands. Propagation by suckers or seed (berries). Similar to buckthorn but has no thorns. Liked by brimstone butterflies; birds enjoy fruit.

Ash (*Fraxinus excelsior*) Native tree with light, open appearance. Rapid growth in right conditions but very fussy in choice of site: likes moist but well-drained fertile loam, neutral to alkaline (dominant on lime-rich loams); dislikes waterlogged and thin soils. Shade-tolerant in early life; wind-tolerant. Coppices freely. Strong, resilient, shockproof wood much in demand for quality sports equipment, furniture, tool handles; also cart-wheel rims, oars, coach bodies, hurdles, walking-sticks. Easily cleft or bent into shape. Excellent firewood. Mature trees important for lichens and mosses; beetles, fungi, woodpeckers and other hole-nesting birds. Quick-decaying leaves make good field layer. Seeds (keys) eaten by birds and small mammals.

Aspen (*Populus tremula*) The native 'trembling' tree with quivering leaves. More often a thicket of suckers than single trees (seed has very brief period of viability). Damp heavy clays, marshy areas. Timber for pulpwood, ply, veneer, and prime matchwood poplar abroad. Good for insects, birds, deer browse. Known in Wales as 'the tree of the woman's tongue' because leaves never stop moving. Interesting colour patchwork on individual leaves in autumn.

Beech (*Fagus sylvaticus*) Large native tree, lovely light green foliage in spring, rich brown in autumn. Creates dense shade in woodland and is itself shade-tolerant. Best on dry, deep, well-drained, light, fertile soils especially over chalk or soft limestone and especially in southern England. Seedlings need shelter from sun and frost (for example, birch or coppice hazel as nurse crops). Good, close-grained hard wood with even texture important for furniture, veneer, turnery. Cleft when green. Bends easily for bentwood furniture. Very good firewood. Beechmast eaten by small mammals and birds; lots of fungi and lichens, also rare orchids in beech-woods.

Beech, southern (*Nothofagus procera* and *Nothofagus obliqua*) Introduced fairly recently and showing promise as timber trees. Sheltered sites on clay or sand. Fast-growing but not always cold-resistant. Fairly strong wood for furniture, panelling, pulpwood, firewood.

Birch, common (*Betula pendula*) The well-known native silver or warty birch. Dainty tree casting only light shade, and not shade-tolerant. Pioneer species especially on sandy heaths after burn-offs; tolerates wide range of soils with preference for lighter, drier types. Wood for turnery, ply veneer; very good firewood. Often planted as nurse crop. Bark for waterproofing woodland shelters; brushwood (coppiced) for besoms and horse jumps. Grows better in Scandinavia where birches are used in furniture-making. Rich insect life; birds include tree pipit, woodpeckers, chaffinch, redpoll.

Birch, downy or hairy (*Betula pubescens*) Another native birch, with peeling bark and downy twigs; more upright than common birch. Tends to be on moister sites than common birch – tolerates wet, acid, exposed upland, damp peaty moorland. Timber as common birch; wildlife as common birch, also attractive to bees. Both birches best grown in groups.

Blackberry (*Rubus fruticosa*) Well-known bramble, either an annoying weed or a useful wildlife habitat. Calcareous to neutral clays and loams. Spreads by self-layering of long shoots. Good for birds (food and nesting), many insects, and basic deer browse.

Blackthorn (*Prunus spinosa*) Native shrub, major hedging species (thorns vicious and wounds can become septic). White blossom on bare twigs in spring. Calcareous to neutral clays and loams. Suckers form thickets. Fruit (sloe) for sloe gin; wood for knobbly walking sticks and cudgels. Good for butterflies; also good nesting thicket for nightingales in south.

Box (*Buxus sempervirens*) Evergreen native shrub or small tree. Best on dry, lime-rich soils; native in south-east England but rare in wild; shade-tolerant and can be grown under beech. Too rare to harvest but the hardest wood grown in Britain; bright orange-brown, used for finely calibrated rulers, scales, carving, wood-engraving. Good firewood. Valuable protection for roosting birds, game and other wildlife.

Broom (*Cytisus scoparius*) Spineless shrub on neutral to acid sands. Handsome flowers attract butterflies. Originally used for broom-making.

Buckthorn (*Rhamnus cathartica*) Bush or small tree, not always thorny. Neutral loams, clays. Black berries. Used as medicinal purge. Visited by brimstone butterflies.

Buckthorn, sea (*Hippophae rhamnoides*) Tall-growing shrub, densely thorned; branches thickly covered with orange berries which, although shunned by birds, are rich source of vitamins and are widely harvested in Russia. Not a member of the buckthorn family but an oleaster. Suckers form dense thickets on sand dunes.

Butcher's broom (*Ruscus aculeatus*) Small evergreen shrub, stiff stems with hard, sharp, spine-tipped 'leaves' which bear little white flowers, turning into orange-red berries. Woodland understorey species in southern England, forms thickets from which plants can be divided for planting. Formerly used for cleaning butchers' slabs and blocks.

Cherry, bird (*Prunus padus*) Native tree, medium height, with long racemes of flowers. Moist neutral or slightly acid well-drained loams; more common in north than south. Black fruit stripped by birds and small mammals. Flowers give important source of early nectar for bees and insects. Good firewood. Attractive in landscape.

Cherry, gean or wild (*Prunus avium*) Confusing Latin name for a native species which is not the bird cherry! Grows much taller than the latter. Fruit ripens through yellow and red to purplish; can be bitter or reasonably sweet. Delicate flowers, good autumn foliage colour. Vigorous, frost-hardy, light-demanding, wind-firm. Moist fertile soils, calcareous loams best (often associates with beech); prefers woodland edge for light and space. Suckers into thickets. Small but valuable market for high-quality timber: furniture, veneer, turnery, inlays, pipes, musical instruments. Very good firewood. Fruit eaten by birds, seeds by hawfinch. Also used as graft stock for domestic cherries.

Chestnut, horse (*Aesculus hippocastanum*) Well-known candles-and-conkers tree introduced in 1616. Large, vigorous and long-lived; easy to raise from seed. More ornamental than practical; white, smooth, soft wood used only for items such as trays and toys. Flowers for bee nectar.

Chestnut, sweet (*Castanea sativa*) Prime coppice species but can also become large tree with characteristically twisting trunk. Southern counties for coppice and saw timber: prefers warm, sunny aspect and moderately fertile light soil – does well enough on acid sandy sites. Not for frost pockets or exposed positions. Larger logs can develop shake, especially where water-table fluctuates. Mainly coppiced for fencing (very durable heartwood good as oak); readily cleft, or as roundwood. Wired paling fences; hop-poles; walking-sticks (easy to form). Saw timber for furniture, coffin boards. Main wildlife value lies in fact of coppicing but also nut crop.

Small Woods and Hedgerows

Crab apple (*Malus sylvestris*) Native fruit tree, very pretty with flowers and fruit. Calcareous loams and clays. Flowers provide useful nectar; apples feed birds, mammals; many insect species. Useful in hedgerows.

Dogwood (*Cornus sanguinea*) Red-stemmed native shrub in south (rare in north, introduced in Scotland) with fine autumn colouring and black berries. Calcareous to neutral clays and loams. Wood once used for skewers.

Elder (*Sambucus nigra*) Native shrub or small tree in same family as guelder rose, wayfaring tree and honeysuckle. Deeply furrowed bark, pithy twigs. Flat flower clusters, heavy bunches of black berries. Grows like a weed on bare ground, very common, calcareous to neutral loams. Suckers from base. Resilient to cutting – can be difficult to eradicate but not appreciated in hedges. Many culinary uses for flowers and berries. Early flowers good for insects; berries for birds.

Elm, English (*Ulmus procera*) Lovely large hedgerow tree, traditional part of the landscape until devastated by Dutch elm disease. Evidence of sucker regrowth now: tend to survive for perhaps twenty years only. Wide range of soils, usually calcareous to neutral. Timber resolutely resistant to splitting – interlocking grain is uncleavable; mallet heads, stool and chair seats, wheel hubs, coffin boards, packing cases for heavy machinery. Long-lasting in water if kept permanently wet – good for waterpipes, dock baulks and so on. Provides nest holes for wide variety of birds, fodder for livestock and for caterpillars of comma, large tortoiseshell, white letter hairstreak. Tendency to shed big branches without warning.

Elm, Wych (*Ulmus glabra*) Native elm, very large leaf, low-branching, sometimes as shrub in hedgerows. Less prone to Dutch elm disease. Calcareous. Timber and wildlife similar to English elm.

Gorse (*Ulex europaeus*) Evergreen thorny shrub, scented flowers. Withstands exposure and cutting. Neutral loams and sands (western gorse, *U. gallii*, on acid loams, clays). Nesting for linnets; good for insects.

Guelder rose (*Viburnum opulus*) Large native shrub; white flowers, translucent red berries, colourful autumn foliage. Neutral to calcareous damp clays and loams. Insects on flowers; fruit appreciated by birds and woodmice.

Gum, Alpine snow (*Eucalyptus niphophila*) Hardiest of the eucalypts. Often multi-stemmed; dark green foliage.

Gum, cider (*Eucalyptus gunnii*) Fast-growing, large, hardy; the most widely planted eucalypt in Britain. Grey-green to glaucous leaves.

Gum, shining (*Eucalyptus nitens*) Less hardy, very fast-growing, quite large. Good timber and firewood.

Hawthorn, common (*Crataegus monogyna*) Native thorny shrub or small tree, principal species for hedging (quickthorn). Flowers while in leaf (as opposed to blackthorn, which flowers on bare twigs). Can withstand shade and regular cutting. Calcareous to neutral loams, clays. Hard, fine-grained wood for small decorative work, turnery, carving, rake tines, tool handles, knobbly walking-sticks. Good firewood. Red berries relished by many birds (especially thrush family) and woodmice; more than 150 insect species attracted to hawthorn flowers; good nesting crown if a tree.

Hawthorn, Midland (*Crataegus laevigata*) Similar to common hawthorn; can withstand shade very well. Neutral, calcareous, clay. Used for hedging. Wildlife similar to common hawthorn.

Hazel (*Corylus avellana*) Native many-stemmed shrub or sometimes small tree; coppices readily and can withstand shade – often grown under standards. Needs sunshine to produce nut crop. Neutral to slightly acid loams, clay. Suckers freely from stool base. Used to be major coppice species: pea-sticks, bean-poles, faggots, spars, wattle fencing, sheep-hurdles, cratewood, large baskets, walking-sticks and crooks, hedging-stakes, fish traps and all manner of useful items. Bends and cleaves easily. Good firewood though small. Good for wildlife: nuts for birds and mammals, cover for song and game birds, habitat for spring flowers, early pollen for insects. Nuts are very nutritious.

Holly (*Ilex aquifolium*) Native evergreen shrub or tree with waxy leaves restricting loss of water. Withstands deep shade and cutting. Well-drained neutral to acid soils. Heavy white wood is close-grained and very hard: turnery, inlays, fine carving (for instance, chess pieces), sticks. Good firewood with very high heating power, and can burn green because of low water content. Deer browse, nesting cover, berries for birds. Most plants either male or female, therefore some never have berries. Berry formation depends on warm, dry, sunny summer in *previous* year.

Honeysuckle (*Lonicera periclymenum*) Twining woody plant, not a native but very common in hedges and woods. Scented flowers if climbing but not if spreading. All soils. Bees and insects on flowers; birds on insects and tight red berry clusters. Useful for training up stems in walking-stick coppices to give character.

Hornbeam (*Carpinus betulus*) Tree native to south-east England in some ways similar to beech but not closely related. Trunk fluted or angled. Quite vigorous, tolerates shade, severe cold and drought. Heavy soil, neutral to acid; best on silt overlying heavy clay. Strong timber too hard for some uses; traditionally for ox yokes, mill cog-wheels, butchers' chopping blocks, turnery. Still used for piano mechanisms. Very good firewood. Slow to grow but will coppice. Known as the hawfinch tree – the bird loves its winged seeds; also other birds and small insects but not particularly good for insects.

Lime, common (*Tilia × europaea*) Large tree with big, irregular bosses on trunk, often seen in avenues; hybrid of large-leaved and small-leaved limes. Moist, well-drained and moderately fertile soil, avoiding acid peat. More of an amenity tree than for plantations. Tends to attract leaf aphids; flowers good for bees and insects, which attract woodpeckers; dense sucker shoots from base provide good nesting cover.

Lime, large-leaved (*Tilia platyphyllos*) Another big tree, and a native; bright green foliage, ribbed fruit; vigorous. Light fertile soils with high pH: does well on deep or shallow soils over chalk or limestone. Lime wood is soft and white; used for fine, delicate carving, turnery, perhaps pallets, piano keys, hat blocks, shoe lasts; bark fibre for rope; flowers for lime tea. Wildlife as common lime.

Lime, small-leaved (*Tilia cordata*) Not quite as large as other limes, native species locally common in ancient woodland (useful indicator); pretty foliage small and birch-like, bluish undersides; swollen bosses. Grows well with ash; shade-tolerant and usually vigorous. Soils and uses as large-leaved lime but also good for coppicing; often planted as understorey in shelter belts or mixed broadleaf woodland. Good honey tree, and woodpeckers suck the sap – good tree for conservation purposes.

Maple, field (*Acer campestre*) Medium-sized native tree or shrub, often seen in woodland, coppice and hedgerows; bright yellow autumn foliage. Calcareous clays and loams – common on lime-rich sites in south and east; alkaline preferred but will tolerate wide range; very hardy, and freely self-seeding coloniser. Hard, smooth, creamy-brown wood for turnery – bowls, spoons, dishes, tool handles, also stakes. Good for wildlife: insects on flowers (but not on leaves), keys eaten by small mammals. Rare in north and west, but our only native maple.

Maple, Norway (*Acer platanoides*) Introduced larger tree; lots of yellow flowers on bare twigs in April, good autumn colour; vigorous. Prefers alkaline soil, deep and moist, but will also grow on neutral to acid soils in high rainfall areas of west, and throughout Scotland. Hard, strong, smooth wood widely used in Europe for furniture, turnery and carving, but not really a timber tree in Britain (sycamore grows bigger and better).

Medlar (*Mespilus germanica*) Small, spreading tree, pleasant autumn colours, quite large flowers, round green fruits eaten when rotting (bletted). Ornamental. Open, sunny position, any well-drained and reasonably fertile soil.

Mulberry, black, white (*Morus nigra* and *Morus alba*) Hardy, slow-growing small trees established here for more than four centuries. *M. alba* is the silkworm tree; *M. nigra* bears edible fruit rather like loganberries in appearance. Deep, well-drained, rich loams with adequate moisture; site protected from north and east winds.

Oaks (*Quercus* spp.) Our native oaks are the pedunculate (*Q. robur*) and the sessile or durmast oak (*Q. petraea*), both large and familiar trees. Pedunculate has long-stalked acorns, leaves have rounded basal lobes and are stalkless; sessile conversely has stalkless acorns, stalked leaves, and generally better growth, crown, foliage and timber. Pedunculate does best on richer, heavier, neutral to acid soils but does not like very free or poor drainage, exposed sites or frost pockets; sessile more tolerant, typically seen on lighter acid soils of north and west. Timber of both is traditionally esteemed for strength and durability of heartwood; close-grained, hard, cleaves readily when green, can be steam-formed; used for veneer, furniture, fencing, building, charcoal, spelk baskets, turnery, carving, spokes, rungs; bark for tanning; good firewood too. Outstanding for wildlife: richest of all our trees in insects and birds; acorns for birds, mammals, insects (and pigs!); lichens and mosses – in fact, the native oaks are vital for wildlife. Other oaks include American red (*Q. borealis*); cork (*Q. suber*); scarlet (*Q. coccinea*); red (*Q. rubra* – red autumn foliage, pale yellow in spring, fast-growing even on moderately fertile soils; rather featureless wood for furniture, firewood and so on – not as good as native timber); Turkey (*Q. cerris*, introduced in 1735 and now naturalised tall tree of great vigour, fast-growing and handsome, straight trunk, rough bark streaked tangerine, long narrow leaves, mossy acorn cups, but poor timber in British climate though highly esteemed in Turkey for fencing, furniture and building); and the unusual evergreen holm oak (*Q. ilex*, introduced in the sixteenth century, able to live for 250 years, creates very dense shade which suppresses everything beneath it, very wind-firm and totally resistant to salty air, thus ideal for coastal planting; very strong, hard, dense wood is difficult to work – decorative carving or firewood).

Small Woods and Hedgerows

Plane, London (*Platanus* × *acerifolia*) Pollution-tolerant species from chance cross between oriental plane and American plane (*P. occidentalis*), widely planted in cities. Timber similar to beech – hard, strong, easily worked in any direction, but not durable out-of-doors: furniture, carving, veneer (lacewood). Seed hairs can irritate eyes.

Plane, oriental (*Platanus orientalis*) Introduced in the early seventeenth century, now well-established very large tree which seldom manages to set seed.

Poplar, balsam (*Populus balsamifera* – eastern – and *Populus trichocarpa* – western) Sweet-smelling, sticky gum on bud scales is very noticeable in spring. Usually ornamental only, but hybrids for timber in west of country (Fritzi Pauley, Scott Pauley, balsam spire) but not on exposed sites, high altitudes, shallow soils, acid peats or heathland and never stagnant water (kills off all poplar species). Timber as black poplar.

Poplar, black (*Populus niger*) The true black native is very rare and most today are hybrids (*Populus* × *euramericana*) with very exacting site requirements: sheltered situations, rich alluvial or fen soils (well-drained and well-watered – never stagnant); not suitable for west and north. The native species is tall and fast-growing but not long-lived though hardy and reliable; likes rich, moist, neutral silts or gravelly loams and needs light. Timber for cable drums, boxes, crates, pallets, fencing, veneer. Poplar wood is heavy when felled but very light when seasoned; supple, resistant to splitting, and was deliberately planted for matchwood (but now all imported); also strawberry punnets, cart bases, wheelbarrow bases, pulpwood. Wildlife as aspen.

Poplar, grey (*Populus canescens*) Natural cross between white poplar and aspen: vigorous, hardy, high-domed tree with heavily ridged black and silver bark, silvery spring foliage, yellow autumn leaves; strong roots and suckers. Disease-free, resistant to salt winds. Prefers moist, light loam, or shallow soil over chalk; wild in southern England and Wales.

Poplar, Lombardy (*Populus nigra*, 'Italica') Introduced in 1758, the familiar columnar poplar for shelter belts, screens and ornamental plantings. Grows fast when young but not long-lived, and useless timber full of knots.

Poplar, white (*Populus alba*) Well-established poplar with white, downy twigs, buds and leaf undersides; creamy bark. Naturalised only in southeast England; tends to produce suckers and form thickets, especially on coastal cliffs and sand dunes (resistant to salt winds); useful for binding clay cliffs.

Privet (*Ligustrum vulgare*) Tall semi-evergreen shrub (loses its leaves very late), scented white flowers, shiny black berries; tends to spread in a tangled thicket of suckers. Calcareous loams and clays. Good game cover, also hedges; some insects, birds take fruit. Common in south (especially on chalk); rare in north, introduced in Scotland.

Robinia or locust tree (*Robinia pseudoacacia*) Leguminous tree with profuse flowers – quite happy on poor soils and useful for disguising slag heaps and spoil. Golden wood is hard, strong and naturally durable but trunk twisted and fluted; used in America for fencing, tool handles, cart shafts. Root nodules fix nitrogen. Sends up strong suckers.

Rowan or mountain ash (*Sorbus aucuparia*) Small native tree in the *Rosaceae* family (also includes whitebeam, wild service, bird cherry, gean, etc.): white blossom, scarlet berries, 'ash' leaves. Grows in all sorts of unlikely places (seed carried by birds and dropped in rocky crevices); frost-hardy and able to stand exposure. Light-textured mineral soils – avoid poorly drained sites. Wood is strong, hard, tough, easily worked, but too small for industrial purposes – originally used to make rune tablets, spinning-wheels, country furniture, tool handles, mallet heads, cart shafts, platters and bowls; also good firewood. Flowers attract a few insects; fruit relished by birds, especially thrush family. Useful tree for woodland edge.

Spindle (*Euonymus europaeus*) Native shrub or small tree – very obvious in the hedgerow with its shocking coral-pink and yellow fruit. Calcareous to neutral loams but usually on limestone. Wood used to be made into spindles and butchers' skewers. Alternative host for bean aphids: do not use in hedge near bean or beet crops.

Spurge laurel (*Daphne laureola*) Evergreen shrub with dark, glossy leaves clustered at top of stem; small yellow-green flowers, black berries; little branched stems. Calcareous soils in English woodland; rare in Wales, introduced in Scotland.

Strawberry tree (*Arbutus unedo*) Native evergreen but only hardy in south and west England or coastal areas in Ireland, Scotland and Wales. Leathery, waxy leaves on a low bush (but can also be a small tree); scented heatherbell flowers; strange 'strawberry' fruits which birds like but people do not ('*unedo*' means 'I eat one only') and full of small, hard seeds. Wood is hard and tough but small – main outlet seems to be carved souvenirs of Killarney – it grows wild only in the west of Ireland, liking mild, wet winters and preferring hot, dry Mediterranean summers.

Sycamore (*Acer pseudoplatanus*) Known as plane in Scotland; large tree which grows like a weed – hardy everywhere. For good timber (felled at 100 years old) grow on fertile soil, preferably lime-rich and well sheltered, and protect from squirrels. Although an unpopular tree with conservationists and farmers, it can produce very good timber with the property of not staining cloth or tainting food, therefore used for kitchenware and cloth rollers; medium hard, close-grained, pale cream with a clean appearance, also strong and hardwearing for use as table-tops, chopping-boards, rolling-pins, furniture, spoons, turnery. Specialist outlets include veneer and violin-backs. Can be cleft; easy to carve when green. Good shelter species – very wind-firm and does not mind exposure; bees appreciate nectar.

Walnut, common (*Juglans regia*) Introduced to Britain by the Romans, does best in warm summers in south, especially in sheltered site with southerly aspect. Well-drained, moderately fertile, neutral soil; avoid heavy clay or sand. Open-grown trees can produce valuable veneer; rich grey-brown timber with lots of variety in it for high-class furniture, carving, bowls, platters; naturally durable, mechanically strong and very stable – also used for gun-stocks. Late into leaf, and the leaf juices will stain your fingers brown (used by gipsies for a false tan). And, of course, there are those protein-packed nuts, if you are lucky.

Wayfaring tree (*Viburnum lantana*) Rather weak shrub with downy leaves and twigs, fragrant flowers similar to those of related guelder rose, berries. Quite common on chalk scrub in south. Not very good in hedges, but birds take fruit and insects attracted to flowers.

Whitebeam (*Sorbus aria*) Native tree with a silvery look – attractive white foliage and flowers, red berries. Mainly in southern England on limestone and chalk; useful for woodland edges. Fair turnery wood, good firewood. Flowers and leaves for insects; fruit for birds and small mammals. Also Swedish whitebeam (*Sorbus intermedia*), widely planted.

Wild service tree (*Sorbus torminalis*) Rare native tree in same family as rowan and whitebeam. Maple-like leaves, rough bark, very handsome; crimson autumn foliage, dark brown spotted fruit (eat when bletted – 'chequers'). Prefers heavy neutral clay or calcareous. Major problem with parasitic wasp infecting 80–90 per cent of seeds. Good for birds and insects, and attractive in the landscape – rare in old woodlands and very worth preserving.

Willow, almond (*Salix triandra*) Shrub or small tree with smooth, brown, peeling bark; coppiced for basket rods when grown on best agricultural soil, well watered and well drained. Willow wood is exceptionally lightweight and very tough; the slender rods split into thin bands and are very pliable while moist but set into firm shapes when dry and seasoned, thus excellent for basketwork.

Willow, bay (*Salix pentandra*) Native shrub or small tree with glossy leaves, rugged grey bark, shiny twigs, sticky fragrant buds. Damp fertile loams – moist alluvials. Good for moths, bees and willow warblers; terrible firewood.

Willow, crack (*Salix fragilis*) Sizeable, fast-growing native tree with fragile twigs which readily snap off and eventually root as new plants. Moist alluvial soils. Rich insect fauna; also favoured for fraying by deer.

Willow, cricket bat (*Salix alba* var. *coerulea*) Local variety of the white willow, and always female. Specialist crop growing only in ideal conditions for manufacture of cricket bats and artificial limbs (wood is resistant to impact).

Willow, goat (*Salix caprea*) Native shrub, widespread and common in damp situations and at waterside. Brittle wood, really used only for clothes-pegs. Excellent for insects: food plant for purple emperor caterpillars (rare butterfly today); livestock enjoy leaves and young shoots.

Willow, grey (*Salix cinerea*) Very useful for wet places in association with alder; similar to goat willow but narrower leaves and hairy twigs.

Willow, osier (*Salix viminalis*) Shrub with long, straight, flexible branches grown on short rotation (annual or biennial harvest) for basketry. Very long, narrow leaves with silky grey undersides.

Willow, white (*Salix alba*) Large native tree with characteristic hairy silver leaves. Vigorous. Moist alluvials, by stream or pond, often planted at riverside for rough baskets and hurdles. Very good for moths, bees and willow warblers.

NATIVE CONIFERS
Juniper, common (*Juniperus communis*) Shrub or small tree growing wild; ornamental; mainly on southern England's chalk downs or on open hillsides further north. 'Berries' used to flavour gin. Browse for deer; fruit for birds. Reasonable firewood.

Pine, Scots (*Pinus sylvestris*) Useful timber tree for a wide range of conditions, especially light or sandy soils; not so good for higher elevations or coast. Very frost-hardy and does well in drier regions. Fairly slow-growing compared with introduced conifers but reliable, with good strong timber for fencing, planking, packaging, pallets, mine props, chipboard, telegraph poles.

Yew (*Taxus baccata*) Very primitive conifer with red berry-like fruit. Shrub or small tree with potentially very valuable timber if grown straight. Veneer, furniture, carving – lovely grain and colours, and a 'hard' softwood. Shade-tolerant. Poisonous to livestock (foliage and seed).

OTHER CONIFERS

Wide range of conifers introduced in last hundred years or so, either for fast-growing timber or for ornamental and screening purposes. Briefly, here are the ones most commonly grown today. Note that they are listed by their English names which are often misleading: for example, the incense cedar is not a cedar but a cypress.

Key: T = timber   S = screen/shelter/hedge
      O = ornamental   C = Christmas trees

Cedars:

Atlas (*Cedrus atlantica*) (also a blue type, var. *glauca*) — O

Deodar (*Cedrus deodara*) — O S

Incense (*Calocedrus decurrens*) (a cypress) — O

Cedar of Lebanon (*Cedrus libani*) — O

Western red cedar (*Thuja plicata*) (a cypress) — O S T

Cypresses:

Arizona (Smooth) (*Cupressus glabra*) (powder blue) — O

Italian (*Cupressus sempervirens*) — O

Lawson (*Chamaecyparis lawsoniana*) — O S

Leyland (× *Cupressocyparis leylandii*) (cross between Nootka and Monterey cypresses) — S

Monterey (*Cupressus macrocarpa*) — O S T

Nootka (*Chamaecyparis nootkatensis*) — O

Sawara (*Chamaecyparis pisifera*) — O

Swamp (*Taxodium distichum*) (a deciduous redwood, lakeside planting) — O

Firs:

Caucasian (*Abies nordmanniana*) — O C

Douglas (*Pseudotsuga menziesii*) — T

Grand (*Abies grandis*)   T
Noble (*Abies procera*)   T C O
Silver (*Abies alba*)
(serious problems
with aphids, no
longer planted for
timber)

Juniper:
Chinese (*Juniperus*   O
chinensis)

Larches (all deciduous):
European (*Larix*   T
decidua)
Japanese (*Larix*   T
kaempferi)
Hybrid (× *eurolepis*)   T

Pines:
Austrian (*Pinus nigra*   S
var. *nigra*)
Bhutan (*Pinus*   O
wallichiana)
Chilean (*Araucaria*   O T
araucana)
(the monkey puzzle
tree)
Corsican (*Pinus*   T
nigra var. *maritima*)
Lodgepole (*Pinus*   T
contorta)

Monterey (*Pinus*   S T
radiata)

Redwoods:
Coast (*Sequoia*   O
sempervirens)
Dawn (*Metasequoia*   O
glyptostroboides)
(deciduous)
Giant sequoia/   O
Wellingtonia
(*Sequoia giganteum*)

Spruces:
(Blue) Colorado   O C
(*Picea pungens*)
Norway (*Picea abies*)   C T
Serbian (*Picea*   O
omorika)
Sitka (*Picea*   T
sitchensis)

Hemlock:
Western (*Tsuga*   T C
heterophylla)

Ginkgo:
Maidenhair tree   O
(*Ginkgo biloba*)
(very primitive
deciduous conifer)

GLOSSARY

Agroforestry A combination of trees and plant crops or livestock on the same piece of land.

Ancient woodland A site which has been woodland continuously since at least 1600 AD.

Beating up Replacing newly planted trees which have failed.

Besom Yard broom made of bundled birch twigs.

Bodger Itinerant chair-maker, especially one working in a beechwood.

Brashing Cleaning the lower trunk (usually up to above head height) by removing branches.

Broadleaf Description which distinguishes dicotyledon trees from needle-bearing gymnosperms or conifers. Most of our native trees are broad-leaved, and can be either deciduous or evergreen. Their timber is described as hardwood, which distinguishes it from the softwood of conifers, although not all broadleaves have harder wood than conifers.

Butt The trunk or stem of a tree up to its first branch.

Cambium Thin layer of growing cells, capable of division to form new cells, adding concentric cylinders of new growth which thicken the stem by pushing outwards towards the bark.

Canopy The mantle of branches and leaves of adjoining trees: that is, the uppermost 'storey' of the woodland.

Cant One of the sections of a coppice, harvested of its poles on a regular basis. Other terms include 'coupe'.

Cleaning Taking out unwanted shrubs and saplings among a young plantation crop.

Clear-felling Removal of the whole crop as one.

Cleft Split down the grain rather than sawn.

Conifer Group of trees which, in contrast to broadleaves, have narrow needles or scale-like leaves, scaly buds, resinous fragrance and, in most cases, woody cones (though juniper and yew, for example, have fleshy berries, and the alder, a broadleaf, has fruit rather like cones). The majority are evergreen. Conifers are gymnosperms rather than dicoty-ledons, and their timber is known as softwood, even though some species have quite hard wood. Conifers have a simple structure and growth pattern, and as a group they grow fast on poor soils even in harsh climates.

Coppice To cut tree stems close to the ground so that the tree's original stump produces several new shoots which can be harvested again after a few years.

Cord A locally variable measurement of a stack of logs, usually 8 × 4 × 4ft; also (as a verb) to cut wood in appropriate lengths and stack it in a cord.

Coupe *see* **Cant.**

Crown A tree's canopy of branches and foliage.

Deciduous Shedding all leaves periodically: that is, not evergreen. Most of our broadleaves are deciduous, and the larch is a deciduous conifer.

Enrichment Filling in gaps in a wood or plantation with new plantings or by encouraging natural regeneration.

Epicormic shoots Secondary growth from adventitious buds, usually on the trunk or on large old branches.

Evergreen Retaining green leaves throughout winter. Individual leaves are shed at intervals as they age and can live for anything from one to fifteen years.

Faggot Bundle of twiggy growth used as fuel for ovens.

Feather Untrimmed standard.

Green Freshly felled; not yet seasoned.

Hardwood Timber of broadleaf species, whether deciduous or evergreen, and whether or not it is actually harder than the timber of coniferous (softwood) species. Commonly used as an adjective to describe broadleaves.

Heartwood Inner core of a stem (trunk or large branch): that is, wood no longer carrying sap and effectively 'dead'. Very durable in some species (such as oak), liable to decay after felling in others (for instance, many softwoods).

High forest Woodland in which the majority of trees are full-grown timber specimens, generally with a high, closed canopy.

Hoppus foot Measure of volume of a log, based on length and quarter-girth at the log's midpoint. (See Appendix IV.)

Layer To propagate a new plant by bending and pegging down a shoot from a parent plant so that it can take root.

Log Roundwood large enough for the sawmill: that is, with a minimum diameter of 18cm overbark and a minimum 3m length of clean stem.

Lop-and-top Branches and foliage which do not form part of the log: that is, all the growth from the point at which the tree first branches. Can be valuable for firewood.

Maiden Young tree which has not been cut back, particularly the original growth of a tree which will subsequently be coppiced.

Muka Dried ground-up mixture of pine needles, petioles, deciduous leaves and small twigs used as a feed for livestock.

Nurse Quick-growing species planted with slower-growing timber crop to draw up the more valuable trees while they are young.

Nut Fruit with woody shell containing a kernel.

pH Measure of the acidity or alkalinity of soil (or of water and solutions). With soil, a pH of 6.6–7.3 is neutral; less than 6.6 is acid (4.5 or less is

Small Woods and Hedgerows

very acid), and more than 7.3 is alkaline (9 or more is very alkaline). The scale ranges from 0 to 14.

Pit-planting Planting into a pit of cultivated soil.

Pole Young tree or coppice growth below the size of saw timber but large enough to be harvested as coppice or thinnings.

Pollard High-level coppice: that is, tree cut at above head height (beyond reach of livestock) so that it can produce a new crop of shoots. Also a good method of ensuring that a waterside tree does not become top-heavy or take too much light from a pond.

Provenance The source – that is the place where the original stock from which a plant is propagated was grown.

Pulpwood Small roundwood, perhaps 2–3m long, destined to be converted into wood pulp for the production of paper or board.

Quarter-girth Measure used in estimating the volume of a felled log: a quarter of the log's circumference at the mid-way point of its length.

Roundwood Timber as it was grown: that is, not yet squared by sawing. Small roundwood has a minimum diameter of 7cm but is less than the 18cm diameter required for a saw log.

Sapwood Wood carrying the sugars (manufactured from atmospheric carbon dioxide and water, captured by the tree's leaves or needles), the energy from which fuels the tree's metabolic activities. Living sapwood resists decay, but felled sapwood is not very durable. The proportion of sapwood surrounding the heartwood varies according to the species; for example, it is very thin in oak and sweet chestnut.

Saw logs Timber acceptable to a sawmill – that is, long, straight, clean stems of good quality at least 18cm in diameter and at least 3m long after felling.

Shake A disorder seen in some species: for example, ring shake in sweet chestnut, in which the wood splits along the annual rings – not apparent until the stem is felled.

Shrub Woody plant with several stems rising from the ground or from near ground-level naturally (that is, not coppiced), as opposed to the single stem of a maiden tree. Some species might develop as either a shrub or a tree, according to circumstances.

Silvopastoral Term defining a system in which tree-growing is combined with livestock enterprises on the same site.

Slabwood Sawmill offcuts: that is, the barked outer lengths of the stem sawn off when the log is squared up.

Snedding Removing branches and snags from a felled stem.

Softwood The timber of a coniferous tree, regardless of whether or not it is in fact softer than the hardwood timber of broadleaved trees. For example, yew wood is very hard.

Spile A pale, i.e. a stake split out lengthways from a coppiced pole for fencing.

Stag-headed Description for a typical old oak in which many of the crown's branches have died back and protrude, bare of bark and leaves.

Standard Tree with a clean stem at least 1.8m long; either a young transplant, or a tree being encouraged to grow to maturity as timber.

Stem Trunk.

Stool The stump of a coppiced tree, from which the new crop's shoots grow.

Thinning Selective removal of individual trees within a crop to improve the growth of the remaining trees.

Timber Stems suitable for sawing into planks, etc.

Transplant Plant which has been lifted and replanted in the nursery in order to encourage the development of a good root system so that the plant will grow well in its final station.

Tree Woody plant with single main stem or trunk in natural (uncoppiced) growth.

Treen Small items made from wood: for example, spoons, bowls, carved knick-knacks.

Tree shelter Protective tube for newly planted or regenerated trees which guards against browsing predators, deters weed growth around the tree and creates a microclimate to encourage the tree's development.

Turnery Art of producing wooden articles with the aid of a lathe – for instance, tool handles, bowls; art of shaping wood to a curved transverse section.

Undercut Plant whose taproot has deliberately been severed to encourage the development of fibrous root system.

Understorey Trees whose crowns are below the canopy of the dominant tree crop, often coppice under standards.

Veneer Thin sheets of top-quality wood peeled or shaved from timber of the highest quality, generally from clean trunks of large diameter.

Wattle Panel of woven rods, often of hazel.

Whip Young tree with slender, unbranched stem, perhaps 1m tall.

TERMS FOR DEER

SPECIES	MALE	FEMALE	YOUNG
Fallow	Buck	Doe	Fawn
Muntjac	Buck	Doe	Fawn
Red	Stag	Hind	Calf
Roe	Buck	Doe	Kid
Sika	Stag	Hind	Calf

Groups of deer are generally termed herds, but a group of roe is a family or bevy.

BIBLIOGRAPHY

ACKERS, C. P.: *Practical British Forestry* (Oxford University Press, 1947)

BECKETT, K. and G.: *Planting Native Trees and Shrubs* (Jarrolds Colour Publications, 1979)

BLYTH, JOHN, *et al.*: *Farm Woodland Management* (Farming Press, 1987)

CHIVERS, KEITH (ed.): *History with a Future: Harnessing the Heavy Horse for the 21st Century* (Shire Horse Society, 1988)

EDLIN, H. L.: *Collins Guide to Tree Planting and Cultivation* (Collins, 1975)

EDLIN, H. L.: *British Woodland Trees* (Batsford, 1945)

EDLIN, H. L.: *Trees, Woods and Men* (Collins, 1956)

EDLIN, H. L.: *Woodland Crafts in Britain* (Batsford, 1947)

ELEY, GEOFFREY: *Wild Fruit and Nuts* (EP Publishing, 1976)

FREETHY, RON: *The Making of the British Countryside* (David & Charles, 1981)

GREAVES, VALERIE: *Hedgelaying Explained* (National Hedgelaying Society)

HART, CYRIL E.: *Practical Forestry for the Agent and Surveyor* (The Estates Gazette, 1967)

HART, ROBERT: *The Forest Garden* (Institute for Social Inventions)

HIBBERD, B. G. (ed.): *Farm Woodland Practice* (Forestry Commission Handbook 3, 1988)

HILEY, W. E.: *Woodland Management* (Faber & Faber, revised 2nd edition, 1967)

HILL, JACK: *The Complete Practical Book of Country Crafts* (David & Charles, 1979)

HILLS, LAWRENCE D.: *The Good Fruit Guide* (Henry Doubleday Research Associates, 1984)

MABEY, RICHARD: *Food for Free* (Collins, 1972)

MAXWELL, SIR HERBERT: *Trees: A Woodland Notebook* (James Maclehose & Sons, 1915)

PACKHAM, J. R., and HARDING, D. J. L.: *Ecology of Woodland Processes* (Edward Arnold, 1982)

PETERKEN, G. F.: *Woodland Conservation and Management* (Chapman & Hall, 1981)

PETERKEN, G. F.: *A Method for Assessing Woodland Flora for Conservation Using Indicator Species* (*Biological Conservation*, 6, 1974)

POLLARD, E., HOOPER, M. D., and MOORE, N. W.: *Hedges* (Collins, 1971)

RACKHAM, OLIVER: *Ancient Woodland: Its Vegetation and Uses in Britain* (Edward Arnold, 1980)

RACKHAM, OLIVER: *Trees and Woodland in the British Landscape* (Dent, 1976)
SEYMOUR, JOHN: *The Forgotten Arts* (National Trust/Dorling Kindersley, 1984)
SLEE, BILL: *Alternative Farm Enterprises* (Farming Press, 1987)
SPARKES, IVAN G.: *Woodland Craftsmen* (Shire, 1977)
WIDDOWSON, R. W.: *Towards Holistic Agriculture* (Pergamon Press, 1987)

BRITISH TRUST FOR CONSERVATION VOLUNTEERS:
   Woodland Management
   Fencing
   Hedging
CENTRE FOR ALTERNATIVE TECHNOLOGY:
   Tools and Devices for Coppice Crafts (1977)
COUNTRYSIDE COMMISSION:
   Various publications
FARMING AND WILDLIFE TRUST:
   Schering Farm Conservation Guide (1988)
   Various leaflets and booklets
FORESTRY COMMISSION:
   Numerous publications, but especially:
   Wildlife Rangers Handbook
   Forestry Practice (Bulletin 14)
   Nursery Practice (Bulletin 43)
   The Landscape of Forests and Woods (Bulletin 44)
   A Key to Eucalypts in Britain and Ireland (Bulletin 50)
   Seed Manual for Ornamental Trees and Shrubs (Bulletin 59)
   The Yield of Sweet Chestnut Coppice (Bulletin 64)
   Farm Woodland Planning (Bulletin 80)
   Conifers (Booklet 15)
   Broadleaves (Booklet 20)
   Managing Small Woodlands (Booklet 46)
   Coppice (Leaflet 83)
   Practical Work in Farm Woods (FC/ADAS joint leaflet pack)
INTERNATIONAL LABOUR OFFICE, Geneva:
   Fuelwood and Charcoal Preparation (1985)
NATURE CONSERVANCY COUNCIL:
   Forestry Operations and Broadleaf Woodland Conservation
   Hedges and Shelterbelts
   Nature Conservation and Agriculture
   Managing Farm Woodlands
   Tree Planting

INDEX

Access *see* Extraction
Ackers, C. P. 22
Advice, sources of 12
Agroforestry 138, 139–40, 184
Alder 19, 32, 33, 34, 35, 36, 52, 65, 66, 70, 80, 93, 95, 170–1
Alder buckthorn 38
Almond 34
Amadou 114–15
Amphibians 155
Ancient woodland 38–40, 184
Ash 15, 18, 19, 21, 22, 33, 34, 45, 52, 57, 60, 64, 65, 66, 80, 82, 85, 93, 107, 108, 113, 135, 171
Aspen 34, 38, 65, 171
Assessment 13, 17, 31

Bagging (seeds) 69–70
Barberry 113
Bark, peeling *see* Peeling
Bark, uses for 110–12
Bark scorch 24
Bark stripping 45, 47
Bats (*see also* Conservation) 154, 155–6
Beanpoles *see* Hazel
Beating up 59, 184
Beech 15, 17, 18, 19, 33, 34, 41, 45, 52, 57, 60, 63, 64, 65, 66, 70, 93, 113, 135, 171
Beech, southern 33, 52, 80, 95, 171–2
Bees 141
Besoms 109–10, 184
Bilberry 38, 113
Birch (*see also* Brushwood) 15, 18, 19, 22, 33, 34, 45, 52, 64, 65, 66, 70, 80, 93, 95, 112, 172
Birds, wild (*see also* Conservation) 151–4
Blackberry 72, 113, 172
Blackthorn 65, 66, 72, 108, 113, 135, 172
Bouffier, Elzeard 16
Box 34, 65, 71, 135, 172
Brashing 23–4, 184
British Horse Society 144, 161
British Trust for Conservation Volunteers

26, 88, 100, 129, 155, 158, 162
British Trust for Ornithology 151–2, 162
Broadleaf *see* Hardwood
Broom 65, 113, 135, 172
Browsers (*see also* Deer, Livestock, Rabbits) 24, 44–8, 81
Brushwood 109–10
Buckthorn 65, 135, 172
Bundling 103
Burning off 42
Burred oak 24
Butchers broom 66, 71, 173
Butterflies (*see also* Conservation) 156–7

Callus 23, 60
Cambium 130–2, 184
Campbell, Dr Alastair 114
Cants 82, 184
Carter, Robin 106
Cattle *see* Livestock
Centre for Agricultural Strategy 94
Charcoal 95–9
Cedars *see* Conifers
Chequers *see* Wild service tree
Cherry 15, 19, 33, 34, 38, 52, 57, 65, 66, 72, 108, 113, 173
Chestnuts *see* Horse chestnut, Sweet chestnut
Chips, chipping machines (*see also* Energy crops) 15, 95, 110, 112
Christmas decorations 118
Christmas trees 12, 116–18
Cleaning 23
Cleaving 103
Common Ground 140, 162
Conifers (*see also* Softwoods) 15, 17, 18, 19, 23, 28, 32–6, 35, 45, 52, 57, 64, 65, 66, 93, 95, 113, 135, 181–3, 184
Conservation 12, 13, 14, 19–20, 21, 26, 40, 82, 86, 125–7, 147–8, 151–7, 167
Consultants 11–12, 13–14, 16
Contractors 30
Cooper & Sons 107

Co-operatives 30
Coppice (*see also* various species) 21, 25, 37, 57, 79–90, 91–115, 119, 154, 184
Cotoneaster 65
Cordwood 88, 185
Cork 112
Councils, local 12, 40, 132, 158, 162, 167
Countryside Commission 61, 132, 158, 160–1, 162
Crab apple 19, 34, 38, 52, 72, 93, 113, 174
Crafts 105–6, 150–1
Cranberry 113
Cricket bat willows 119–20
Crooks 109
Currants 38, 65
Cuttings 55, 76–7
Cypresses *see* Conifers

Dartington Trust 22, 162
Deer (*see also* Browsers) 24, 45–52, 81, 141, 148–9, 187
Derelict woodland 21
Diameter at breast height (DBH) 27, 169
Dogwood 65, 135, 174
Dormancy (seeds) 63, 66–7
Drainage 36–7

Edible produce 113, 151
Elder 65, 113, 135, 174
Electric fencing 48
Elms 19, 34, 38, 45, 65, 66, 93, 174
Elmhirst, Dorothy and Leonard 22
Energy crops 90, 94–5
Enrichment 21, 25, 185
Enterprises 9–12
Epicormic growth 24, 185
Eucalypts 35, 52, 65, 80, 95, 121–3, 174–5
European Farm Development Group 162–3
Exposed sites 36
Extraction 26, 30, 83, 86

Fairfax, Michael 106
Farm Diversification Grant Scheme 160
Farm Woodland Scheme 159

Farming and Wildlife
    Advisory Groups 12, 14,
    110, 125, 153, 155, 163
Feathers 55, 185
Felling 26–7
Felling licences 12, 27, 166
Fencing (products) 15, 99–
    105
Fencing (protective) 44, 47–
    8
Fertiliser 36
Financial aid *see* Grants
Firewood 15, 30, 91–4
Firs *see* Conifers
Foliage 115, 123
Forest Crafts 106–7
Forest gardens 139–40
Forestry Commission 10,
    11, 14, 17, 26, 30, 34, 43,
    47, 90, 108, 141, 148, 149–
    50, 156, 158, 163, 166, 167,
    168
Foxes 149
Fraying 46–7
Fruit 113, 114, 140
Fuel 91–9
Fulcher, Raf 137
Fungi 114–15

Game (*see also* Deer,
    Pheasant, Shooting,
    Wildfowl) 145–9
Game Conservancy 146–7,
    163–4
Games, woodland 149–50
Goats 141, 143
Gorse 65, 135, 174
Grants 10, 21, 158–61
Grass 42–3
Greenhouse effect 20
Group felling 24–5
Guelder rose 38, 65, 71, 113,
    135, 174
Gums *see* Eucalypts

Hair 49
Hampshire Wildlife Trust
    61
Hardwoods 14, 15, 185
Hares *see* Rabbits
Hart, Robert 139–40
Hawthorn 34, 38, 52, 65, 66,
    71, 93, 108, 113, 135, 175
Hazel (*see also* Coppice) 22,
    25, 33, 34, 65, 66, 80, 82,
    83, 90, 104–5, 105–6, 107,
    108, 113, 135, 175
Hedges
    Aging 124–5
    Laying 129–32
    Planting 134–7
    Shapes 127–8
    Trimming 125–9
Hedgerows 124–37, 155
Hedgerow trees 14–15, 132–
    3

Height assessment *see*
    Measurement
Hemlock *see* Conifers
Henry Doubleday Research
    Association 136–7
Herbicides 42
Hiley, Wilfrid 22
Hills, Lawrence D. 137
History (site) 38–40
Hoeing 42
Holly 19, 33, 34, 38, 52, 65,
    66, 71, 93, 108, 135, 175
Honeysuckle 135, 175
Hooke Park 23
Hoppus foot 28, 169, 185
Hornbeam 19, 33, 34, 38, 52,
    65, 66, 80, 93, 135, 176
Horses 24, 37, 77, 141, 143–
    4
Horse chestnut 19, 33, 35,
    52, 64, 65, 93, 135, 173
Hurdles 104–5
Hypericum 71

Judas tree 35
Juniper 34, 65, 66, 71, 113,
    181

Laburnum 35, 36, 65, 135
Landscape 37–8
Larches *see* Conifers
Laurels 35, 135
Layering 83, 84, 185
Laying, hedge 129–32
Legislation 10, 166–8
Limes 18, 19, 22, 33, 34, 38,
    52, 65, 66, 71, 80, 93, 113,
    176
Livestock 43, 81, 127, 141–
    3
Local provenance 61, 186
Locust tree 35

Maidenhair tree 65
Maintenance 59–60
Makepeace, John 22–3, 106,
    165
Management 22–30
Manpower Services
    Commission 88
Manure 44
Maples 33, 34, 35, 38, 45,
    52, 65, 66, 71, 80, 135, 176–
    7
Markets 12, 15
Mats *see* Spats
Measurement 14, 26, 27–30,
    168–70
Medlar 34, 65, 113, 177
Men of Trees 12, 16, 164
Merchants 30
Mice 69, 70, 74
Ministry of Agriculture,
    Fisheries & Food 30, 132,
    158, 159, 160, 164
Mistletoe 115

Monks Wood Experimental
    Station 124, 161
Muka 113–14, 185
Mulberry 35, 65, 177
Mulching 42, 43–4
Multiple land use 138–57
Myrobalan *see* Plum

Nash, David 106
National Agricultural
    Centre 150, 164
National Farmers Union 30,
    164
National Hedgelaying
    Society 130
Nature Conservancy
    Council 40, 152, 154, 155,
    156, 161, 164, 167
Neglected woodland 13, 21,
    22
New woods 31–60
Nitrogen fixation 36
Njonjo, Chief Josiah 16
Nurses 56–7, 185
Nuts (*see also* Edible
    produce) 113, 114, 185

Oak 14, 15, 18, 19, 33, 34,
    35, 36, 38, 45, 52, 57, 60,
    64, 65, 66, 81, 82, 85, 93,
    99, 100, 113, 135, 177
Oakford, Anna 143
Oleaster 35
Opportunity forestry 22
Orchards 140, 141, 145
Organisations 161–5
Osiers 90, 118–19

Palings 103–4
Parkland 14–15
Parnham Trust 22–3, 164–5
Partridge 146–8
Pea boughs *see* Hazel
Peach 34
Pear, wild 34, 65, 72, 113
Peat 36
Peeling 88, 100–3
Pheasants 44, 47, 141, 145–
    7
Pigs 43, 141, 142–3
Pine *see* Conifers
Pine, Scots (*see also*
    Conifers) 15, 19, 34, 45, 52,
    57, 64, 71, 181–2
Planes 18, 19, 35, 65, 178
Planning permission 12
Planting 53–8
Plum 34, 65, 135
Pointing 103
Pollarding 81, 186
Ponds 147–8
Poplars 15, 18, 19, 22, 33,
    34, 35, 55, 65, 66, 77, 93,
    95, 120–1, 178
Poultry 141, 144–5
Power lines 27

Index

Preservatives 99–100
Privet 65, 66, 72, 135, 179
Project Silvanus 165
Propagation 61–78
Pruning 23, 60

Quince 65

Rabbits (*see also* Browsers) 44–7, 48, 81
Rackham, Oliver 20, 133
Raised beds 73–4
Refrigeration (seeds) 69
Regeneration, natural 24, 40, 77–8
Registered Source 61, 167–8
Renovation 13–21
Reptiles 155
Restocking 20, 21
Rhododendron 23, 135
Robinia 36, 65, 179
Root collar 55, 58
Root systems 36, 58
Roundwood 23, 28, 186
Rose, Julian 142–3
Roses, wild 38, 65, 72, 113
Rowan 34, 52, 65, 66, 72, 113, 179

Sap 26
Saw logs/planks 14, 15, 28–30, 186
Sea buckthorn 65, 113, 123, 135, 173
Seale-Hayne Agricultural College 114
Seed
    Collecting 62–4
    Sources 61, 62–3
    Sowing 67–8, 70–2, 73–5
    Storing 67–72
    Types 65
Seedlings 54, 75
Set-aside 10, 40
Shake 89, 186
Sheep *see* Livestock
Shelter belts 133–4
Shire Horse Society 143
Shii-take 114
Shooting 21, 145–9

Sholto Douglas, James 138–9
Silvopastoralism 138, 141–3, 186
Site assessment 38–40
Site preparation 40–1
Site of Special Scientific Interest (SSSI) 20, 167
Slee, Dr Bill 114
Sloe *see* Blackthorn
Slopes 37
Softwoods (*see also* Conifers) 15, 16–17, 100, 186
Soil 31–3, 89, 185–6
Spacing 55–6
Spats (tree) 43
Species, indicator 38–9
Species, introduced 31–2, 34–5
Species, native 31, 34–5
Spellerberg, Dr Ian F. 155
Spindle 65, 66, 72, 135, 179
Splitting *see* Cleaving
Spruce *see* Conifers
Spurge laurel 38, 179
Squirrels 45
Stakes *see* Fencing
Staking 58
Standards 55
Standing crop 28–30
Stratification (seeds) 68–9
Strawberry tree 34, 65, 179
Stumps 21, 53
Stumping back 59
Subsoil 37
Sweet chestnut (*see also* Coppice) 15, 18, 19, 21, 22, 33, 34, 36, 52, 57, 64, 65, 66, 81, 82, 89–90, 93, 99, 100, 107, 108, 113, 173
Sycamore 15, 18, 19, 33, 34, 45, 52, 57, 60, 64, 65, 66, 81, 93, 95, 135, 179–80
Systems 9

Tate, Elizabeth 137
Tannin 111
Thinning 24–5, 59, 75
Timber Growers UK 30, 165
Trails 150

Training 26, 155
Transplants 54–5, 187
Tree guards 49
Tree Preservation Orders 20, 27, 166
Tree shelters 49–52
Tree spats 43
Tulip tree 35

Undercutting 54, 75–6, 187

Veneer 14, 15–16, 187
Voles 43, 46
Volume *see* Measurement

Walking sticks 12, 107–9
Walnut 15, 19, 33, 34, 52, 63, 65, 113, 180
Watercourses/tables 27, 36, 37
Watermark disease 120
Watts, Edgar 119
Wayfaring tree 65, 135, 180
Weeds 24, 41–4
Weight (*see also* Measurement) 28
Whips 55, 187
Whitebeam 34, 52, 65, 66, 72, 113, 135, 180
Wildfowl 147–8
Wildlife *see* Conservation
Wildlife & Countryside Act 167
Wild service tree 34, 38, 62, 65, 66, 72, 113, 180
Willows 12, 19, 33, 34, 55, 65, 66, 77, 81, 90, 93, 95, 118–20, 135, 137, 143, 180–1
Windblow 17–20
Woodland Grant Scheme 158–9
Woodland produce/uses 9, 10
Woodland Trust 12, 158, 165
Wright, C. N. 119

Yattenden estate 117–18
Yew 18, 33, 34, 52, 65, 72, 93, 113, 135, 182
Yields 14